The Secret Millionaires' Club

by Adrian Frost

First published by Scott and Pine Publishing in 2023.
ISBN 978-1-7395385-0-7

Find out more at www.authorfrost.com

For Mum.

(Sorry about the occasional swear word.)

Part One

1

Democratic Republic of the Congo. October 2018.

The driver was easy to spot. Tall and broad, he dwarfed the other dozen or so lean, excited men holding up cards in the chaotic arrivals hall of N'djili Airport. He cracked the briefest smile of welcome, or perhaps relief, as David approached him. He said something which David recognised as being in French, but it was too fast for him to understand.

'Parlez-vous Anglais?' asked David.

The driver shrugged.

'Long drive, long drive,' he said and grabbing David's two large bags, he cut a swathe through the crowds of insistent porters, taxi drivers and hotel touts to a capable-looking truck in the car park.

'Not far to the river, though? I thought the river would be the quickest way?' asked David casually, trying not to sound like he knew better than the driver. 'To Yepi? Isn't the boat quicker? That's what Monsieur Bertrand told me...'

The driver shook his head. 'Long drive, long drive,' he repeated and handed over a tattered roadmap.

David felt disappointed. He'd watched a *National Geographic* documentary about it and was looking forward to a river trip. More than that, the sudden change in the plan made him nervous. Monsieur Bertrand, the charity organiser, had stressed the area was safe, and that the local guide he was meeting would look after everything. But the words in the travel insurance documents that David had been reading on the plane were fresh in his mind. 'Conflicts can evolve quickly. Monitor the local media for signs of unrest and avoid areas where demonstrations may happen.' Perhaps something had happened to make the river trip unsafe.

Perhaps he shouldn't have come. David was a teacher from Nebberton High School, whose pupils had raised fourteen thousand pounds to help build a new school in Yepi, a small mining town, a hundred and fifty miles west of the capital. Some might say that transferring the money to the charity's bank account, which had been done weeks ago, was enough. They might see a trip out to present a cardboard cheque as an unnecessary and patronising gesture. But David felt it was so important, he funded the trip himself. He wanted to forge a link between the two schools, to show both sets of kids that they were, in some small way, connected. Too many of the world's problems came from a feeling that people who lived far away were somehow different from those at home. Their circumstances might be wildly different, but people were fundamentally the same.

As they travelled, David traced out the circuitous route on the map with his finger. It really was going to be a long drive. It was hard to gauge, not knowing the road conditions, but maybe four hours. Or eight? Or sixteen? He became alarmed. If it was going to be a long haul, where would they sleep? Would the driver keep on through the night? He looked like he was capable of it, David thought.

At first, the road felt like any busy national highway, with multi-lane traffic, advertising hoardings, and street-side markets and cafes. Then they turned off to a narrower road which set out with good intentions of tarmac and kerb stones, but here and there reverted to baked mud and loose rocks. At times it faded almost out of existence, or transformed into deep rutted mud fields, but the driver seemed to know where he was going and kept a pace that impressed and scared David in equal measure. Either the man had faith in the truck's rugged engineering or else a total disregard for safety. David couldn't establish which it was because the driver was mostly silent, probably concentrating. There were certainly a dangerous number of pedestrians for such a major trunk road; children on their way home from school, men guiding animals, and people using the road as a general meeting place, and in some places, a market.

David settled down into his seat, occupying his mind by looking for photo opportunities, as he knew he would have to make a presentation to the school children on his return to Nebberton High. He didn't want that slideshow to be a series of clichéd and condescending pictures of Africa. He wanted to capture images that showed the people here were just the same as those in the Midlands, back home. All the same, when he saw a trio of tall women carrying bundles of laundry on their heads, he couldn't help reaching for his smartphone camera.

Despite the unfamiliar surroundings, despite the cultural shift, despite the alien landscape and tropical vegetation, after two hours of travelling, the journey became monotonous. David felt ashamed of himself. He felt guilty to be a spoilt northern European who still harboured unreal and stereotypical expectations. They were in wide open country now, with gently rolling hills. He mentally rehearsed a question for his driver that he knew he wouldn't have the nerve to say out loud. 'Do you think we will see..... I wonder, do you ever see... how difficult would it be... do you think we will see... an elephant?'

So far, it had only been goats and cows. At last, David saw something that qualified as a photo opportunity. It was a herd of about twenty antelope, close to the road. David asked the driver to pull over so that he could get a good steady shot. The driver looked puzzled. 'Non, Monsieur. Not allowed to shoot the animals.' But while David tried to correct the misunderstanding, they passed the antelope, and the opportunity was gone.

The sun was now dropping low in the sky, and David wondered again where they would stop for the night. His attempts to find out were only met by the driver's familiar mantra 'Long drive, long drive.' But then a short while later, seemingly in the middle of nowhere, the man turned to him and said, 'You want pictures of animals, yes? We try this road.' They turned off the main trunk road and onto a rutted mud track that led into bushier vegetation. David felt that as they drove deeper and deeper into wilderness, his chances of an encounter with one of the Big Five were increasing; although the fading light meant that his chances of a decent photo remained small. The truck slowed down to a halt.

'You wait in the truck, please. I see it is safe.' The driver grabbed a rifle from the back and started walking ahead, looking all around him. A bird flew from the bush, but David couldn't see what it was. The driver stopped, turned around to face back at the truck. He raised his rifle, took aim, and shot David through the windscreen.

2

Message: 4 March 2019

Jenny. I'm continuing to observe the birds we spoke about. They don't seem to pose any threat, but I think we should keep the field study going. They don't seem aware that I am watching them, although I've got reasonably close to them, and from time to time I've actually sat amongst them to hear their birdsong and chatter. At the moment this seems to be inconsequential twittering. But I hope to pick up a better understanding of their habits over the next couple of weeks.

Will send further reports. Robin.

That'll do. It's just for another couple of weeks. I deserve a break anyway. And who knows? There may be something in it.

3

Jason Tranter's boss, Malcolm, popped his head round the door.

'Morning, Jason. Small meeting room in ten minutes. Rather important.'

Something about the look on his boss's face made Jason take his feet off the desk. By the time he'd sat up, though, Malcolm had disappeared again. Jason stared at the door as thoughts raced through his head. He couldn't remember ever seeing Malcolm look so serious before. Was today going to be the day Jason had simultaneously been waiting for and dreading? Was he going to be fired? Had he got time to make a coffee?

Jason felt flushed and clammy. The thick ginger beard he'd grown to conceal his blush-prone skin did nothing to hide the fact that the tips of his ears had turned pink. He turned to his array of computer screens and tapped at his keyboard in a nervous torrent. The company website that he managed appeared on the screen. PKR Aerospace—Excellence Through Traction. He clicked through to the Products page, which listed a range of high precision aviation parts; a gallery of gaskets, shaft clamps, flanged bushes and other items that Jason had no idea about. And there, near the bottom of the page, a photo showing three tins of custard.

He keyed in the commands to remove the photo. He'd added it three days ago in response to a dare set by his mates at the pub. It was the latest in a range of random items, starting with a plastic model aeroplane and including at various times a Star Wars action figure, a paddling pool, and a pair of underpants. Until today, Jason had been quietly confident that these rogue items would never be discovered, as hardly anyone ever visited the site. It was confirmation, if he needed it, that his job was pointless.

He walked over to the back of the small office to make himself a drink. A shot of single origin Ethiopian ground coffee might help him stay sharp for whatever Malcolm was about to say to him. He reckoned he could claim that the site had been hacked and that he'd already sorted out the problem. Malcolm would have no way of disputing this. For a Head of Digital Services, he had a very limited understanding of computer networks and web hosting. It didn't matter, because neither did the senior management team. This was a light engineering factory on the outskirts of Wolverhampton. There was a wealth of expertise on sheet metal working, circuit boards and electronic components, but the website was a 'dark art' and left to Malcolm and, by extension, Jason.

Jason had been quick to exploit the situation when he'd joined as a graduate entrant eight years ago. He'd persuaded Malcolm that the smell of metalwork and the sound of drills and lathes was not conducive to the Silicon Valley-style atmosphere they were trying to create. They'd commandeered a couple of small rooms at the top of the factory and, over time, had furnished them with gigantic monitors, padded swivel chairs, a coffee machine and a basketball hoop. The seen-it-all-before engineers and sales managers that ran the company had gone along with it out of a sense of curiosity as much as anything else. But times change.

'Corporate restructuring,' said Malcolm, as soon as they were in the small meeting room. 'Our team axed. Immediate effect. Operation outsourced to an external agency. Not too bad for me—lots of opportunities. Really sorry for you, though, Jason. Twenty-eight days' notice, I'm afraid.'

Jason was used to Malcolm's tendency to speak in phrases rather than sentences, especially when he was feeling awkward. He stared at his boss in disbelief, but not in dismay.

'Is this because of the stuff on the website?' asked Jason. 'Because I think I've tracked down how it is happening...'

'Website fine,' interrupted Malcolm. 'Fantastic, actually. In fact, caught the eye of rival company; their CEO asked our CEO which agency they used. Bingo! Our CEO finds out that there are agencies that can do this stuff cheaper than you and I can. Bit of a shame, really, but there you go. There *we* go.'

Jason felt relieved, but also a bit disappointed his pranks had gone unnoticed. He couldn't even claim bragging rights for sabotaging his own career. His dismissal was down to a chance conversation. It all seemed so random. What was he going to do now?

'Malcolm, I've got thirty days' leave owing to me. I'm not sure how I can squeeze that into twenty-eight days' notice?'

'God, yes. Terrible! Take it all as leave. They've agreed to recompense you for the two days extra.'

'But... I mean, surely you'll want me to do some handover... to someone. Who did you say is taking over our work?'

'Yes. No. Not a problem. Agencies. Better if you just clear your desk today. Really, don't worry. Use the time to get yourself sorted. You'll be fine. Should arrange a drink this evening. People will be sorry to see you go.'

When Jason had started at PKR, the people on the shop floor had viewed him with suspicion, but he'd become popular over the last few years, first with the drawing office, and latterly with some of the engineers. So a few stalwarts re-arranged their evenings to accompany Jason for a drink at The Sunbeam, followed by a curry at The Dosa King. Some even took him up on the offer of a nightcap after that. As they left the last bar, just after midnight, Stuart, his best pal and fellow hipster, had thrown an arm over his shoulder and said in a slurred voice, 'Epic night, Jason!'

The next morning, as he sipped his breakfast coffee, his phone buzzed, his National Lottery app alerting him that tonight's EuroMillions draw was a rollover, with an estimated 150 million pounds jackpot.

'Oh, sugar, the syndicate!' he thought, and reached for his phone to call Dawn, the receptionist at PKR.

'Oh, hello, Jason. Get you — ringing back already! Can't keep away from us, can you? Sorry I couldn't make it out last night, love. Our Tracy's poorly. What is it, love? Have you forgotten something?'

Jason explained he had forgotten to collect all the syndicate's numbers for the week. Graciously, he said that he was happy to carry on running the lottery club, even though he'd left the company, as he had the spreadsheet and the phone app and everything. Besides, it would be a way of keeping in touch.

'Awww! Aren't you a love? That is sweet of you, darling, but no, don't you worry. It's all sorted. "Goods-In" Graham has said he'll do it. It's taken care of, Jason, so you don't have to worry.'

'Oh, okay,' said Jason, trying not to sound snubbed. 'Well, I suppose I could just send my numbers into Graham then. I mean, it's alright me still being in the syndicate, I mean after all...'

'Thing is, Jason, no.' Dawn interrupted. 'We did talk about it, and I didn't see why not, but on the whole, people felt the syndicate should just be for PKR employees. It just starts getting complicated otherwise. You understand, love, don't you?'

4

'Toast is on the table,' Helen called up the stairs. 'Thirty minutes and counting, no screens until you're washed, dressed and fed.' There was no answering sound. 'And you've got to get your bags ready and water bottles filled.' she added. 'It's now less than thirty minutes and you're going to be late.' Two stifled groans finally acknowledged the message.

All the electrical appliances in the kitchen were on the go. The toaster was singeing the final pieces of toast, and the kettle had been boiling for the last three minutes. Its broken thermostat prevented it from automatically cutting-out, and the threat of it boiling dry and burning out the element was a real and present danger. The washing machine started its second spin cycle with a high-pitched wail that meant a bearing was wearing out. Every wash seemed to Helen like an added bonus before the thing finally gave up the ghost and forced her to look for a new second-hand machine. If David had been here, he would have had a go at replacing the bearing. He might have even succeeded, but that wasn't going to happen now. She'd have to lean on her brother, Vincent, for what seemed like the thousandth time since David had died. She wondered how long she could keep imposing on Vincent and his family. Accompanying the screech of the spinning clothes, Helen heard the low-frequency buzz of the electric shower, indicating that one of the boys had made it to the bathroom before his rival. The galloping footsteps coming down the stairs meant that twelve-year-old Luke had lost the race to his fifteen-year-old brother, Brett.

'Get the post, Luke,' Helen called, but not soon enough.

'Sorry,' replied Luke as he entered the room, sat down and grabbed toast in one graceful move.

Helen didn't react. She went into the hall, picked up the post from the mat, and returned to the kitchen, switching off the kettle, which had just boiled dry and now needed filling again. Two bills, an envelope marked 'Crisis! Urgent appeal' and a letter she didn't recognise.

'Your football shirt is in the dryer, don't forget it. What time do you need picking up tonight?'

Luke, with a mouth full of toast, made a noise that suggested he didn't understand the question.

'You've got football tonight and you're having your tea at Ben's. What time am I supposed to pick you up?'

Luke shrugged and held up nine fingers while he chewed toast.

'Eight,' corrected Helen. 'And you need to be ready to leave when I come to pick you up. I'm not hanging about talking to Ben's mum.'

That awful woman. Okay, not really awful, but over-sincere. The way she grabbed Helen's hand, and stared into her eyes while saying how 'truly, truly sorry' she was. That sort of prolonged, invasive eye-contact would have made her feel uncomfortable at the best of times, but a week after David's death, when she had started to see people again, it had made her feel somehow inadequate, as if she was being shown how to 'do grief properly'. Helen found she actually drew more comfort from friends who were a little awkward or shy, because that echoed how she was feeling herself, and it seemed like an acknowledgement that something terrible and momentous had happened, and nothing would ever be the same again. Which felt like the truth. Now, even after five months, Ben's mum was still greeting her with sorrowful, sympathetic, 'poor you' smiles while her other hesitant and embarrassed friends were talking more freely and naturally again.

The two bills were for car insurance and water, and looked impossibly large. David and Helen had never really worried about money; they both worked, they lived simply and there was always enough to get by. Now that she was solely responsible for the family finances, every outgoing expense seemed like a threat. She winced but told herself that there was probably enough, and they'd be alright. The Urgent Crisis Appeal was another matter, though; this time she would have to wait and see. She pinned the unopened envelope to an overloaded cork-board by the fridge and chose to obscure a photo of a half-built building in a rainforest clearing that she didn't want to see again but couldn't bear to tear down from the board.

The half-built building in that photo was the start of a new school in the Kasai region in the Democratic Republic of the Congo. The picture showed workmen adding a bright yellow tin roof to a basic construction of breeze blocks. Looking at it triggered a familiar and painful set of questions and regrets. How had David originally heard about the project? Was it from some friend? She couldn't remember. Why had she and David worked so hard to raise funds at the school where they both taught? They'd raised over fourteen thousand pounds. That was more than any other fundraiser in the school's history. Why couldn't it have been like the annual appeal for school library books and raised a measly fifty quid? Most painful of the questions; why did David decide he had to present the money in person? Here, she at least had an answer. David wanted to make a link between the two schools. It seemed like a way for everyone to benefit. The children in Kasai would get equipment for their school and the pupils of Nebberton would get closer contact with another part of the world and would see that their actions could make a tangible difference. And although dwarfed by those two lofty ideals, the publicity associated with the trip would have done no harm to David's profile and his chances of becoming Head of Department before the age of forty.

As she obscured the photo with the appeal envelope, her thoughts flew back to a time that they had shown it to a neighbour. It was the day when David was packing, and the neighbour had dropped round to lend him a suitcase. 'How proud you must feel!' said the neighbour, and they had vigorously insisted that it was all down to the kids at school and their generous parents. But Helen had caught a glance from her husband and they both instantly knew they were sharing an embarrassingly powerful surge of pride in themselves, their energy, their tenacity, their persuasiveness. His eyes twinkled and his nose wrinkled in the characteristic way it always did when he laughed. That glance, Helen thought, marked the very point when she had loved him most and she had loved him for nearly twenty years.

Their elder son, Brett, came down the stairs and the younger son, Luke, ascended towards the bathroom. They passed wordlessly in the hall. Helen poured a mug of tea for Brett and looked at the remaining letter from the morning's post. The envelope looked official. Her name and address had been printed, but there were no corporate or government logos decorating the envelope. She screwed her eyes up, slit open the envelope, and scanned the letter. It was from her solicitor and suddenly she realised.

'Oh crikey, the estate!'

Sorting out her husband's affairs was always going to take a long time. It had taken seven weeks just to get the officials in the Democratic Republic of Congo to issue a death certificate. That was just the start of the process. Luckily, most of their modest savings were in joint accounts, so she had access to them. But things like his pension took longer to sort out, and, as the solicitor had said, he needed to check whether there were any old building society accounts from his boyhood or premium bonds or things like that. It all took time.

Feeling slightly cheap, Helen scanned the letter for the total figure. It didn't make sense. She had to read the figure several times, and her eyes started to blur. It was... it couldn't be... it said thirteen million, five hundred and something. Thirteen million...!

'The complete and utter bastard!' was all she could say.

It was a couple of hours later when she realised she had indeed misread the letter. Her husband had, in fact, left her one hundred and thirty-five million pounds.

5

It was Friday night, so it was The Pig at Hambourne. Even though it was Jason's local and he could easily walk, tonight was his night to drive. His friends lived a little further away, but they all agreed it was the best pub for miles, so they took it in turns to be 'designated driver'. It wasn't a gastropub; the food was pretty basic, but it was a cosy, friendly bar and the beer, specifically Hank's Best Bitter, was a real craft ale and worth travelling for. He picked Sultan up first. His first words to Jason on climbing into the passenger seat were, 'Well, what is a badger, anyway?' in an accusatory tone. Jason smiled. Some things don't change; this was going to be a good night.

Twenty minutes later and Jason, Sultan and Stuart were sitting around their favourite table, talking rubbish. They stood out from the other regulars in the pub, who were mostly older couples. The three friends were in their early thirties, and the barman, who prided himself on his lack of cultural sensitivity, had nicknamed them 'The Taliban' on account of their all having beards.

'No, man. Honest to God, I had never heard of it. Badger? I honestly thought it was a pervert. Really, I did. I thought it was a name for a type of deviant sexual predator or something. Whoever heard of an animal called a "badger"? I sent the kid to report to the headmaster!' And then, burying his face in the palm of his hand, 'Oh man, what did I do?'

Stuart said, 'Hang on there... you thought a badger was... what?'

'... Yeah, a pervert. Well, I dunno, do I? You know, one of them persuasive sexual predator men.' Sultan grinned as his friends looked incredulously at him. 'I mean, it's a thing, innit? Like, you hear people say "He was badgered into it" or "I've been badgered into doing such-and-such". I dunno, do I?'

'Unbelievable,' said Stuart, shaking his head slowly.

Sultan continued. 'So this kid says, "Sir, your hair looks like a badger's" and I think he's being homophobic or racist, or something. So I sent him to see the headmaster. Ha ha ha! I'll probably get a complaint.'

Sultan had a white streak in his thick black hair, which, combined with his above-average height, added to his striking looks. When people told him he looked like a young Omar Sharif, as older generations frequently did, he stared at them hard and said he didn't know who that was. Then he would give a smile that made him look exactly like Omar Sharif. Some people would ask him about his ethnicity, again it always seemed to be older people who were interested in this, and he would ask them to guess. Most would tentatively suggest he was Asian, but he delighted in telling them he was born in Canada. He claimed he had run away from home in Northern Alberta to come to the West Midlands.

Neither Stuart nor Jason believed that Sultan had grown up in Canada. Nor did they believe he didn't know what a badger was. He was a maths teacher; a good one by all accounts, and part of his classroom shtick was to appear ignorant about everything, except maths. Pulling apart one of Sultan's wild stories or outrageous opinions was traditional fare for a Friday night at The Pig. Despite this, Jason was itching to tell Sultan the news about his redundancy. 'So.....', he said loudly, and paused for dramatic effect.

'What you up to then, Stu?' Sultan asked, deliberately taking the wind out of Jason's sails.

Of the three of them, it could be said that Stuart had the most significant beard. Longer and more unkempt, it was really the defining feature of his appearance. Sultan's beard came and went; he had one of those faces that you had to think really hard about to remember whether or not he even had a beard. Jason's beard was part of an overall set of features that combined to make a 'tall Scottish-looking guy', but Stuart was more frequently described as 'that bloke with the beard.' He was into gadgets and photography and combined the two hobbies into an occasionally lucrative side-line; aerial drone photography. Tomorrow, Stuart was invited to be a wedding photographer. His clients were getting married at two thousand feet above the ground in a hot-air balloon. Stuart was to use his remote-controlled drone to fly next to the balloon and capture the big event from a unique vantage point.

Jason asked whether his remote control drone would have the necessary range. A hot-air balloon can move pretty fast and pretty unpredictably. Might it not suddenly be a couple of miles away and out of range?

'No, that's it. I'm going to be operating the drone from inside the hot-air balloon basket with the couple. So cool.'

'Cool?' queried Sultan. 'I'm imagining the wedding video. Romantic music, panoramic views. We see the majestic shape of the hot-air balloon. We close up on the basket and we see the beautiful bride, the dashing groom, the minister or whoever is actually marrying them, and Stuart, his tongue sticking out in concentration, wiggling his little joystick, operating the drone camera. Well, that will be one for the couple to treasure!'

'I'll actually be hiding down in the basket, not visible to the camera. I can operate the drone without seeing it—I'll be seeing what the camera sees.' But Stuart's explanation struck Jason and Sultan as even more ridiculous and they rocked back on their chairs, laughing. The hilarity attracted the attention of a woman who was sitting on a stool by the corner bar and who, up till now, had been distracting two regulars playing darts.

'Hey Sarah. You've got to hear this' Sultan said as she walked over to join them. So the breaking of Jason's news was put on hold once more while Stuart's plans for the weekend were recounted again. Then Sultan found a way of re-introducing his badger story for Sarah's further amusement.

Sarah was a year or two older than the three friends. To say that she was a regular at The Pig was to do justice to the word. She was there every night. She always arrived alone but knew everyone and always found herself someone to talk to. Somehow this made the three young men slightly wary of

Sarah, as if she was slightly louche; the sort of woman their mothers wouldn't approve of. But Sarah didn't drink much, and always went home alone to her flat a few doors away. They supposed Sarah just found the pub and its customers more entertaining than being alone in front of the television. She enjoyed Sultan's story.

Jason cleared his throat to gain attention so that he could finally announce his news about being made redundant, but Sultan, sensing the opportunity to wind Jason up, didn't give him the chance. 'This drone then, Stuart. You allowed to fly it next to a balloon? I thought that there were rules about drones and aircraft and stuff. Like that Gatwick Airport business.' Gatwick Airport had been in the news the previous year because sightings of nearby drones had forced the airport to close temporarily, just in case there was a terrorist threat. Stuart leaned in and whispered conspiratorially. Apparently flying a drone at a height of a thousand feet, which would be the likely altitude of the balloon ride, wasn't strictly legal, but the balloon pilot was cool with it, as long as Stuart kept the drone well away from the balloon.

Sarah looked concerned. 'I don't know, Stuart. It's dangerous, I reckon. And it's a criminal offence to endanger the safety of an aircraft in flight.'

The tip of Stuart's nose blushed a deep red. 'I won't endanger... it's not dangerous... it's only a small one.'

'Easy, pal,' said Sultan. 'I bet you say that to all the ladies. Eh, Stu?' He turned to Jason at last. 'So, what about you, mate? What you doing this weekend?'

'Well, I've been made redundant!'

Sultan stared for a moment, but didn't look surprised. 'Now that is cool,' he said.

Half an hour later and Jason was standing alone outside the pub in the car park. It was getting stuffy in the pub and the questions about what he was going to do with his time were making him feel uncomfortable. At one time, this would have been a fag break. Jason didn't smoke anymore but didn't see why that should stop him from taking himself out of situations from time to time and just standing outside in the cool night air.

His pocket buzzed, and he reached for his phone. There was a notification from his lottery app.

'Christ! I've won,' he thought. The notification read 'Congratulations! You are a Lottery Winner!' He swiped it to find out how much he had won. His eyes scanned the page that came up but couldn't see the amount anywhere. In the past, he'd won a fiver a couple of times and once, the night-changing sum of forty-eight pounds, but this screen looked different. He read the words instead of scanning, 'You must ring this number as soon as it's safe to claim your jackpot total.' He spoke the last three words out loud.

There was a flutter in his chest now. This was a decent win, more than a hundred, more than a grand maybe. He'd have to share it with the syndicate... except he wouldn't, because they'd thrown him out of the syndicate. Oh, this was sweet. He wasn't sure he wanted to ring the number there and then. He could savour this feeling a bit more. But he knew he couldn't go back into the pub and tell Stu and Sultan he'd won the lottery without knowing how much.

Fifteen minutes later, and the bar seemed noisier than when he'd left it, and everyone seemed a little more drunk.

'Oh, you still here then? Sarah got you a coke,' Sultan said. They were nearly at the end of their pints. 'Think it's your round, next Jason. You alright, mate? You look weird.'

Jason felt weird. He knew he was smiling. He knew he couldn't stop smiling, but his eyes were burning and strangely on the edge of tears.

'Yeah, good. Thanks Sarah, Um... just had some good news.' His voice was cracked and high-pitched.

'No! They taken you back on?' asked Stuart.

Jason's mind raced. This was a turning-point moment. He'd won the jackpot. *The* jackpot. They couldn't confirm the total figure yet, but the estimated figure was.... well... He didn't want publicity; he knew that. He wasn't sure why, but he just didn't want everyone to know. Not yet. Still, he had to tell someone. He had to tell Stuart and Sultan. And Sarah, as he guessed he couldn't really ask her to leave the table.

'I've just won on the lottery!' he said with a lowered voice. 'I can't believe it. But I bloody have, though. Don't know how much quite, but it's good, it's more than... a hundred grand.' The figure was whispered, partly because Jason didn't want to be overheard and partly as an involuntary reaction, because it was a lie. Okay, not exactly a lie; the figure the woman from the lottery had mentioned was indeed more than a hundred grand. Much, much more. And although Jason wanted his friends to share in this brilliant, breathtaking news, something inside wouldn't let him share the full extent of this life-changing win. Not yet.

Sultan and Stuart took some convincing, even of the lower figure.

'Lying bastard!'

But something about Jason's nervous restlessness and tightened vocal chords rang true.

'Drinks for everyone, then?' suggested Sultan.

'Look, I'm just not sure yet, right? The woman from the lottery... I spoke to her... it's a shared prize. They don't know how much yet exactly.' It wasn't a shared prize. He was the sole ticket holder on a rollover week. 'I'm just going to go easy for now, till I find out properly.' He paused and shuffled on his seat. He lifted his coke to his lips and put it down again. 'Sod it, we'll get taxis tonight. I need a drink.'

With fresh pints in front of them, the talk turned inevitably to the effect of sudden changes of fortune on the lifestyle of a young, single male.

'Go travelling, mate,' was Sultan's advice. 'The world is your lobster. I'd hit it big time.'

'Definitely, America,' said Jason 'And Europe, of course. Not sure really, I'll have to think about it.'

'What about new wheels? You've got to get new wheels.' Stuart suggested.

'Maybe. But not day one. Cars aren't my thing.'

'What is your thing, Jason?' Sarah's voice was steadier, calmer than the others. Jason noticed she wasn't forcing suggestions on him, and he was grateful for the space to think.

'You know, that's what I'm going to have to think about. I really don't know. I'm going to have to think hard about it. It'll be great to have money, but at the moment, to be honest, I think I'm feeling a bit overwhelmed. I have this stupid feeling that as soon as I start spending, it will all disappear. It's mental, but the only thing that keeps popping into my head is something that I've always wanted but never thought I'd have enough money that I could afford to waste it on... but I am. I'm going to get a seriously good coffee machine.'

They laughed.

'That's it! Tech!' Stuart was enthusiastic again. 'Gadgets! All of them. That's what I'd do. I'd get a house full of the best gear. Computers, music systems, TVs, cameras, stuff! Everything!'

'Yeah, but it's not about stuff though, is it Stuart?' Sarah interrupted. 'It's what you do with your life. It's about opportunities. That's what Jason needs to think about. What does he want to do in the world? Like Sultan said, the world is his... "lobster". You could start your own business, Jason. Anything. Give it all away to a good cause, train to be something different, whatever you like. It's up to you, isn't it? Take your time to decide.'

6

Jason had to wait until Monday to meet the Lottery Winners' advisor. It was all explained to him during the trembling phone-call in The Pig car park on Friday night. The lottery company would send their representative to visit him at his home, but it needed to be done on Monday when the banks were open. He'd need to have two forms of identification ready so that they could open a private bank account. The advisor could bring some money with them if he needed some urgently, but Jason had said that he didn't need any. The lady on the phone call said that in that case, all he had to do was sit tight until the meeting on the Monday and write his name and address on the back of the winning ticket and keep it in a safe place. Jason pointed out that he didn't have a winning ticket; he had played the lottery through an app on his phone. The lady laughed and said that was perfectly fine.

Now, back at his house in Hambourne, Jason had already forgotten most of the details of that call. It worried him that he didn't have an actual lottery ticket and he printed out a screenshot from his phone, just to be safe. He found his passport and his driving licence, and put them with his printed ticket and his phone on the table by his bed. He told himself that those few things were the proof he needed, that he had indeed won the lottery, and he was who he said he was. They were safe by his bed; he could reach out and touch them. But were they really safe? If someone else got hold of them, could that person claim they were Jason Tranter? He couldn't quite see how they could, not unless they looked like the photos in his passport and on his driving licence. But hang on! He didn't think he looked like those photos himself anymore, not since the beard. This triggered another worry. If necessary, he would shave off his beard. He checked he had his razor, loaded it with a fresh blade and added it to the collection of items essential to proving his identity. These were too important now to just sit on his bedside table, so he hid them in his sock drawer. Then he remembered hearing that the sock drawer was the first place burglars looked in a house for valuables. He put the items into a plastic bag and put them in the freezer compartment of his fridge, but then worried that his phone would stop working and quickly retrieved them. He was being stupid. No-one was going to break into his house. No-one knew about his lottery win except Sultan, Stuart and Sarah, and he could trust them; he'd known them for years. Well, Stuart and Sultan anyway.

He thought about Sarah. He didn't really know much about her. Conversation in The Pig rarely delved into people's personal lives. They talked rubbish mostly; jokes, films, music, computers and gadgets. Sarah always played the rôle of the outsider to the group, indulging their geekiness, sometimes faintly mocking them. Jason realised he knew nothing about Sarah's own interests, or her job, or her background, or family, or anything. Despite that, he instinctively felt he could trust her. But what if she let his news slip out to anyone else?

He passed the night with these worries dancing and multiplying in his head interspersed with alternate periods of dozing and staring fixedly at his passport, driving licence, ticket, phone and razor. It was only in the morning that he realised he hadn't thought once during the entire night about how he might enjoyably spend his fortune.

When he finally rose and prepared his morning coffee, he remembered how, in the pub last night, the only thing he could think of on his wish list was a fancy coffee machine. His head felt clearer now. He put his passport, driving licence and ticket into a zip-up pocket and went into Birmingham. Jason spent his Saturday shopping for a fully automatic "bean to cup" coffee machine. He found a specialist shop with an agreeable, attentive assistant who demonstrated a few different models and let Jason taste the results. He opted for a top-of-the-range machine that even had a screen which showed impressive looking graphs as the steam built up the required pressure to force the hot water through the coffee. It delivered the best-tasting espresso he'd had in his life and he was careful to buy exactly the same variety of bean, with the same roast, as well as a few other bags of coffee for variety. After getting everything back home, he set up the machine, played with the settings, and tasted the results. He couldn't quite get the same sublime taste he'd experienced in the shop, but it was pretty good.

Glancing at the clock, he was shocked to see how late it was. That night, he slept surprisingly well, considering the amount of caffeine he had on board.

Jason visited his parents on Sunday, something he did most Sundays. Today, it immediately struck him how old-fashioned and meagre everything seemed. Nothing much had changed in that house since he'd left home for college over ten years ago, but it suddenly felt like a museum to him. An old arrangement of dried flowers stood by the phone on a hall table. In the kitchen there was a shelf with a neat array of labelled jars containing decanted groceries: muesli, flour, rice, dried pasta. The cupboards contained the same products it had done all those years ago. Change was not encouraged in the Tranter household. Jason remembered an episode from his childhood when he'd read a book which described a cool American kid raving over 'milk and cookies'. It sounded like the most sublime treat ever. He'd asked his mum if she could get some cookies, so they could try them. He remembered being taken aback by his mother's cruel laugh. 'We don't have cookies in this house, Jason. "Cookie" is just American for "biscuit". We have biscuits in this house. Digestive biscuits because they're good for your digestion. You can try them with milk if you like, but don't dunk them. You won't like it if your biscuit goes soggy and drops in your milk.'

Jason didn't mention the coffee machine or the lottery win. His parents were mildly concerned to hear that he had lost his job, but it wasn't their habit to enquire much about their son's life. Jason sometimes wondered if he was a disappointment to them.

On Sunday night, he had a phone call from Stuart. 'Are you okay, mate?'

'Yeah, fine thanks,' answered Jason, impressed that his friend was taking time to check. 'It's all a bit weird, but yeah... fine.'

'Cool. Right, I'll come right out with it then. I'm on the scrounge.'

'Oh, bloody hell, Stuart! Now look...'

'Listen, Jason, it's not what you think. It's business. The drone photography.'

'Oh, yes, how did the balloon wedding go yesterday?'

'Well, that's it. It had its good points and bad points. I got good shots, really impressive actually, especially as the wind was gusty and it was a bit of a bumpy ride at times. Bad points? The landing was bloody awful. We were dragged in the basket at high speed across a field of cabbages or something. The smell was something rotten. And what with that, the turbulence earlier on, and the fact that I was still a little hung over from Friday night, I threw up, didn't I? All over the drone. It's buggered.'

'Oh, Stuart! What about the bride and groom?'

'They saw the funny side, thankfully. They've got their pictures. I avoided getting any sick on her dress. They're well pleased. The balloon guy, too. He was dead impressed... with the drone, I mean. He said he's got another wedding next weekend and asked me if I can join him. So there you go. I need a new drone for next weekend. My credit card's maxed out, or I wouldn't ask, mate. It's only a loan...'

Jason agreed. He knew that Stuart's photography was a big deal for him. He'd often talked about quitting PKR one day and turning his hobby into a career. Jason wanted to help him, if he could. But he also thought to himself, 'Only three people know about my win, and I'm already being tapped up. I'm telling no-one else.'

The Lottery Winners' advisor arrived promptly on Monday morning. To many people, travelling the country handing out fortunes to lucky people would seem like a perfect job, spreading happiness wherever you go. Gwen was the wrong person for the job. She spoke with the enthusiasm of someone who had been on the road for five hours, travelling up the M1 and M6, in nose-to-tail traffic past Birmingham in the morning rush hour, to arrive in Hambourne for a ten o'clock meeting.

'Well, Jason, this is the five hundredth time I've made someone a millionaire and I can honestly say that this time is just as exciting as the first. Having looked at your proof of identification, I can confirm that you are a lucky lottery winner. Let's have a look at the final total for you... so that's one hundred and fifty-three million pounds, two hundred and fifteen... bloody hell that is a big one... two hundred and fifteen thousand, seven hundred and thirty pounds and seventeen pence. Well, Jason, it's not my biggest, but it's up there.'

Jason had imagined that she'd have brought champagne with her, but none seemed forthcoming. He felt obliged to make her a cup of coffee while she started unpacking a laptop and sheaves of paperwork. Time to show off the fully automatic 'bean to cup' coffee machine.

'To be honest, Jason, a milky instant will do me.'

They spent the next two hours trying to connect Gwen's laptop to the internet and creating a new bank account for Jason. She explained that this was just a temporary deposit account. She gave him a list of private banks and wealth advisors and recommended that he selected one and get in touch as soon as he could. 'They're all good on that list. St John's, Delta, Ensignia, P&Q. So really just pick one you like the sound of and go with that. If it were me, I'd go with Pitt's, cos it just makes me think of Brad Pitt, but that's just me. I'm not allowed to advise you in any way.'

Finally, she was finished, and she packed up her laptop and papers. 'I'll just say this Jason, I think you're doing the right thing. About the publicity, I mean. The world is full of scrounging bastards and you're best to get shot of them. Now, you won't hear from me again. I just wish you all the very best.'

Jason thought it was the only time she had made eye contact throughout the entire session, and he found himself touched by the sincerity of the wish. Her expression was more of pity than of congratulation.

Left alone, Jason felt both deflated and elated at the same time. The visit had been an anticlimax; no champagne, no outsized cheque, no fanfares, just Gwen's rather lacklustre monologue and a lot of form filling. On the other hand, it was now sinking in that he now had an enormous amount of money. An unimaginably enormous amount, in fact, and he thrilled to its possibilities. Random images flashed through his head; fast cars, flash clothes, beautiful women, exotic places, expensive hotels. He wasn't sure that was quite the world he wanted, but it might be nice to try it. He also thought, more nobly, about the good he could do with his money. It was pleasant to imagine himself becoming a Bill Gates-type philanthropist. He was certain only of one thing; that his decision to avoid publicity was the right one. It wasn't that he was wary of Gwen's 'scrounging bastards'. It was more that he didn't want things to move too fast. For as long as possible, he wanted to stay as Jason Tranter. He didn't want to be defined by his fortune. Not yet.

7

'I'm sorry, Brian, I'm going to say it. She killed him. I always knew she would. We both knew it. I always said that woman was trouble from the moment he brought her home. It was the fault of that blasted university. I say 'university'... Middlesex. It's a polytechnic; I don't care what they call it. A hotbed of socialists. When David left Wellington, he was a wonderful, respectable boy and within weeks of being at that place, he'd hooked up with all kinds of I-don't-know-what sort of people. You shouldn't have let him go, Brian. It's your fault, really. I said all along that he should retake his 'A' Levels and go to a proper university, but no, you were happy for him to traipse off to Middlesex and waste his time studying geo-politics or some nonsense. He'd have been better off not going to university at all. I said at the time, "Why go to university anyway, when you've got a perfectly good job waiting for you in the family firm?" He wasn't thick, after all. You'd have found him something at the firm. He could have learnt the ropes. But Middlesex? It wasn't suitable at all. They let anyone in there. Do you know who went to Middlesex University? I'll tell you who went to Middlesex University. Alan Carr, that's who. The one off the television. Yes... that one. But that's not the half of it. They have people from all over, and David just wasn't used to people from those circles. I mean, there were boarders at school who came from overseas, of course, and I'm sure they were perfectly nice. But I doubt if David had even so much as talked to an Ethnic Person before going to Middlesex. When he phoned home to say that he'd met a girl called Helen, well, I just naturally assumed... I mean, you do, don't you? But it's not that, you know it's not. Nigel, Katie, you know I'm no more racist than... anyone. Live and let live. But I could see through her. Oh, she may have talked about "diversity" and "equal rights" but she was sniffing out money alright, take it from me. She knew she was onto a good thing with David. He didn't flaunt his money, did he, Brian? Quite the opposite. He seemed almost ashamed of it, the clothes he wore, that dreadful flat he took with her and her friends in the second year — appalling! Oh, Katie, if you could have seen it, it would have made you shiver. But she knew all along that she was onto a good thing with David. We warned him, didn't we, Brian? We said "It's your choice, David, but we won't support you if you go on mixing with that sort". But he didn't listen, Nigel. Boys don't listen, do they? Next thing we knew, she was pregnant. Can you believe it? I was furious. That was the last time he had any money from us, wasn't it, Brian? "No!" I said. "You've made your bed, you can bloody well lie in it!". You think I was being unkind, Katie, but I was just trying to show him the mistake he'd made. He should have left her and her baby and come back to us, where he belonged. She'd have thought nothing of being a single mother — they're all at it. But he stuck with her, bringing up a baby in their final year at college. Ridiculous! And then, of course, the next thing we know is they're applying to be teachers. I think that was the final straw. We hardly spoke after that. It was just too awkward, do you see? She'd changed him. I think we were an embarrassment to him, with our nice home and comfortable lifestyle. They took on some pokey little semi-detached house in Luton, or Bedford, or somewhere. I've never been there, but you went, didn't you, Brian? I couldn't have borne to see David struggling like that. We decided to lay down an olive branch and offer them a way out. We would set them up here, in the village, nice house, job with the firm, but they threw it back in our faces. Said they were happy where they were leading their own lives, "giving something back to society". As if a career in packaging isn't giving something to society! People need cardboard boxes, Nigel. Even the homeless people end up sleeping on cardboard boxes sometimes. But no, teaching was their thing. "Do-gooders", that's what they were. Holier than thou. It makes me cross. And they weren't content with helping our own. They had to start helping people in Africa, of course. Well, I suppose they were helping her own. So David goes over to Africa and gets himself shot. My boy. My lovely boy.

'I'm sorry, Nigel. Sorry Katie. This is the first time we've had anyone... since... it's been six months now and I thought I was getting better, but I'll never get over it, never. Oh dear! There. That's better. I really am so sorry. Brian, top up Nigel and Katie's drinks and I'll pop into the kitchen and bring out desserts. There's a Tarte Tatin, and a Pina Colada Cheesecake that's rather fun.'

8

As far as Sultan, Stuart and Sarah were concerned, Jason had won two hundred thousand pounds. That was what he eventually told them, and to a certain extent, that was what he told himself. The actual figure was too much for his mind to cope with, whereas a notional fortune of two hundred thousand was enough to explain why he wasn't desperate to look for a new job, why he had a swanky new coffee machine, and why he might change his lifestyle modestly. Modesty was an idea that Jason clung to for the moment, without really understanding why.

Sultan thought Jason could do better than modest changes, particularly regarding his clothes.

'You dress like shit, bro. Seriously,' was his judgement.

Jason didn't argue. 'I do want to buy a couple of decent suits, actually. I thought I might go into Birmingham –'

'Suits?' interrupted Stuart 'You're a man of leisure, now! You don't need suits!'

'Yeah, but what I'm thinking is that I might do my own start-up, — don't ask me what. Web design, consultancy, I really don't know. But I thought it might be cool to go to some trade fairs, see what other people are doing, get some ideas. And I'd want to look the part.'

'Don't go to Birmingham. I know a tailor in Dudley that will do you proud, mate. Trust me.' Sultan always knew someone, and in this instance, his advice paid off nicely. A couple of weeks later, Jason had three made-to-measure suits he was really pleased with. After one fitting he popped next door to an old-fashioned barbers, and came out with a haircut and beard trim that looked like something fresh off the pages of a men's lifestyle monthly, rather than from the Readers' Photos page of Survivalist Magazine. Jason really looked the part of a young internet entrepreneur, and he loved the fact that he had achieved this look in Dudley.

Jason's real motivation for wanting to smarten up was that he had arranged an appointment at the private bank he had chosen in London. He'd spent a couple of days scouring the websites of all the private banks on the list Gwen had given him. At the end of the exercise he was none the wiser and was close to going with Pitt's Bank, but he couldn't bear the thought that Gwen could take credit for the decision and worried that she might get some unethical kick-back so instead chose the bank one higher on the list: Perry's on the Strand.

Four weeks after his lottery win, Jason took the train down to London to visit his private bank and talk to his wealth advisor. He decided to travel light. It would spoil the effect of his smart suit to carry a scruffy rucksack. He didn't have a smart briefcase, and he didn't know what he would carry in one, anyway. All he carried were his wallet and his new phone, with which he was very pleased. Along with the suits and the coffee machine, it was one of the few significant purchases he had made since his win. It was all he needed to entertain himself on the journey. He had films, podcasts and music to listen to, but on the way to the station he suddenly became nervous about using up all the charge on his phone too early in the day; he was going to need it to navigate him to Perry's on the Strand, so he didn't dare use it on the outward journey.

So despite the novelty of a comfortable, quiet, spacious, almost empty, first class carriage, Jason was bored. He jealously eyed the one other passenger in the carriage, a young man across the aisle, leafing through a copy of *GQ* magazine. 'Surely too young to be travelling first class,' Jason thought. Something in his magazine was making the young lad smile to himself. The smile irritated Jason, who felt annoyed that this youngster, still bearing the remnants of teenage acne, looked more comfortable than he did in a first class carriage. He felt the urge to let this young Herbert know who was who. It was the first time since winning the lottery that he had wanted to flaunt his millions, but he couldn't quite think how to do it. And then again, it struck him that there was something about the way he had come into his fortune, by winning it on the lottery, that was ever so slightly demeaning. Presumably, this puppy-faced, erstwhile teenager was riding first class on the back of an impressive job in the City, probably a better position than Jason had managed in his own career. Perhaps aware that he was being stared at, the young man looked up from his magazine, and Jason turned his head as nonchalantly as he could, to avoid eye contact.

GQ wasn't a magazine that Jason would normally read, but he was delighted when the train pulled up at Coventry Station and the young man got up to go, leaving the magazine on the seat. Jason jumped up with indecent haste as soon as his adversary had left the carriage, seized the magazine, and settled back to read an illustrated appraisal of the ten best dressed couples at the Cheltenham Festival this year. A short while later, to Jason's horror, the youth returned from the buffet car carrying a coffee and a croissant. He looked at Jason, reading his magazine, and smiled condescendingly.

Jason stammered, 'Oh, sorry, I thought...'

'It's okay' said the man-boy, annoyingly. 'Read on. I'd finished.'

Jason stared at the pages and started flicking through them without reading. He was glad that his beard hid his flushed cheeks. When he had calmed down, he started making sense of the article in front of him. It was a piece about the top ten, must-have spy gadgets. There were listening devices, tracking devices, devices for jamming listening and tracking devices, and camera drones. Jason recognised the model that he'd helped Stuart buy a fortnight ago.

Perry's Bank on The Strand was a venerable institution, tracing its roots back to the coffee shops and trading houses of the eighteenth century, but the facade it presented to Jason today, as he stood across the street, was a modern concoction of glass and steel. He decided he liked the overall impression of the building. It was much larger than his old high street bank in Dudley, and that, he felt, was appropriate for a serious private bank. The steel frame that supported the panels of blue-grey glass looked sturdy and substantial. The design spoke of openness and modernity. Perry's logo, etched into the glass above the door, was discrete and stylish. This was a bank that chimed with Jason's millionaire-hipster credentials. 'Oh, man!' he thought, as he crossed the road and saw a vast atrium behind the glass frontage. 'Trees. And a waterfall? Really?'

Entering the bank through the revolving glass door, Jason could hear the water crashing down ten metres from a ledge in the internal stone wall to a small pool, under-lit by powerful spotlights. The waterfall dominated the whole of the left-hand side of the hall. It was framed by two indoor trees and a cluster of tropical plants, surrounding the pool. In contrast, on the opposite side of the hall was a single reception desk, behind which sat a smart woman in a pin-stripe suit. The shine on her blonde hair and her flawless make-up stood out to Jason, who had never seen anyone so meticulously turned-out, not even in the pages of *GQ* magazine. At the moment, she was talking to a young man, who leant over the desk towards her in an over-familiar way that seemed inappropriate to Jason. The receptionist didn't seem to mind though, and she laughed as she handed the young man a pass card. As he turned and made his way to the lifts, Jason saw the youngster's face and felt a sudden nausea as he recognised him as the annoying man-boy from the train, whose magazine he'd inelegantly pinched. Jason looked down at his shoes, but not quickly enough to miss a moment's eye contact, which told him that the boy had recognised him too.

How bizarre that the man he'd shared a carriage with from Wolverhampton should work at this very bank! Jason didn't like it at all. He thought how typical it was that after that mix-up with the magazine, the fates would conspire to double his embarrassment. Oh well, perhaps it would provide an amusing story for The Pig.

'Good afternoon Sir, can I help you?' The receptionist's voice brought his attention back.

'Hi, I'm Jason Tranter. I have an appointment.' He had to raise his voice to be heard over the waterfall.

'Ah yes sir, an appointment with Mr Richards. Very good. Mr Smethwick will show you to Mr Richards' office.'

Mr Smethwick appeared, genie-like, from a door just behind the desk. A short, stocky man, in his mid-fifties, he had close-cut, dark, curly hair that showed faint tinges of ginger, especially around his sideburns. He wore a smart, dark blue jacket with gold braiding on the cuffs and lapels. He had a deep, smoker's voice with a hint of a London accent.

'Mr Tranter, sir? Pleasure to meet you. The name is Smethwick. Just this way, sir.' Smethwick's twinkling blue eyes weighed up Tranter as he gestured towards the lift. 'Your first appointment, is it, sir? Up in London for the day, is it?'

'Er, yes,' replied Jason, wondering how much personal information the bank's doorman had access to. How did he know it was a first appointment? And how did he know he didn't live in London? Did all the staff here have free access to personal information? Even the man-boy? If so, he didn't think much of private banking. Jason felt apprehensive as Smethwick led him to a waiting area facing a row of five offices, all with closed doors.

'You're in safe hands with Richards, sir. Very capable hands, I should say. I'm no expert myself sir, but if I know Richards at all, he'll have you fixed up with a mixed portfolio comprising equities, fixed interest securities and a selection of off-plan property investments in no time at all. But as I say, I'm no expert myself. Now I think he's just finishing some business, so if you wouldn't mind just taking a seat. May I get you a cup of tea or a coffee, sir?'

Jason accepted the offer of a coffee, thinking it would be an excellent test; he had certain expectations of a private bank, and a cup of instant coffee would fall well short of those. The questionable taste of a waterfall in the lobby, and the apparent indiscretion of the doorman, were making him doubt the wisdom of choosing Perry's. He was reassured, though, by the arrival of a full-bodied espresso with a velvety, golden crema.

Jason savoured his coffee and took in the surroundings. He noticed that the office door that he was waiting in front of had a sign saying 'Richards' and nothing more. No 'Mr' or initial, just 'Richards'. Perhaps it was some old-school banking tradition, thought Jason, but he noticed that none of the other offices in the row had such stark labels. 'Mr B. Jones', for example, not only had his name but also a job title, 'Senior Client Manager'. Richards' door opened, and Jason heard the tail end of a conversation. A loud, impatient voice was saying '... So I expect I'll see you out there, young man. Now, we'll close it there; I have a gentleman waiting to see me.'

Jason stood up suddenly, spilling the cup onto his suit trousers as he did so. Jason let out a yelp of pain, which doubled as an expression of surprise. The person leaving the office was, humiliatingly, the man-boy. He left the office with a confident walk, looking like he owned the place and, noticing the growing coffee stain on Jason's trousers, gave an irritating smirk.

Richards approached Jason with a businesslike, polite smile, extending his hand in welcome. He was a tall man with fantastic hair. Jason was aware of strong, well-manicured hands and a subtle hint of cologne. A brief smile matched the perfect white of his shirt. 'Richards. Welcome to Perry's. How unfortunate! Smethwick, can you get Mr Tranter something to sponge his trousers, please? Please, sit down, Mr Tranter, if that's comfortable. Let me just get your file.' His voice was rich and sonorous, like an actor's.

Jason took his seat on a comfortable black leather chair and took the time to regard Richards' hair. Jason appreciated good barbering, and this was exceptional. Thick and dark with silvery streaks, it swept in natural waves that looked incapable of ever being out of place. It framed a serious-looking face, with a strong jawline and a distinctly prominent nose. The overall impression was that of a model you might see in a business advert on an airport wall.

Smethwick re-appeared with a selection of wipes and towels to deal with the spilt coffee. Despite the discomfort and embarrassment of his wet trousers, Jason felt re-assured again.

Richards was a commanding presence; he embodied the word 'executive', and Jason felt in awe of him. Jason recognised that, deep down, he needed to feel this level of respect for his private banker. It felt like the proper way of things.

Richards found Jason's file and scanned it quickly. He put it down and looked hard at Jason for a few seconds before speaking. 'Mr Tranter, as I was saying, welcome to Perry's. We're very pleased to have you as a customer. I don't need to tell you that you are an extremely wealthy man, and I can see that this amount of money will be rather new to you. Do you have any plans regarding what you would like to do with your money?'

It was a question that he should have been prepared for but wasn't, and now he found himself making up an answer on the spot. 'I'm in the early stages of establishing a new start-up business,' he said, repeating the lie he'd told Sultan and Stuart. 'Technology,' he added, lamely.

'Ah, very interesting. Which area?' Richards asked, leaning forward.

'Security, surveillance, drones,' Jason's voice rose higher. 'Who am I trying to kid?' he thought. He cleared his throat and said, 'I haven't totally decided yet, Mr Richards. To be honest, all I've done is help a mate out by buying a couple of drones with cameras. I haven't told hardly anyone about my money yet. I'm overwhelmed by it all, to be honest. But while I'm coming to terms with it all, I want to make sure that the money is safely invested, if you understand me?'

'I think I do understand you, Mr Tranter. I think I do. I think you are wise not to tell people about your circumstances. The sort of wealth that you find yourself with brings with it concerns about one's personal security. One is suddenly a target for every kind of thief, fraudster, or kidnapper. Be on your guard, Mr Tranter. Trust no-one!' Richards paused, and stared silently at Jason for another few moments, as if to make sure his words had sunk in. He started again, this time speaking quickly. 'Now, if I understand you correctly, you require a discrete set of instruments to protect a structured portfolio of assets. Whilst you have a low appetite for speculative risk, you want to ensure that your capital is employed advantageously by making full use of our high-touch investment engineers. I assume you want to minimise your fiscal liabilities as far as can be achieved within a compliant prevailing framework? Of course you do. Who wouldn't? But my question, Mr Tranter, is this: what degree of liquidity do you require? How much exposure to equities in preference to bonds?'

'Er.. I don't know. I mean I....'

Richards leant in across the desk and lowered his voice. 'Of course you don't know, Mr Tranter. You have literally no idea, do you? I could be talking a different language to you, couldn't I? You've come into what I expect you call a "shed-load" of money and you have absolutely no idea what to do with it.' He relaxed and sat back again. 'But don't worry, Mr Tranter. You are not alone. Most of my clients are exactly the same as you. The difference is that they think they know what they want. I have a little test, you see. I'll spout out some financial jargon just like I did a moment ago. Some people will pretend they understand. Some will even come back with their own jargon, trying to impress me! They think they already know what's best for them and they are almost always wrong. I have a devil of a time just preventing them from blowing their entire fortunes. It's perfectly reasonable that you don't know what you want to do with your money, and there is no need for you to rush into any decisions. We can ensure that you have a comfortable income without unnecessarily eating into your... substantial... capital. Then, when you do make up your mind about which direction you'd like to go, I can help you do that efficiently. Whether you want to pursue your idea of an aerial surveillance company, which I think is a very good idea, by the way – just the right time, I think – or whether you decide to live a life of idle luxury, whilst growing your fortune still further through a range of investments, or whether you want to find a way for distributing your wealth to philanthropic causes, or do a combination of all of those things, Perry's can help you.'

Richards paused for a while and looked at Jason with a concerned expression. Jason felt prompted to say something, but wasn't sure what. Before he formulated any words, Richards continued. 'You may be wondering whether you've selected the right bank in Perry's? I imagine it was a hard decision, if you know absolutely nothing about finance. I mean, how would you judge? Absolutely no frame of reference. All I can say is you just have to trust that you've made the right choice. Look at me and decide whether you can trust me. I'm afraid you really can't do any more than that. Do you trust me, Mr Tranter?' he said, leaning forward over the desk.

Jason found himself saying 'I do' and afterwards wasn't sure whether he'd been intimidated into saying it or whether he actually did trust this larger-than-life personality. There was the hair. He trusted the hair.

'Excellent! That makes all the difference. You won't live to regret it, Mr Tranter. This business idea of yours... you say that you have a friend that operates these surveillance drones? Well, the thing to do would be to set up a limited company, employ him and let him take care of things. Stay out of the day-to-day stuff, Mr Tranter, but keep a lookout for ways to develop and expand... if that's what you want to do. I have colleagues here who can take you through all the paperwork. You'll be surprised how effortless it is, and it will hardly impact your capital. Have a think about it. In the meantime, we must make sure that capital is working for you.' And then quickly in a lower voice, 'The value of your portfolio can go up and down, an income is not guaranteed, and you may lose your original investment. I'm obliged to say that, Mr Tranter, and now I'm going to spend the next thirty to forty minutes describing the details of the various funds and investment options that I'm going to recommend for your money. You're going to find it rather dry, I'm afraid. Can I get you another coffee?'

Despite another shot of caffeine, Jason found it hard to concentrate over the next half hour. He felt a growing acceptance that he was just going to have to trust the integrity of Richards and of Perry's. But his mind wandered back to the conversation that he'd had with Mr Smethwick as he led him to Richards' office. It still bothered him that the standard of privacy wasn't quite what he was expecting. How had Smethwick, a glorified concierge, known that this was Jason's first meeting? How had he known that he'd travelled up to London 'for the day'? As the meeting finished, Smethwick returned to lead Jason back to the entrance door and Jason tackled him.

'Thank you, Mr Smethwick. Can I ask you something? Before you brought me to Mr Richards' office, you suggested to me that this was my first appointment and asked me if I was in London "for the day". To be honest, I was a bit surprised. I thought details about my meeting and where I lived would be confidential, and I got the impression that you knew about me already. I wouldn't make a big deal about it, but you expect a certain amount of confidentiality from a bank like this, don't you?. Why do you assume I'm "up to London" for the day? How do you know I don't live in London?'

'Oh, I am sorry, Mr Tranter sir.' Smethwick looked genuinely embarrassed. 'That was very presumptuous of me, I'm sure. Very presumptuous. It's just that I recognise all Mr Richards' regular clients and it's always a pleasure to meet a new one. That was how I guessed it was your first appointment. And the London thing? Well, it's just the suit, you see, sir.'

'My suit?'

'Well, you'll think I'm very weird, sir, but it's something I take a bit of an interest in, you see. I noticed straight away that it's a very fine suit, sir, and I can tell it's a bespoke suit, skilfully tailored, if I may say so. But forgive me for saying sir, it's not a

London suit, is it, sir? I'm no expert myself sir, but I did notice the jetted pockets, and I was just trying to think which of the London tailors would use a jetted pocket on a suit of this style, with this fabric? I just couldn't think that any of the London tailors would ever... I mean to say... May I ask where...?'

'It's from a tailor in Dudley, in the West Midlands, actually.'

'Dudley! Well, I never!' Embarrassment turned to joy in an instant. 'That's a first for me, sir. A real first. Would you believe that's where my family comes from? The Black Country. That's where my grandfather, Arthur Smethwick, came from. I still have family there, Mr Tranter, and a lot of contacts. If ever you need anything, sir, up in those parts, or in London, let me know. Tickets for shows, restaurant tables, hotel suites, anything at all. I have a few connections. And having money, sir, changes all the rules.'

Jason walked out of Perry's, very conscious that he was a rich man, and the realisation terrified him. Perhaps Richards' words — *'Be on your guard, Mr Tranter. Trust no-one!'* — had spooked him. The simple act of stepping out the door of a private bank identified him as a member of an elite, a target even. Inside the bank he had been enjoying the feeling of business-like calm and the courtesy extended to him by its staff. Outside, everyone seemed to be in a hurry and the pavements weren't wide enough any more. Faces were blank or scowling. A woman standing on the kerb was shouting a stream of profanities into her mobile phone. The stop-start traffic was impatient, engines revved and brakes squealed. Jason didn't know which way to walk, but he started walking eastwards along the Strand anyway, just hoping to get out of this busy stretch.

A man came towards him, chugging a collection box. 'Refugees,' he said impatiently, but Jason wasn't sure whether he was raising money to help them or to get rid of them. Jason swerved the guy, but stepped over the legs of a man wrapped in a sleeping bag, stretched out across the pavement. 'Oi! Mind me dog, you bastard! Spare us some change?' Jason put his hand in his pocket, but was feeling too rushed and confused to stop and actually give the man any money, and his legs carried him further up The Strand.

A man on a motor-scooter had pulled up to the kerb and was trying to attract his attention. 'It's no use asking me directions,' Jason thought and carried on walking. But the scooterist, dressed in a long coat and a black helmet with a full-face visor, just rolled forward ten metres, and waved again, beckoning Jason to come over. Jason pretended to ignore him and instead, took advantage of a temporary gap in the traffic and crossed over to the central reservation of the road. The traffic on the other side was too busy to cross, but while Jason waited, he could see from the corner of his eye that the scooterist had given up and driven on.

Jason completed his crossing and paused, looking into a shop window, while he gathered his thoughts. It was a little shop selling antique postage stamps and first day covers. It seemed a world away from the banks and branded retailers on the rest of the Strand, and the hipster in Jason wanted to go inside and soak up the musty atmosphere, but then a familiar engine-note forced its way back into Jason's consciousness. The scooter again, and now it was heading towards him. It must have u-turned further up the street.

Jason was positively scared now. Why was he being pursued like this? He walked quickly back westwards along the Strand again and, after a few metres, saw a better chance to get rid of his pursuer. There was a narrow pedestrian alleyway to his left, with steps at intervals. He darted down it, hoping not to be seen by the man on the scooter.

The high graffitied walls of the empty alleyway did nothing to calm Jason's nerves. This would be exactly the wrong place to be cornered if he was being followed on foot, but scooters only came down steps like that in films; he was safe again. Still, he kept looking back over his shoulder as he made his way down the alley, checking that no-one was following him. There was a bar halfway down the alley and he thought about taking a drink, but a man standing just inside the door looked like he was there to scare customers away rather than drum up trade. Jason took out his phone from his jacket pocket to Google the shortest way back to Euston. Thankfully, the alley was actually leading him closer to the Embankment tube station, where he'd be able to get a direct line. He quickened his pace again and walked purposefully to the end of the alleyway.

The man in the long coat and black helmet with full-face visor wheeled his scooter across the exit of the alleyway. Jason froze. The man took off the helmet. It was Smethwick.

'Glad I caught you, sir,' said Smethwick, almost casually. 'I think you may have dropped this in the office during the business with your trousers, sir.' He handed Jason a business card. Jason looked at it. It was a beautifully printed card with a picture of a small bird on it, and the black and white mosaic of a QR code and nothing more.

'Sorry, no... don't recognise it. Not mine, I'm afraid. I'm sorry you've gone to all this trouble. Thank you, though.'

'No trouble, sir. I think you should keep it all the same, sir. Richards and I both think you should keep it, sir.'

Smethwick pulled his helmet back on, revved the engine of his scooter, and sped away.

'Enigmatic bastard,' thought Jason.

9

Helen was disappointed by the way her solicitor was behaving. When she and David had first met him to set up their wills, Mr Jarrold had seemed such a lovely, amiable man. Much nicer than the man from the firm they had approached previously, who had struck both of them as distinctly 'civil'. That was the word that they used when they suspected someone disapproved of their marriage. It happened less often as the years passed, but Helen and David were very sensitive to 'courteous disapproval' and they had a shared policy of not tolerating it. Mr Jarrold was a much better choice. He was warm and friendly and talked to both of them equally, not concentrating solely on David, as so many people did. When David died, Mr Jarrold ('Helen, please, call me Arthur') had been a wonderful support. He'd taken on everything, dealing the UK Foreign Office, the Congolese Police, and even the Hospital in Kinshasa where David's body had been taken, and handled the tortuous business of getting a death certificate from the Democratic Republic of the Congo efficiently as anyone could, in Helen's opinion.

But now, sitting in Jarrold's office, trying to understand the shocking news that her husband had assets worth over a hundred and thirty million pounds *that he had never told her about*, Helen felt a distinct lack of empathy from the solicitor.

'I'm sorry, Mrs Yarnley, I really don't have much more information I can give you. I've never experienced anything like this. Your father-in-law wrote to inform me that David had some private funds and that he'd made the necessary arrangements to wind these up and have the final balances sent to me, as executor. I assumed these would be childhood savings accounts and suchlike. I did not expect offshore accounts based in the Cayman Islands! I'm finding it hard to comprehend how your husband managed to conceal this fortune from you, yet alone why.' He spoke in a clipped voice and didn't look her in the eye. He tidied some papers on his desk as he spoke, and Helen got the impression that he wanted the meeting to end.

'But Arthur, I don't understand. Couldn't this offshore trust give you any information at all?'

'Not yet, Mrs Yarnley. They've said that they will not discuss matters with me, even though I am the legal executor of your husband's will,' Jarrold explained. 'So far, they have given me the very barest information, just the sum...' he paused and looked at the figure in the letter in front of him, raising an eyebrow to show that he still found it hard to believe the amount. '... the considerable sum involved and have said that they will contact you directly to discuss the next steps.'

Suddenly, Helen understood. 'Oh my God! Arthur! I've just got why you're acting so weird. I'm so sorry, I hadn't even thought about it! You're acting as executor on a fixed fee basis, aren't you? You must regret not holding out for the percentage deal. I remember when we made our wills, David insisted on going for the fixed fee, even though it looked more expensive. Oh, look... this is awkward. I can see it's not really fair. I'm sure we can arrange...'

'Helen, please,' interrupted Jarrold. 'It's nothing of the sort. I'm disappointed you should think such a thing. If I'm "acting weird" it's because, in my professional opinion, this is all highly irregular. Now, I've no evidence at all, but my instinct tells me that there is something deeply suspicious about this money of your husband's. I'm concerned that you are going to have to be extremely careful and I suggest you take independent advice, no matter what the people from the trust say. Believe me, I'm not thinking about the size of my fee. I'm thinking about you. It's essential, especially now, that you realise that there are more important things than money. Integrity is priceless.'

The meeting ended more amiably; Helen agreed she would wait to hear from the offshore trust and that she wouldn't hesitate to call Arthur Jarrold if ever she needed him.

'In fact, there is something you could do for me.' She handed him the photo of the school taken from her kitchen cork-board. 'Would you mind finding out what has happened to the school project that we were supporting? I want to make sure it's all taken care of. The contact details are all on here.'

'Of course, I understand, Helen. Leave it with me,' said Jarrold, tucking the photograph into his folder. 'But I have to tell you that this may be the last thing I do for you. I'm retiring at the end of next month, and I'm winding down all my accounts, but if I can ever provide any advice or help, in a personal capacity, please let me know. I'll give you my home number.'

'Oh Arthur! That is really very kind of you. I feel embarrassed now — I'm so sorry I suggested you were pissed off about the fee, Arthur. That was bad of me,' she said as she left the office.

As the door closed behind her, Arthur Jarrold mentally calculated what two per cent of a hundred and thirty-five million pounds would have amounted to and snapped his ballpoint pen in two in a mixture of surprise and ruefulness.

A letter arrived for Helen the following day. She ripped it open and started reading.

Dear Mrs Yarnley,

Please allow us to offer our deepest condolences on the sudden death of your husband, David. We recognise what a terrible time this must be for you and we sincerely wish to assist you in any way that we can. The news of your husband's portfolio will have come as a great shock to you and we will be in touch again with you shortly to discuss the matter and help you decide on the best course of action. We have informed your late husband's executor, Mr Arthur Jarrold, of the total amount of funds in the account. Please confirm whether you are happy for us to divulge other details of the account to him, or whether you would wish to see those yourself. In the meantime, please find enclosed a letter written by your husband in 2004, to be passed onto you in the event of his death, in accordance with his Expression Of Wish. There is also an additional note from 2006, which we have also enclosed.

Helen saw that there was another envelope enclosed, with just the word 'Helen' in her husband's familiar handwriting. As she opened this envelope, carefully this time, she let out a low, anguished moan. She read:

To my dearest Helen,

Gosh, this is a tough one to write. If you're reading this, it means that either there's been some terrible clerical cock-up or else I'm no longer alive. In either case, I'm truly, truly sorry.

Helen, honey, I love you more than anything in the world. I hope you know that. I've always told you that our love is the most true and precious thing in the world and I mean it forever. It hurts me (and I guess it's going to hurt you even more) that something so true and precious should be undermined by a lie. It's a well-intentioned lie, or at least I think it is – you may have your own opinion. Please don't judge me too harshly.

You know my parents don't approve of us being together. My mother, in particular, has been horrible to you and I can never forgive her. Actually, it hurts me more deeply than I've ever let you know. I know you nearly gave up on me because you thought it was unfair to come between me and my family. I couldn't let that happen. Let me say it again. You and Brett are the most important things in the world to me. I made a choice, and I chose you. I couldn't let you know how much that choice actually hurt me. Despite their mad, bigoted opinions, deep down I still care for my parents, even if we're not really on speaking terms anymore.

But last year, my dad broke silence and contacted me. I thought it was strange because Dad has always taken the back seat in all family matters. Not surprising when you think of what Mum is like. He asked to meet up and stressed that I shouldn't let you know we were meeting. I assumed at first that this was another attempt to lure me away from you and tempt me to take up a role in the family business. But I was wrong.

I met Dad in London (I told you I was going to a gig with Mike... sorry again!). He told me an amazing story. It turns out that the guy is loaded. Seriously loaded. I always knew that our family was pretty well off. You don't get a Wellington education without substantial dosh in the bank. But Dad is actually in a different league and he never told us. He made some spectacularly smart investments in the nineties and put his money in an offshore account. Here's the fun part. He had a plan to set up a new life with the only other person who knew about this secret wealth, Ingrid, his secretary. I just about remember meeting Ingrid once when I was a small boy. Rather glamorous, as I remember. The old bastard was all set up to do a runner, leave his family behind, and live with her in the Bahamas or somewhere, when he found out that Ingrid was shagging someone else, his under-manager, as it happened. He told me he had a sort of awakening at that point. He came to the realisation that you can't trust anyone, anyone at all. Ingrid had proved untrustworthy. His under-manager had proved untrustworthy and he, himself, had proven to be untrustworthy. He looked around himself and saw a world full of liars and cheats. (It was the time of Thatcher, Archer, Aitken and all that lot, remember!). He decided that there was actually only one person who he trusted, and that was Mum! By that time, although he found her pretty hard work, being so fussy and stuck-up, he recognised and valued her loyalty and decided that he would stick with her and me.

And so we went on, a respectable middle class family, living in a respectable village in Berkshire. But all the time, Dad had his secret stash of money squirrelled away in offshore investment trusts and schemes that only he knew about. The money grew and grew as he invested in internet start-ups and so on. He told me he'd bought into eBay really early on, which turned out to be a remarkably good move from the old boy. But he never really spent any of the money. He said that the money that the family business was bringing in was enough for him, Mum, and me. We had everything we needed, he said, and that was true. My parents were happy – they had the golf club, their friends from the village, the dinner parties and so on. Dad felt that if he let Mum know about the money, the truth would come out about Ingrid and he didn't want that to happen. He actually told me he was scared of the money and that he reckoned that if ever he came clean about it, Mum would insist on moving up in the world, and want an even posher house, and start wanting to mix with some of the titled parents of my chums at school, the minor royals and all that set. He hates the idea of that. Once or twice a year, when Mum gets too much for him, he spends a crafty few days away in the Cayman Islands or some island in the Mediterranean somewhere. His 'business trips'. I think he enjoys watching his pile grow, playing with the investments as a hobby, but never spending any of it.

Now, Helen, what do you make of all that, I wonder? I imagine you'll be pretty annoyed. All that money sitting there doing nothing when it could be doing some good. That wouldn't sit well with you, I know. But again, I ask you not to judge too harshly. Because I've kind of done the same thing.

At that meeting in London, about a year ago, Dad told me he wanted to hand some of the money over to me. I promise you, I objected, as you would expect me to. But he said that it would all come over to me at some point anyway, when he passed away, and he wanted me to get used to the idea sooner rather than later. He said he wasn't trying to lure me back into the fold. There were no conditions that came with the money, except that Mum must never know.

So why haven't I told you all about this? There's no simple answer to that. I keep thinking I will tell you, and then I chicken out. The truth is, just like my dad, I'm scared of this money and what it could do to us. I'm so proud of the life that we have made together, by ourselves, without money from my parents or anyone else. It feels honest and true. That's the background I want Brett to grow up in. But now there is all this money and I can't work out what to do. I'm frightened that you'll think differently of me, see me as part of the system that we want to change, see me as still being tied to the Yarnley family. I'm frightened that you'll leave me.

Part of me wants to give the whole lot away, but even that is an enormous responsibility that I don't think I'm ready for. How do you make sure that the money you give away actually goes where you intend it to? I need time to think about it. I'm going to keep the money secret for now. A sort of 'wealth management' company, called Rara Avis, will manage for me. They operate from London, although most of the money is actually in an offshore account in the Cayman Islands and in various investments. I know what you're thinking!!! All the times we've got so angry about tax-dodging millionaires keeping their money in offshore tax-havens. It doesn't sit easy with me, believe me, but on the other hand, I'm not keen on the current government getting their hands on forty per cent of it and squandering it on their mad schemes. Rara Avis keeps track of my money for me, ensures that it's safe and can also arrange discrete, anonymous payments, should I need to make any. In a couple of years, I reckon I'll have come to terms with it and I'll be able to tell you all about it and we can decide together where to go from there. I'm writing this note though because should anything happen to me, Rara Avis has instructions to pass on the money to you.

So if you are reading this... as I say, either there's been a terrible mistake or I'm no longer alive. What can I say? How many times have I told you 'I love you more than a million pounds!'? Well, it turns out it is true.

David x

There was another note.

Helen,

A couple of years later, and I'm still not brave enough to tell you about this money. I have found a way of feeling better about it, though. Whenever you and I decide that there's a cause that's worthy of our time or money, even on our tight budget, then I am also making an anonymous donation as well. It still feels creepy, but it's stopped me feeling like a complete miser!

Last week, you told me you are expecting our second child. We are both so unbelievably happy and I just can't bear to do anything that will upset the apple cart. I've decided that the money will stay a secret for a while longer. Maybe we'll need this money. I don't know whether our teachers' salaries are going to be enough if we keep on having babies!

I watched a dad teaching his girl to ride a bike in the park the other day. The girl was just starting to pedal without stabilisers and she didn't know that her dad was still running behind, waiting to catch her if she fell. It felt like us. There's this big safety net, but I'm keeping it secret so that we don't rely on it being there.

All my love

David X

10

'You two? In business? God help us! Seriously?' Sultan found the news that Jason and Stuart were setting up a business together highly amusing. 'What are you going to call yourselves? "Boys With Toys R Us"?'

'It will be Stuart's business, really,' Jason explained. 'He's the one with the gear and expertise. I'm just providing some backing to get him going, some promotional materials and stuff. I'll just be a sleeping partner.'

'And I'm sure he'll find that a great comfort when he comes home after a long day being blown about in a hot-air balloon,' Sultan mocked. 'You two can cuddle up and...'

'Very funny,' said Jason. 'You're just jealous of my *Dragon's Den* lifestyle. A man of my means likes to help budding entrepreneurs like Stuart here.'

'A man of your means? You may have won a fortune, but all you've bought yourself so far is a couple of suits, a new phone, and a coffee machine. What is wrong with you, man?'

Jason felt Sultan had a point, but still tried to defend himself. 'Hey, there's no rush, is there? I know what you'd have done. You'd have gone and bought a new house in one of them gated communities where the footballers live, wouldn't you? But personally, I don't want a twenty-one-year-old brat and his spray-tanned girlfriend for my next-door neighbours, thanks.'

'Steady on, mate — you've only won a couple of hundred grand. I don't think you're quite in that league.'

Jason realised he'd nearly let slip the extent of his real win. He'd have to be more careful. Since his visit to Perry's, he'd become a bit more accustomed to his wealth, and now he was finding it harder to remember that his friends from The Pig thought he'd won a much more modest sum. Perhaps he'd have to let them in on the truth at some point.

Sarah asked Stuart what he'd spend money on, if he had any.

'On my mates, obviously... What finer way to spend some cash is there?'

Sultan agreed, 'Spot on. We pass this way but once, Jason. Spread a little happiness as you go by, you tight bastard!'

'Well, since you mention it, it's my birthday, a week on Thursday. Dinner's on me. I'll pick you up and take you all somewhere decent. Try and scrub up, Stuart, there's a lad. Might be somewhere where they have a dress code. Thursday alright with you, Sarah?'

It was awkward. Sarah wasn't really part of the gang. She'd never been with them outside The Pig, but since the night of the win, she'd spent more time with them, sitting in their usual corner.

Sarah said, 'Thanks, Jason — but you don't want me slowing you lads down. You have a good night.'

'No, join us,' said Jason. 'They'll behave better if we have female company.'

'Alright, if you're sure,' said Sarah. 'Great. Thanks, Jason!'

Jason spent the next few days doing the busiest research, planning and preparation that he'd done since he left work.

Since before then, come to think of it. He rang round the swankiest restaurants in Birmingham, but none of them seemed to have a table free on his birthday and none of them seemed bothered that they couldn't accommodate him. They didn't try offering alternative dates, and seemed affronted that anyone could expect to get a table with less than a month's notice. After three such nonchalant refusals, Jason thought perhaps he was being stupid. Perhaps there was a way for a sufficiently wealthy person to get a table, he thought, if he pressed harder. It went against the grain, but on his next attempt, he tried to be a bit more persuasive.

'Oh, that's a shame. It's a special occasion, you see. Are you sure there isn't a way that you could make a table available? No? No way at all? Can I put it another way? How much would it take to make a table avail... No? Of course not. No, I didn't mean to suggest anything. Sorry, goodbye.'

He was losing hope and had visions of ending up at Nando's, after all. He liked it there, but he had set rather more impressive expectations. There was only one top-notch restaurant left on the *TripAdvisor* listings of the best restaurants in Birmingham and it was the number one on the list, 'Jack's'. It was the establishment owned and run by Jack Tang, the TV celebrity chef, who had recently starred in his own foodie travel show, exploring South East Asia. It was the place celebs frequented when they were in Birmingham, and there were often hopeful paparazzi hanging outside around closing time. He remembered what Smethwick had said, 'Having money changes all the rules'. He rang Perry's and asked for Mr Smethwick. A few minutes later, a table in Birmingham's top restaurant was secured.

The next task was to get a car for the evening, something with 'wow factor'. Again, Mr Smethwick was able to recommend a company that rented elite sports cars, and Jason browsed their website. It was a field he knew nothing about. The Daimlers, Bentleys, and Porches all looked impressive, but the models displayed on the website were all black or grey. If he'd been looking to buy a car for his permanent use, these would have appealed, but Jason was possessed by a growing desire to break out of his usual conservative habits and make a statement. Although the red of the Ferrari appealed to his aesthetic sensibilities, the yellow Lamborghini Huracan seemed more ostentatious, and that drove his decision. Also, apparently, it ran on 'petrol and pure adrenalin'.

He rang the company and made the arrangements. The salesman quickly detected that Jason was a newcomer to the world of supercars. He asked about Jason's driving experience and patronisingly suggested that a Bentley or an Audi might be more appropriate. Jason, however, was not to be talked down.

'Actually, I'll take it for the whole week. I'll get some practice in.'

The salesman now sounded nervous and listed the extensive terms and conditions, the liability arrangements and nine thousand pounds deposit required. None of these dissuaded Jason, who was now enjoying the discomfort he was causing the man.

'That's great, mate. I'll transfer the money straight away. Just one last question: does it take unleaded or diesel?' There was a silence. 'It's alright, only joking, pal.'

A couple of days later, a car transporter delivered the bright yellow sports car, which looked ridiculously out of place in the Hambourne avenue where Jason lived. He sensed curtains twitching. The delivery man took Jason through the driver's controls, but Jason found it difficult to concentrate. His mind was on the stupid blunder he had made. The car was, of course, a two-seater. Not the vehicle he needed to take his three friends on a posh night out.

Later that afternoon, he summoned up the courage to take the Lamborghini for a spin. It was a difficult start, and he stalled twice before leaving his street. He wasn't used to such fierce acceleration, and his clutch control was lacking. An elderly man with a greyhound stood on the corner of the road, watching and laughing. Jason wound his window down.

'Alright, John?'

'Having a bit of trouble, are you? That's quite a fancy car...'

'What, this? It's just a courtesy car they've lent me while I'm getting me Ford Focus fixed.'

It took a few miles of country roads, but Jason gradually grew accustomed to the car and started to enjoy himself. At first, it annoyed him that every time he stopped at traffic lights, there seemed to be some hopeful buck in a BMW or Golf GTi trying to force him into a racing start. But after a couple of times of proving how effortlessly the Lambo could deal with such competition, he relaxed and just concentrated on perfecting a smooth ride. When he got home, he rang up Donington Park race track and booked himself in for a day's training. 'I could become a petrol-head, after all,' thought Jason.

Thursday arrived, and Jason drove to his parents' for a birthday lunch. Steak and kidney pie, oven chips and tinned sweetcorn, his childhood favourite meal, and Jason was touched. His parents bombarded him with all their news, mostly about the bowls club and minor ailments, and paid scant interest to Jason's affairs. His mum did ask him whether he'd found another job yet, but didn't seem bothered that he hadn't.

'Don't worry, take your time, love. We'll always help you out if you're stuck.'

He felt guilty that he hadn't told them about his money, but correctly guessed that they'd be more worried for him if they knew he was a millionaire than they were about him being unemployed. Jason didn't mention the car, and it was only as he went to leave that they saw it. 'I've just borrowed it,' he said. 'I'm taking someone out tonight.'

'Ooh, they must be someone special!' said his mum.

'Just you be careful, son,' added his dad in a quiet voice. 'Those low sports cars, they'll do your back in.'

He picked up Sarah at seven-thirty. Both of them did a double-take; she at the magnificent yellow sports car, he at her evening wear. At The Pig, she usually wore jeans and a hoodie. Tonight, she had her hair done up and was wearing a classy black dress under an expensive-looking coat. She wouldn't look out of place in the Lamborghini.

She hesitated before lowering herself into the passenger seat, however. 'Er, Jason, I thought you drove a Ford Focus?'

'Yeah, normally,' said Jason. 'This is a hire car. Birthday treat to myself.'

'And I thought Sultan and Stuart were coming?'

'They are,' said Jason. 'I hired the wrong car by mistake. I've arranged for a taxi to pick them up, though. Well, a limo actually.'

'Oh my God! How much does this cost to hire, Jason?'

'A lot. But don't worry. Money is no object tonight. Anyway, I'm glad I did. Anything less would look shabby next to you tonight.' Jason felt embarrassed as soon as he had said it. That was so cheesy! He never spoke like that.

Sarah smiled. 'Thanks Jason, that's very nice of you.'

The Thursday night traffic made the drive into Birmingham a stop-start affair. Jason's cheeks were still glowing for a long time after his initial compliment and he wanted to make sure that Sarah didn't think that there was any ulterior motive behind his choosing to take her, rather than Sultan or Stuart, in the sports car. Sarah was very interested in where he'd got the car from, and asked him how long it had taken him to get used to driving it. Jason tried to keep his answers cool, but was conscious that he was probably sounding offhand. He hadn't thought it would be so difficult to get the tone of the conversation right. Things got easier as they noticed the car was attracting the excited attention of pedestrians on the side streets of Birmingham.

'I suppose they think that we're celebrities or something,' said Jason.

'Well tonight, Jason, I feel like one and I am going to bloody well own it!' laughed Sarah.

They pulled into Cornwall Street and a tall man standing outside Jack's saw the approaching car. He nodded to Jason and removed some plastic cones from the street directly in front of the restaurant and signalled for Jason to pull into the space. 'Totally cool, Jason,' Sarah murmured.

'Yeah, and I didn't even have to use my nan's blue badge,' said Jason with a wink. 'Impressive, what a little phoning ahead can achieve,' he thought. As he manoeuvred the car, a white stretch limo pulled up behind them.

'Get out of here, man! I do not believe it!' Sultan approached them as Jason held the car door open for Sarah. 'What a pile of junk! I mean, seriously, get a Ferrari, bro! I'm glad we ended up with the stretch limo option — even if it felt like school prom night, with Stu as the worst prom date ever.' As usual, Sultan's insults and easy conversation helped the evening flow.

The four did their best not to look or act out of place in a restaurant where their fellow customers were dressed in corporate suits or rock-star chic, and the staff all looked like they could all hold down alternative careers in films or modelling. There was an easy ambience to the place, and they were shown to a table in a quiet alcove, which meant that when nobody was looking, they could snigger at the menu, which boasted items such as Earl Grey bacon, and something described as 'painted beef'.

Stuart said 'Oh, I get it. The number after each menu item is the number of calories, yeah?'

'No, Stu. That's the price, but don't worry about it, okay?' said Jason. The menu was always going to be a challenge for Jason. Despite happily self-identifying as a hipster, Jason did not have an eclectic taste in food. Except for pizza, he distrusted any food that his mum had never served him. His ideal meal in any restaurant would comprise roasted meat with some sort of potato and one other English vegetable, with as little interference from a chef as possible. Happily, there was something that almost fitted the bill.

'I'll have the pan-fried Sedgley pork tenderloin, with rhubarb compote, pommes dauphinoise and seared carrots, please. Only could I have it without the rhubarb compote, and could I get a side order of fries, please?'

The others were a bit more adventurous, but as so often, Sultan faced a very restricted vegetarian choice.

'I guess I'll have the butternut squash thing please, mate, seeing as it's the only item that didn't involve killing something.'

'The quinoa and grilled halloumi with micro-salad is another vegetarian option, sir.'

'No, offence mate, but do I look like a micro-salad sort of guy?'

On the whole, the four behaved themselves. When the wine waiter came to take their drinks order, Jason confessed they were all out of their depth and bravely asked him to choose wine to complement his guests' menu choices, while he stuck with mineral water. 'Whatever you think goes best, mate.... only don't take the piss, obviously.' He didn't regret his choice to drive and not drink. He was feeling high on the amount of money he was splashing out. It was an unexpected pleasure to spend without constraint.

Stuart announced that this was a double celebration.

'I've taken voluntary redundancy from PKR. It's not a vast amount, so don't expect me to offer to split the bill, Jason, but it will mean I can put some money into the surveillance business and concentrate on it full-time.'

Sultan and Sarah cheered, but Jason bit his fingernail and furrowed his brow. Had his involvement in Stuart's affairs encouraged him to take a reckless decision? The amount of money that Jason was investing in the business was an insignificant fraction of his wealth, so it wouldn't matter to him if the business flopped. But if Stuart had given up the security of a job at PKR, a failure could be a disaster for him. On the other hand, thought Jason, with his backing there really wasn't a worry of failure, so he relaxed again. It was wonderful how money could make problems go away. He smiled and said, 'Nice one, mate.'

The food, when it arrived, was fantastic, and the service was impeccable. Jason's pork arrived with a separate little dish of the rhubarb compote, which Sarah persuaded him to try. He screwed his face up as he tasted the tiniest smidgeon, but had to admit that it was good and ended up eating all of it. Handing over control of the wine choices turned out to be a good move, and all the staff seemed to relax. Before the desserts arrived, their waiter brought little dishes of chestnut and armagnac sorbet.

'Just an *amuse-bouche*, Chef's speciality. It's on the house.'

Stuart ended up eating all four dishes.

After their meal, they were relaxing over limoncello digestifs that the sommelier had brought, including a non-alcoholic version for Jason.

As they took their first sips, the waiter returned and said, 'Mr Tang is on the premises tonight and wondered if you'd mind if he dropped by to say hello?'

In fact, the four had just been lamenting the fact that they hadn't recognised any famous people so far, so they would have certainly agreed. They didn't need to, because Jack Tang was hard on the heels of the waiter. He lived up to the label of 'celebrity'. His eyes were brighter, his teeth were whiter, his hair was shinier than anyone else in the room. His blemish-free skin seemed to glow in the subdued lighting, and he smelled more as if he had just emerged from a spa treatment rather than a busy kitchen. He was just a little shorter than they had remembered him from seeing him on television.

'Hi guys — I hope everything's been okay for you this evening?'

They murmured their approval; of course it had.

'It's just that I don't think we've seen you here before and I like to make personally sure that everything is top dollar for our latest friends.'

'Well, you're charging top dollar, so I guess it would be, thanks,' said Stuart. It was at this precise moment that the friends realised that normally quiet Stuart was drunk. He'd intended the remark to be in the spirit of cheerful banter, but it came out awkwardly.

'Whoa! Fair point!' Tang held up the palms of his hands and gave a gentle laugh, diffusing the situation. 'I'm guessing that the Lamborghini outside isn't yours then, sir?'

His eyes scanned the other three for signs that they were the owner. Jason sensed that the expensive car had aroused the restaurant owner's curiosity, and guessed that this was the real reason he'd come to chat with his 'latest friends'.

'Oh, I'm just trying it out. It's on loan to me,' said Jason as nonchalantly as he could.

'Then you must be Mr Tranter. Welcome to Jack's. I hope you've enjoyed your meal this evening?'

'We've had a great time, thank you. The food was...,' his mind froze as he tried to think of the appropriate word. '... Bosting.'

It was the only word he could think of, and it made Sarah snort.

'Alright! "Bosting". I'll go with that!' He pointed his smile at Sarah, and noticing that she'd finished her limoncello, said, 'Can I get you another of those, Madam? On the house, of course.'

Sarah accepted. 'Thank you, that's very kind. I saw your show on Cambodia last week, really fascinating.'

In a single movement, Jack Tang leaned over to grab a chair from the nearby unoccupied table, swivelled it round and sat on it, back to front, close to Sarah.

'Oh man! Have you ever been there? You should go. It's amazing. Cambodia really awoke me, you know? You have to get out of Phnom Penh, to the real Cambodia. It's just fantastic.. It's... unreal.'

'So, hang on, which is it? Real or unreal?' asked Stuart. Sultan looked at him proudly.

'There's no stopping him, is there?' said Tang, turning to Jason. 'So what line of business are you in, man? If you don't mind me asking, of course.'

Jason suddenly felt that he was in danger of being exposed as being an imposter. He wasn't going to confess to being a lottery winner, that was for sure. He could legitimately say that he was the owner of an aerial surveillance company, but he knew that if Tang dug deeper, he'd find out that this company was really one man and his camera drone.

'I'm in Technology. Technology Finance,' he added to make it sound less interesting. It worked. Tang turned back to Sarah and talked more about travelling in South East Asia.

The glamour of talking to a real TV celebrity was waning. Sarah kept giving meaningful looks to Jason that could only be interpreted as 'Make this end' as Jack Tang droned on about how he had spent an afternoon with a peasant family on the shores of the Mekong river. Jason caught the eye of the head waiter and asked for the bill. He texted the limo driver to warn him they'd be needing him soon.

Tang said, 'So, you guys going on somewhere?'

For one horrible moment, Jason thought Tang wanted to tag along with them. 'The Pig,' said Jason.

'Umm. I don't know it,' said Tang.

'It's very 'sclusive', slurred Stuart.

'You crack me up, my friend! Listen, I must go. I'll let you enjoy the rest of your evening. It's been really great to meet you,' he said and slipped away.

The bill arrived, and Jason made a point of paying as nonchalantly as he could. It was a good feeling, avoiding the ritual scrutiny and argument over who had eaten or drunk what. But it seemed to make Sultan suspicious.

'Cheers, Jason,' he said. 'Much appreciated. If I ever have a birthday, the kebabs are on me. So. How's "Tech Finance" working out for you, then? Pretty well, I guess, seeing as how you're "trying out" a Lamborghini Huracan. How much would one of those set you back, I wonder? Over a hundred and fifty grand, I reckon. That's a big chunk out of your lottery win, I'd say, my friend. Or is it?'

'Okay. I'm rumbled,' Jason admitted. 'I was about to tell you all anyway, but then Stu's best friend, Jack, came and joined us. It's true. The lottery win was quite a bit more than I told you. I won't say how much — that's between me and my *private* bank. In *London*. Ahem, ahem. Look, the thing is, I know it's a cliché to say, "I won't let it change me". But seriously, it is so, so, weird suddenly having enough money not to worry about stuff. I honestly don't know what's going to happen. But it's meant a lot to me to spend some time with you guys and share a bit of the fun. I understand you won't believe me when I say that this is actually a difficult time for me at the moment, but I really appreciate what good friends you are, and I hope you can bear with me while I sort my head out. Just for a few months, until things settle a bit. Then, of course, you can all just piss off!

'Now, before we leave this fine establishment though, do take a complimentary chocolate! I may be a rich bastard, but I'm not so rich as to turn down free food. And so, let us adjourn to that exclusive, members-only club, The Pig, for a *digestif*. Plus, I could murder a bag of scratchings.'

They each took a wrapped square of chocolate from the table as they got up to go. Underneath the chocolates was a printed card with a logo that Jason recognised. He picked it up and slipped it in his wallet without saying anything.

Outside, back in the Lamborghini, Jason and Sarah were just pulling away when Sarah said 'Um, Jason, I know it's not my place, but I think you should have tipped the doorman — he's kept his eye on the car all evening, and everything.'

'Oh God, yeah. You're right. Good call. I'll just back up a sec. Would you mind passing him this tenner?' He reversed slightly and pulled the rear of the car to the kerb, with the front sticking out into the road slightly. Sarah opened the passenger door, which was longer than she realised, and it struck a cast iron street bollard.

'Oh shit! Sorry. Oh my God, Jason, I am so sorry!'

The drive to The Pig was awkward. Sarah was mortified. It was only the smallest of dents to the door. Jason told her it was all insured and not to worry. He didn't tell her that actually he would lose some or, knowing how these things work, all of his deposit, but it played on his mind. He told himself that it would be a drop in the ocean compared to his staggering bank balance, but somehow that didn't make him feel any better. It was impossible to come to terms with the idea that he could lose nine thousand pounds in a careless incident like that. Not that he blamed Sarah. He blamed himself for not remembering to tip in the first place. Perhaps having money didn't make *all* problems go away.

The nightcap at The Pig was subdued, but eventually redeemed by Sultan's and Stuart's relentless attempts to turn misfortune into mirth. On the way to the pub, Sarah had foolishly texted Sultan details of the incident, so they were prepared.

'Looks like we got here in the *nick* of time, guys. Hope the meal didn't leave too much of a *dent* in your wallet, Jason. Still want scratchings, Jason? Or have you had enough *scratching* for one night?'. And a toast, 'Never mind the bollards, here's to a great night out. Happy Birthday, Jason.'

Later, at home alone, Jason sipped on a twenty-five-year-old malt whiskey, his first alcoholic drink of his birthday, and smiled to himself. He'd had a good evening. He'd enjoyed driving the Lamborghini, he'd enjoyed Sarah's company on the drive to the restaurant, and spending time with the boys was always good. The meal, despite its posh pretensions, had been fun. He'd been impressed by the attention to detail, the friendliness and professionalism of the waiters. The food was really nice, although he'd probably have enjoyed a Nando's just as much. Meeting the celebrity Jack Tang? Well, he was okay, he supposed, but a bit of a dick, really. The dented door incident still made him feel queasy. It was going to take him time to get used to the idea that if he surrounded himself with expensive things, then they would get damaged just like inexpensive things, and they would cost more to put right. But so what? He had enough money to take care of that. Still, it just didn't sit easily with him. All in all, it was a good night, but he wouldn't really want to do it again. An ordinary night out with the lads was the important thing. And Sarah, perhaps.

'I want to enjoy my money, and I want to do it with flair and panache,' he thought. 'And that's harder than I thought it would be. I need advice on how to do "rich" well,' he thought.

It reminded him of Richards and Smethwick from Perry's. And that reminded him of the card he'd picked up in the restaurant, which looked the same as the one that Smethwick had enigmatically given him the street. He took it from his pocket. A picture of a small bird on one side and a QR code on the other. He scanned it with his phone.

It launched a website:

Rara Avis.
'Wealth is the ability to fully experience life.' – Thoreau
Exclusive experiences for the discerning and the discreet.
Interested? Fill out the contact form below.

11

Arthur Jarrold came in from spraying the weeds on his drive. He liked to get weed spraying done early in the morning as he felt that the combination of the chemicals and a full day's sun would work together to 'shrivel up the weedy little buggers', as he liked to put it. Currently, he felt pretty shrivelled up himself. He made a cup of tea and collected the post.

Retirement wasn't suiting him at all. He missed the rhythm of going into the office every day and, most of all, he missed the human contact. In the four weeks since he had retired, he'd had no visitors or callers. The only time he spoke out loud was when he went to the shops. He'd have to do something about this. Join a keep fit class or something. Goodness knows he needed to be fitter. He'd only been out spraying for forty-five minutes, but all his bones ached, and he was noticeably out of breath.

He hadn't been sleeping well either, because the Yarnley case was still playing on his mind. It wasn't the fact that he'd missed out on a potentially enormous commission from sorting out David Yarnley's probate. He could actually laugh at the irony of that. He was comfortable enough with his pension, and he liked a simple life. What was bothering him was that final casual request from David's widow, Helen, to check on the status of the charity project.

He had contacted the Yepi-Kasai School Foundation via the email address that was on the back of the photograph of the half-built school that Helen had given him. The reply had come quickly with a touching email which explained how shocked the Foundation was by the death of David Yarnley and how sorry they felt for Helen. They had named the school, The Yepi-David School in his honour; Yepi being the name of the town in northern Kasai where they had built the school. They were deeply grateful for the fourteen thousand pounds raised by Mr Yarnley and the children of Nebberton High School. They were hoping to have the school opened by the end of the year but were still raising money so that they could hire a couple of teachers.

This had puzzled Arthur. He had now received the closing statement from the offshore bank account where David had stashed away his fortune and it showed a list of recent transactions. These were payments directed to some organisation called Rara Avis, and there were brief notes against each transaction describing their purpose. Most of the transactions were relatively small payments marked 'Hotel' or 'Subscription'. One stood out, however.

A sum of three hundred thousand pounds was earmarked for '*Fondation Kasai Developpement*'. It looked like David had tried to supplement the funds raised by Nebberton High School by making an anonymous donation via this Rara Avis organisation. But if the school had received three hundred grand anonymously, why were they still looking for more funds for teachers? This was a village school in the DRC for roughly eighty pupils, not some multi-million pound academy. This Rara Avis organisation had some questions to answer.

Arthur was a high-street bookkeeper, not a forensic accountant, but with diligence and the time he had on his hands since retirement, he finally found a postal address associated with the bank account belonging to Rara Avis. He had written and explained that he was acting for the estate of David Yarnley and requested an update on the charity donation that David had made to '*Fondation Kasai Developpement*'. And here in this morning's post was a reply.

Arthur sat down with his tea, exhausted from the meagre effort of the morning's gardening, and opened the envelope. There was an A4 sheet with photographs and a brief covering letter from 'Guillaume Bertrand, *Directeur de Fondation Kasai Developpement* ℅ Rara Avis'. This explained that the Foundation 'rarely provides any information regarding anonymous donations', but that in the tragic circumstances of this donation, it was reasonable to provide a report. However, it requested that Mr Jarrold sign a non-disclosure slip and return this in the attached postage-paid envelope. Arthur signed the slip straight away, put it in the envelope and licked the bitter tasting seal.

He looked at the charity report. Unlike the update report received via email, this one was pleased to report that the school was now finished and classes had started. Arthur tried to wash the awful taste of the gum on the envelope with a gulp of hot tea. He looked at the picture in the report, which seemed to be out of focus. Proud men, women, and children stood outside a smart building with a striking red roof.

Confusing. The photo that Helen had given him showed a yellow roof. Had they painted it red, for some reason?

He stared at the photo again. There was definitely something wrong. It seemed to go in and out of focus. He angled the paper towards the light of the window to see it better. His hand was shaking, but he was more and more sure that this was a different school. He stood up to go to the computer to check the email, but the floor lurched towards him, and then he was lying on the carpet with shooting pains in his arms and legs. He tried to call out, but his mouth was dry and his throat was tight. There was no-one to hear him, anyway.

Part Two

1

Message: 17/6/19

Jenny. The birds are used to me now, and I can observe them from close range. One of them is exhibiting interesting behaviour and I am tracking closely. I hope to be able to understand how they mix with other flocks, possibly overseas. Trust this is OK. Robin.

Will he swallow that? I am in so much trouble either way. 'In for a penny, in for a million' as my old granny never used to say.

2

The combination of the drone of the aeroplane jets and the champagne had had the effect that Sarah said they would, and now she was fast asleep. Jason looked at her and felt both reassured and confused. He was nervous about the weekend, but Sarah seemed unflappable. She'd make a great personal assistant for someone, Jason thought.

And this was where the confusion came in. Was she just an assistant, or was she something more? She was, after all, jetting off with him for a weekend in the South of France, and couples that did that sort of thing were usually, well... couples. But she had made it clear that they were to be in separate rooms.

When Sarah met up with Jason, Sultan and Stuart, she was always on the sidelines, amused at the banter of the other three, but not joining in much. Lately, they had spent more time alone together. Stuart was very busy with the drone business, which, as he liked to joke, 'was really taking off'. New contracts and clients were turning up all the time, and Stuart was travelling all over the place, and there was talk of some overseas work. Sultan was even helping him at weekends, which Jason thought was great, although occasionally he felt he was missing out on some fun, and wished he were more than a 'sleeping partner'.

Still, he was enjoying Sarah's company, and they went shopping, enjoyed a couple of lunches out, that sort of thing. She talked more when they were alone together, and Jason enjoyed the fact that, unlike his two pals, she wasn't relentlessly poking fun at everything. She seemed genuinely interested in what Jason thought and felt, and sympathetic to his worries about what he should do with his fortune. He was grateful that he didn't have to hide from her how naïve he felt about his money, even three months after his lottery win. She never mocked him, the way Stuart and Sultan did.

'No, I get it, Jason.' she had said. 'I mean, who hasn't day-dreamed about winning the lottery? We all say that it wouldn't change us, but we're all fascinated by how it might. In one way, we hope it wouldn't, in another way we secretly hope it would. I'm not going to lie, Jason, it's super-cool having a millionaire mate. Being driven around in sports cars, going to posh restaurants, all that. And I won't deny that I'm dead jealous, but I do understand that it must also be very scary for you. So anytime you want to talk, I'm here. Reasonable rates. I'll accept most major credit cards.' She laughed. 'Oh God, that makes me sound like a cheap tart, sorry! I'm just happy to help, that's all. It's dead interesting!'

So, it was natural that when the invitation to the Rara Avis Weekend Induction Event arrived, he had discussed it with her. The almost secretive way that the organisation had contacted him and the service that they seemed to provide had made him naturally suspicious. She made Jason describe in detail everything that had led up to the invitation, including the way Smethwick had handed him the first card, and had said, 'Richards and I both think you should keep it, sir'. And then how the second card had arrived with the bill at Jack's, a restaurant for which Smethwick had helped him get a table.

Jason described how he had scanned the printed code on the card with his phone and it had displayed the Rara Avis website. He had filled out the contact form and the next day he had received an email, thanking him for his interest and urging him to download the Rara Avis app onto his phone. This allowed him to communicate with Rara Avis in a secure way.

Once the app was loaded, there was a message waiting for him.

'Thank you for contacting us. Please forgive the slightly obscure and mysterious way we advertise our service. It will become clear later why we operate in this way. You have been recommended to us as a high net worth individual with a desire to be discreet about your personal wealth. We have over thirty years of experience with clients just like yourself. Note. We are not a bank or an investment company. We have contacts with banks and can help put people in contact with such companies if required. But in general, we don't help people save money, we help people spend it. We are the Secret Millionaire's Club.'

Now the steward indicated the plane was preparing to land and that seatbelts should be re-fastened. Jason reached over to Sarah and touched her shoulder. She woke, stretched, and smiled at him.

Okay, he thought, if they weren't an item, explain that smile. That wasn't a polite 'Oh hello, are we nearly there?' smile. It was surely an 'Oh, I've just been dreaming about you' smile.

He wasn't sure whether the rather jerky landing caused the tumbling feeling in his stomach. He didn't like plane landings; they hurt his ears. His muscles tensed as the noise of the engines grew louder. There were too many new thoughts crowding in for Jason's liking.

Who were Rara Avis, really? Was he about to fall into a trap and be cheated out of his fortune? What were his feelings for Sarah, exactly? More to the point, what were her feelings for him? Did she even have any feelings for him, and if she did, were they just because of his money? Again, the same question came back. Was he about to be cheated out of his money?

'You'll be alright in a moment, Jason,' she said in the reassuring way she had. 'We've got VIP welcome service at Nice, remember? We'll be on our way to the hotel in no time.'

It was Rara Avis who had recommended the VIP Welcome service at the airport. It wasn't cheap, but it took the stress out of landing in an unfamiliar airport, and Jason appreciated the value of that right now. In fact, it had been the attention to detail in the travel arrangements for the induction event that had persuaded Sarah at first, and later Jason, that Rara Avis was probably legitimate and certainly worth investigating further.

'I like the way they've listed absolutely everything; the flights, the limos, the hotel, the trips, everything and put the cost against every item,' she had said as they sat staring at the laptop screen in Jason's living room. 'They claim they aren't marking up the prices and from what I can see, they price everything either at the published rates or slightly below. I guess they must take a commission from the suppliers or something. At the end of the day, it's your money, your decision, but it looks kosher to me.'

'So shall we go, then?'

'We? Hang on, Jason. I can't afford this sort of trip.'

'No. Well, I'll pay, obviously,' said Jason. 'Look, there's no way I'm going on my own. I'd be really grateful if you'd come with me. The invitation says "plus one".'

'Yes, but I'm not your "plus one", am I?' Sarah insisted. 'Oh dear, this is awkward. I'm sorry Jason. I know we've spent some time together lately, but I'm not really looking to be anyone's "plus one" at the moment. We're mates. Is that okay?'

'Sure. That's fine,' Jason reassured her. 'Absolutely. I never meant it like that. But you could still come with me, couldn't you? You're much more sensible than me. You're like my big sister, giving me advice. It's great'

'Little sister, Jason,' she said with mock sternness.

'No, but you're older...'

'Little sister, Jason.'

And so, without any more hesitation or persuasion, here they were, in the first-class cabin of a plane as it taxied towards a terminal at Nice Airport.

When the plane reached a standstill and the overhead lights indicated they could unfasten their seatbelts, they stood up, stretched, and made their way to the exit, which was at the boundary between first and economy class. Jason felt pity for the economy travellers, who were squeezing themselves out of their stuffy, litter-strewn seats only to be held back by the stewardesses until the first class and business class passengers had disembarked.

'Pleasant flight, mate?' said one of the waiting hordes.

'Hiya Sarah! Fancy meeting you here!' said another.

It was Stuart and Sultan, and they were both grinning like idiots.

3

Jason and Sarah were met off the plane by a smart woman from the VIP Welcome service, who found a shortcut through security checks and baggage reclaim, and led to a waiting limousine just outside the terminal. There was a comfortable hour's ride to their destination, during which Jason texted Stuart.

'Bonjour. WTF U2 doing in Nice?'

'Business m8. New client. Very hush hush. *Fermez la bouche!*'

Jason and Sarah decided this must be some sort of prank, but couldn't work out what. Eventually they arrived at the little coastal resort of Cap Sainte Marie, where the gleaming white Hotel Majestic stood behind an avenue of neatly trimmed palm trees. They checked in to their rooms, which were grand and spacious with enormous windows offering sea views. Sarah insisted they checked out each other's rooms as well as their own and it peeved Jason that they had given Sarah the slightly larger room, which also included an enormous vase of fresh-cut flowers.

There was a note left on the bed in both rooms. It welcomed them to the Rara Avis Induction Event and gave them a schedule for the weekend. They had one hour to unpack, rest and prepare for the evening.

Jason, feeling smart in his classic dinner jacket and bow tie, knocked on Sarah's door at seven o'clock. She opened it and, once again, Jason was taken aback by how stunning she looked.

'So, Mr Bond, I've been expecting you.'

'Nice frock, Miss Moneypenny.'

They went downstairs, curious to see what the other prospective Rara Avis members were like. A smart, short woman dressed in a white suit and holding a clipboard greeted them at the entrance to the magnificent ballroom. She had a business-like manner, but a warm, kind smile. Her sunglasses rested on the top of her head, pinning back her unapologetically bleached blond hair. She had piercing blue eyes, bright red lipstick that matched the shade of her fingernails, and an ostentatious necklace. The colour and condition of her skin told of many summers in full sun.

'Hello, I'm Jane Fortune from Rara Avis. Welcome to the Hotel Majestic. Can I take your names?' She had a clear, musical voice. 'Ah yes, Jason and Sarah, separate rooms. I don't really have to ask whether your rooms are satisfactory; I checked them out this morning myself. They're lovely, aren't they? I hope you like them. Now, I'm going to introduce you to a brother and sister couple who've just come down.'

She marched them over to meet the couple who were standing quietly beside a table, nursing drinks and looking apprehensive. They appeared to be the only black couple in the room.

'Vincent and Helen, this is Jason and Sarah. I'm sure you'll find lots to talk about.' Jane Fortune darted back to the ballroom entrance to welcome other guests.

Helen stood out from the other guests, being the only person dressed for the outdoors. She wore a grey padded coat that looked like it was for everyday school-run use and a voluminous red scarf. She looked around the room, and realising the *faux pas*, she took them off and draped them over the back of a chair.. Her blouse and skirt looked interview-smart rather than evening-out-smart, but she carried it off confidently. Vincent was tall and well built and looked hot and uncomfortable in a suit that was on the tight side.

'Alright, mate?' Jason's firm handshake and West Midlands accent seemed to be just the thing to relax Vincent, and he beamed a welcoming smile.

Helen remained reserved. Sarah tried to engage her in conversation about the excellent canapés that smart waiters and waitresses were bringing round on trays, but Helen said. 'Oh, I'm vegan. I've asked and apparently all of them have meat, fish or dairy,' and that seemed to close down the conversation. Other groups of people seemed to be getting on more cordially, and the buzz of conversation in the room grew steadily.

Shortly, Jane Fortune attracted everyone's attention with the help of her pen and a champagne glass.

'Welcome everyone!' The petite woman threw her arms open wide, making a larger-than-life presence.

'We have a wonderful weekend ahead that I know you will enjoy,' she announced, 'And tomorrow we will explain what Rara Avis is all about. But tonight let's relax. Enjoy the drinks and canapés and take this chance to get to know each other. Shortly, we'll cross over the road to the Casino where we have exclusive use of two salons and where we can get to know each other better.'

Jason whispered, 'I have absolutely no idea what to do in a casino. When I've seen them in spy films and so on, I never have a clue what's going on. Do either of you ever...?'

'No. It's not our thing at all,' Helen whispered back. 'It sounds dreadful, if I'm being honest, and I'm not in favour of gambling, anyway. I wonder if we can get out of it?'

One of the messages that had temporarily appeared on Jason's Rara Avis app had been titled 'What to expect'. It had given some advice about meeting the other 'inductees', and had suggested that for reasons of discretion, it was probably a good idea to adopt a 'Don't Ask, Don't Tell' policy about how much money they had or how they had come by it.

Jason was glad that this meant that he was unlikely to have to explain to Helen that he'd won his fortune on the National Lottery. He also remembered advice from the message that had said, 'Typically, our inductees have enjoyed a recent boost to their finances. We aim to create an atmosphere where members can feel relaxed about their newfound wealth and explore the opportunities that now await them. We can't guarantee that all the activities will suit everyone, but we encourage everyone to engage with them. Every year, it surprises people to find that they have a hitherto unknown passion for speedboat racing, a taste for vintage champagne or a deep love of classical opera. Our advice is to *give it a try!*'

'Well, I expect we can just watch the high-rollers,' Jason said.

'So why are you both here, then? How did you make your fortune?' asked Helen abruptly, in what appeared to Jason to be a flagrant breach of protocol. Her eyes locked on to Jason's and he had the feeling that he wouldn't be released until he answered her.

'Um, tech finance,' said Jason. 'It's very boring, really. Just some lucky breaks, I guess.'

'Oh no, that's really interesting,' said Helen. 'That's kind of why I'm here, too. What kind of lucky breaks?'

Sarah saved the day. 'Oh my God! I don't believe it! Don't all look at once, but have you seen who is over there? I'm sure that's Debbie Angelinie.'

'I'm sorry, who is Debbie Angelinie?' asked Helen, pinning Sarah now with her stare after a brief scan of the room.

Jason felt relieved to be let off the hook. Not that he felt Helen was being hostile to the pair of them. She just seemed intensely interested in everything that was going on.

Sarah explained that Debbie Angelinie was the star of a TV reality show based around the world of fashion modelling; '*Cat Walk Queens*'. It was a format where C-List fashion models competed for who could be the bitchiest fashion divas, whilst sporting the most outrageous costumes and being judged by a panel of D-list pundits and fame-hungry fashion designers, with final votes going to the public. Like most reality shows, it worked best when it became a parody of itself, but it had taken a darker turn when Debbie had gone off the rails and apparently taken an overdose.

Helen said that she never watched such programs, but then she quizzed Sarah about what had triggered Miss Angelinie's breakdown and Sarah was happy to supply the low-down.

'Debbie was like the star of the show, because she always said the stupidest stuff. I mean, they set her up in more and more bizarre situations just to see what she would say or do next. One time, she was at the Royal Variety Show, and she accidentally flashed a boob at Prince Charles, that sort of thing. And the cameras would always turn to her long-suffering boyfriend, Travis Smak, and he'd have this over-the-top, horrified look on his face and say stuff like "Oh my days! What has dozy Debbie done now?" It became a meme.'

'Oh, right, I may have seen something...,' said Helen unconvincingly.

'Yeah, well, it carried on for ages like that,' continued Sarah, 'Until they filmed Debbie in a jacuzzi with two Ipswich Town footballers. Travis, being a Norwich City fan, wasn't having any of that. He went ape. There was a big on-screen bust up, and a few days later came Debbie's off-screen overdose.'

'Oh no!' Helen looked horrified.

'Yeah well, of course at first, everyone on Twitter, Instagram, and in the tabloids were all saying how sad it was for her and how terrible it was that the company behind the show had exploited her. They'd obviously put far too much pressure on a vulnerable young girl. Then later, when it turned out the overdose incident may have been staged in order to boost ratings, public opinion turned and suddenly she was fair game again and there was a right media pile-on.'

'Sounds dreadful,' said Helen, 'But she looks okay now?'

There was loud raucous laughter coming from Debbie's corner of the room, where she was standing with someone who could well be Travis, and another couple, one of which looked a lot like one of the Ipswich Town footballers.

'Perhaps our Debbie's turned a corner,' suggested Sarah.

While this was going on, Jason and Vincent both confessed that they had never watched the show and tried, without success, to find some other common interest to exchange small talk about. The conversation was stilted at first. Football? Wrong teams. Cars? Brief interest in the Lamborghini that Jason had hired, but it became obvious that Jason hadn't really paid attention to anything except the music system. Music? Vincent wasn't interested in music much, but had once been to a Coldplay concert and thought he was possibly the only black guy there. They found amusement in their lack of common interests, and Jason and Vincent warmed to each other. It turned out they both liked video games and had similar views on politics, but they both vehemently agreed that they didn't want to talk about that. They ended up talking about nothing much in particular, a field in which Jason was an expert.

Soon Jane Fortune was standing in the middle of the room, tapping on her glass again.

'Ladies and Gentlemen,' she said. 'It's time to move over to the Casino. Now, please don't worry if you are a stranger to the gaming tables. The staff are very helpful and will explain everything, so don't be embarrassed to ask. We have exclusive use of two salons, L'Atlantique and Le Pacifique. In L'Atlantique, the stakes are high — so not for the fainthearted. In Le Pacifique, there is a maximum stake of one hundred euros, which is certainly more my league. Food will also be available in both rooms and the bars in both salons are excellent... I can personally recommend the Martinis. Now, because of the catering, we would just ask you to stick to whichever salon you choose. Remember, that's L'Atlantique for the high rollers, Le Pacifique for the wimps. Only joking! Anyway, whatever you choose, *bon chance, mes amis!*'

There were about thirty or forty diners, Jason estimated. By this time, everyone seemed very relaxed and even though he had only spoken to Helen and Vincent, he already felt a sort of kindred spirit with his fellow inductees. They were a pretty random selection of people. Debbie Angelinie and her pals appeared to be the only twenty-somethings, although it was difficult to gauge the ages of some of the guests, as they had clearly gone for cosmetic interventions. There were more men than women, and all kinds of fashion mistakes on show; Jason felt pleased that his Dudley tailor had done him proud with his perfect-fit, classic dinner suit. In fact, as they were herded over to the Casino, he thought that he and Sarah were the sharpest dressed couple there. Except that they weren't a couple, of course.

'You okay if we try Le Pacifique – the low stakes room?' muttered Jason to Sarah under his breath, as they walked across the road noticing that although it was now dark, the air was still warm. 'When I lose, I want to lose small'.

'That's fine, Jason. Very sensible,' Sarah muttered back, and then with a slight chuckle, 'Cheapskate.'

The entrance hallway of the Casino was lit by an enormous chandelier. Immaculate waiters stood with trays loaded with glasses of champagne, in case any of the party needed refreshment after the fifty metre walk they had just made. It seemed that most of the party did need refreshment. There were signs pointing the way to the two salons. Most of the guests were opting for the high stakes, L'Atlantique.

The first thing that Jason noticed as they entered Le Salon Pacifique was that the walls were lined with slot machines.

How tacky, thought Jason. Surely only American casinos had slots? And perhaps English ones?

The second thing he noticed was that Richards and Smethwick from Perry's bank were standing on the far side of the room.

The room was quiet and lacking the atmosphere of relaxed affluence that had charged the earlier part of the evening. Only six other people followed Jason and Sarah into the room; Helen and Vincent, two men dressed in powder blue velvet suits, that somehow they had not noticed before, and surprisingly, Debbie Angelinie and Travis.

Richards, with a serious look on his face, and his hair in even better condition than when Jason had met him in London, walked up to greet this last pair and guided them over to a corner of the room where he talked to them in hushed voices. Mr Smethwick spoke to the others.

'Welcome, welcome, Mr Tranter, sir. Nice to see you again. This must be Miss Headly, pleased to meet you. My name is Smethwick. Ah, yes and Mrs Yarnley, we've spoken, haven't we? You'll be glad you brought that coat, I think. And Mr Livingstone. Pleased to meet you. I hope you're having a pleasant evening. Which leaves Misters Simon. We've not met before.'

'I'm Spencer, this is Drew. Not much happening in here, is there?'

'Please bear with us, sir. All will be made clear. We'll just be here a short while.'

Sarah tried again to engage Helen in conversation, asking how her flight over to France had been, and where she had flown from. Helen replied that she and Vincent had come by train, on the Eurostar, as it was better for the planet. By digging harder, she learned that Helen came from Dunstable, near Luton, but it was all hard work. Jason listened in, trying to work out whether the woman was deliberately being evasive, or just naturally a private person.

Eventually, Richards and the young reality show stars walked back from the corner of the room to join the others. Whatever the conversation had been about, the pair were now looking very serious, without a trace of the hilarity that they had displayed earlier in the evening.

Richards spoke with his usual commanding tones. 'Very good, ladies and gentlemen. It appears you have all chosen the correct room. Forgive us, but this has been a bit of a test. Membership of the Rara Avis society is a selective process — we have many applicants and only a handful of new entrants are accepted each year. Everybody who was at the dinner tonight was a high net worth applicant, or their guest, of course. Every applicant had expressed an interest in joining our society, which offers a unique service designed to help those fortunate enough to have amassed significant assets make the best possible use of their money in a discreet way.

'However, at Rara Avis, we don't consider high-stakes gambling in a casino to be the best possible use of money, nor do we consider it to be discreet. In choosing the low-stakes Pacifique Salon, you have proven that you share our values, and have made it through the final stage of the selection process. Now, I hope nobody is desperately keen to play roulette or baccarat just now, because we have other plans. Through that door and down the corridor is an exit leading on to the jetty. A fast boat awaits to take you to meet the other members of Rara Avis. I think you'll find it *enjoyable*.'

Richards' habitually ominous tone made it sound more threatening than enjoyable.

For a moment, the eight 'successful' inductees just looked at one another in astonishment, not knowing whether to feel pleased they had got through a selection process or annoyed that they had not been told that they were taking part in one. Sarah was the first to speak.

'Excuse me, where exactly are we going? It's a bit of a surprise, to say the least, to find out that our plans have just been changed like this.' The others murmured their agreement. Richards started to answer, but just then, Jane Fortune bustled into the room.

'Evening all,' she said cheerily. 'Have you told them the good news yet, Mr Richards? I see we have a couple more than we expected.' She was looking at Debbie Angelinie and Travis. 'That's fine, of course. I expect you've had a word with them to check they're absolutely sure they've made the right choice?'

Richards nodded, and Debbie reached for Travis's hand for reassurance.

'Now,' continued Jane Fortune, 'I expect you're all rather shell-shocked, wondering what is going on? I'm really sorry about that. Over the years, we've found that this is the best way of sorting the two groups, even if it involves a bit of subterfuge. But they're only little white lies, I like to think. In fact, I'll let you into a little secret. I've just announced to the other group that *they* are the winners of the selection process and are now members of "The Secret Millionaires Club". They're delighted, of course, and are partying hard. So don't worry about them. They'll have a marvellous time, spend a lot of money, and if past experience is anything to go by, all be broke again in approximately eighteen months' time. The true Rara Avis society that you are about to be inducted into, tend to find their fortunes growing rather than diminishing, so you have every reason to be pleased with yourselves. Now I can see by your faces that you are apprehensive, so let me explain what is going to happen.

'We have two powerful speed boats ready to whisk you across to a luxury superyacht for an exceptional evening. There'll be other members of Rara Avis to meet you, a fabulous meal, and for your entertainment, a very special band will be playing. They're called CCS, which stands for

Counterfeit Counterfeit Stones. I'll leave you to work out who they are. They'll be playing during a scheduled firework display over Monte Carlo, which you'll be able to watch from the deck of the boat. It's kind of special, you could say. Now, after all that, if you're happy, and I really think you will be, we can arrange for all of your stuff to be transported over from the hotel so that you can spend a few nights on the boat. If you thought the hotel rooms were nice, you wait until you see the cabins on this boat. Over the weekend we can cruise the Med, perhaps drop in our own private island, and generally give you an introduction to the opportunities and experiences that Rara Avis can bring you. So if you're all happy with that, you can make your way through to the jetty. If you have any second thoughts, and want to change your mind, you can, of course, just go back to the hotel.'

The eight looked at each other. Jane Fortune's speech was more reassuring than Richards' proclamation, but Sarah still looked uneasy.

Jason spoke quietly to her. 'I guess this sounds okay? I mean, it sounds pretty amazing — shall we give it a try?'

'Jason, it's up to you, but I'm not sure about this,' said Sarah, frowning. 'A bunch of millionaires on an unexpected mystery boat trip, in the dead of night? I don't want to sound dramatic, but they could be kidnapping us, Jason. For all we know, they could be whisking us off to some unregistered container vessel where they keep us until you cough up a hefty ransom. Have you thought about that?'

Then Helen spoke. Jason was a bit taken aback as he thought they were having a private conversation.

'Don't worry. I don't know much about Rara Avis, but I know... knew someone who's been before. I think it will be fine.' She urged them to the door where Debbie and Travis, Spencer and Drew were already leaving.

Like so much lately, the ride in the speedboats was a first for Jason and Sarah. The boats, moored on either side of a short pier, were enormous, black and shiny, with two young lads waiting to welcome the party on board. The women had to remove their shoes before boarding, and Jason and Sarah were unsure of which surfaces it was safe and proper to walk on. Debbie and Travis looked more confident, or perhaps just cared less, and they made a rush to the back seats near the engine. Jane Fortune and Smethwick also joined them on board, looking relaxed.

The two lads appeared to be in sole charge of the boats, which disturbed Jason somewhat. They both had identical black tee-shirts with the words '*Il Capitano*' on the front. Surely they were too young to be in control of any boat, yet alone these monsters? He wondered what sort of background the boys had and how they came to be driving speed boats on the French Riviera at such an early point in their lives, and where the rest of their lives would progress from this point.

The roar of the motors drowned his thoughts out as they cast off and left the shore. He glanced at Sarah with raised-eyebrows as if to say, 'well, this is happening then.'

The others still looked cool about the whole experience, as if this sort of thing happened every day. As they left the harbour, the lights of Cap Saint Marie quickly diminished in size behind them, and a silver pathway of reflected moonlight seemed to suggest the route ahead for the two boats, steadily motoring side by side. The two young capitanos glanced at each other, flashed bright smiles, pulled back their throttles, and started to race. The passengers were pressed into their seats by the sudden acceleration, the engines roared in their ears and their faces felt the drift of cool spray. Everyone, including Fortune and Smethwick, wore broad smiles.

Within twenty minutes, the roar of the speedboat engines subsided as they drew up to the '*Rara Avis*'.

Jane Fortune had described it as a superyacht but it didn't look like a yacht to Jason. It didn't even look boat-shaped. It looked like a floating hotel. They approached the stern, which consisted of a wide platform, about the size of a tennis-court, just inches above the water level. There were comfortable chairs arranged around a four metre wide jacuzzi, behind which were a couple of tables and a bar. Either side of this deck were enormous staircases, with inlaid lighting that would have looked appropriate in a nightclub. These led up to the next deck level, but it looked like there were two or three storeys above that.

'Well,' said Sarah. 'It ain't no dodgy container ship. Bring it on!'

Jason was pleased and relieved that Sarah was no longer so cautious. The cumulative effect of a day which had included a first class flight, VIP greeting service at Nice airport, limo ride to a first-class hotel, a cocktail reception and now, boarding a superyacht, while dressed in his best dinner suit was to make Jason feel that at last he was living up to his millionaire status. He was grateful to Sarah for looking out for him. Her steady, worldly wise approach was one of the reasons he'd invited her on this adventure, but he loved it when she dropped the protective big sister role and they could both relax and enjoy themselves.

Sarah was first to be helped off the speedboat and was quickly leading Jason by the hand up the illuminated staircase, towards the inviting hubbub of what sounded like a stylish party.

As they ascended, they heard a voice saying, 'Hey, everyone! It's the new members.'

They reached the top and Jason recognised the young man in another of the Rara Avis black tee-shirts walking to greet them. It took him a couple of moments to work out where he had seen him before; Perry's. It was the man-boy whose *GQ* magazine Jason had pinched on the train.

4

'Yo!' said the man-boy, 'Welcome aboard the *Rara Avis*.'

He walked towards Sarah and kissed her on both cheeks.

'Philip Nelson. Everyone calls me Pip,' he said, shaking Jason's hand. 'I've seen you before, at Perry's, haven't I? Listen, word to the wise, you want to get your order in for food, like now. I bet you're starving, aren't you? The galley here is amazing. They will literally cook you anything you like. I don't know how they do it. But if you want to eat quickly, I'd recommend the fish grill on the upper deck. It's the freshest fish you'll ever eat, totes delish and super speedy. You do not want to miss the band later.'

'I'm not great with fish, thanks, all the same,' Jason confessed.

'Aw, come on, Jason,' urged Sarah. 'It sounds great, and I am shaking with hunger. Thanks Pip, I'm Sarah, by the way, and it sounds like you've already met Jason?'

Pip laughed as if he found even the sound of Jason's name amusing. 'Come on, Jason. House rules... *Give it a try!* You haven't even tried fish until you've tasted this. Besides, it's kind of my job to make sure all the new guests find their way around the ship and get everything they need. So, to start with, let me be your culinary guide. Oh hello, who's this? OMG!'

By this time, Debbie Angelinie and Travis had reached the top of the stairs and were looking round vacantly.

'Hey! It's Debbie Angelinie, isn't it?' Pip said. 'Philip Nelson. Everyone calls me, Pip.'

'I'm... Rita Peru,' said Debbie Angelinie, in a firm, determined way.

Sarah came to the rescue.'Ooh, I must admit, I thought you were Debbie as well. You look just like her, and isn't this...?'

'Yeah, this is Travis. And I'm Rita Peru. Okay?' she said this with an appealing grin. 'Now, is there some food somewhere? I'm dead hungry.'

Pip Nelson was quick to lead the party to the bar on the upper deck and acted the grand host, in a manner that Jason thought looked pompous in one of such tender years, and was frankly inappropriate for one of the serving staff — he'd expected something more formal. But Sarah and Debbie Angelinie, or Rita Peru, if she preferred it that way, seemed to lap up the attention that Pip lavished on them. It was as if he couldn't decide who to ingratiate himself with the most; he made sure to hold doors for them both, he pulled a seat from the table for both. Jason looked round at Travis to see whether he was resenting this upstart as much as he was, but Travis Smak was wearing the vacant smirk that he always had.

The smirk was like a shield for him against whatever the world threw at him. As a reality star, he had faced all sorts of bizarre situations, on-screen and off. Romantic intrigue in the Big Brother house, challenging dares in the celebrity jungle, compromising pictures in the red-tops, and tough questioning from high-minded reporters; Travis faced them all with the same insolent look he had first perfected as a primary school scallywag. He was known for it. His agent was even trying to copyright it for him.

The fish came, and Jason graciously admitted that it was spectacularly good. Sarah took out her phone to take a picture of him tucking in. Somehow Pip Nelson swiftly got in the frame also, with a practised photo-bombing smile.

'You won't be able to post that for a while,' he said. 'There's no mobile coverage out here. The comms room boys can get you sorted tomorrow if you need it.'

'So we're completely cut off from the world, then?' said Sarah, looking at Jason, but this time her raised eyebrows were complemented by a grin that seemed to say, 'Who cares? We're here now!'

'Kind of,' said Pip. 'Now, eat up. The Rolling Stones are due on in fifteen minutes.' And that seemed to say something about how cut off they really were.

Pip led them up to the sports deck for the concert, explaining that they'd temporarily boarded over the swimming pool on this deck to provide a dance floor for the concert. 'But there's another swimming pool on Deck Two, so don't worry. There are now thirty-one passenger guests on the *Rara Avis*, including yourselves. The Stones have brought about fifteen personal guests, and a handful of the crew also have permission to watch the concert. So an audience of about fifty — pretty niche, yeah?! Enjoy!' and he left them and went to introduce himself to other new arrivals, Helen Yarnley and her brother, Vincent, and the hairdressers, Spencer and Drew.

Jason's personal music tastes would normally have prevented him from going to see something as mainstream as a Rolling Stones concert, but he wasn't going to be sniffy about an exclusive gig like this. Besides, they were legends, and it turned out they could still play really well.

He looked round at the audience. Quite an assortment, but easily divided into two groups. There were some seriously cool-looking people, some with faces that Jason half-recognised. Some of these were dancing wildly at the front, others were nodding heads, still wearing sunglasses at night. These, he assumed, were part of the Stones' entourage. Then there were the others, dressed much more formally, a lot of overweight men in smart evening suits, holding glasses of champagne, self-consciously shifting from one foot to another in time to the music. Their female partners looked younger and more attractive and danced a little more freely, but still in a way that reminded Jason of corporate functions with PKR Aerospace Engineering in Wolverhampton. So these were fellow millionaire members of Rara Avis.

There were exceptions. One guy in a white evening suit and a black shirt seemed to be on his own, but was dancing, arms in the air, like Zorba the Greek, with no apparent regard to the music that was playing. Spencer and Drew, in their powder-blue tuxedos, were clearly having fun, dancing either side of Sarah, who was definitely letting her hair down. Jason stood with Vincent and Helen, who seemed to be taking it all in, like him.

Jason suddenly had the feeling he was being watched, and he turned and looked toward the mixing desk. It wasn't possible! There were Stuart and Sultan, standing next to the sound engineer. Stuart was absorbed in what the engineer was doing, but Sultan was looking directly at him. As soon as he saw Jason's look of surprised recognition though, Sultan wagged his finger, then put it to his lips, indicating that he didn't want Jason to react. Then he made a gesture, suggesting he thought Jason should turn back round and watch the concert. Jason obeyed, feeling a mixture of disappointment that his weekend adventure didn't appear to be as exclusive as he had expected, and excitement about seeing his best mates.

Meanwhile, Debbie Angelinie, or Rita Peru as she seemed to want to be known, and her boyfriend, Travis, had moved to stand by the railings on one side of the deck. It wasn't a great place to see the band, but turned out to be a prime spot to catch the fireworks that started towards the end of the concert, just as the Stones were playing '*Gimme Shelter*'. Rockets were launched from another boat halfway between the *Rara Avis* and the mainland. At the same time, they could see other displays at various resorts along the coast. It made a fantastic scene and for a while Mick Jagger lost his audience, while they turned and looked at the impressive display. Debbie and Travis turned their back on the fireworks and faced the audience. Debbie smiled and posed for the crowd; Jason wondered what was going through her head. Could she possibly think that she was the attraction that was upstaging the Rolling Stones? Travis adopted his trademark foolish smirk. It was impossible to tell what he was thinking, apart from possibly, 'Where the fuck am I? And what the fuck am I doing here?'

5

'Where the hell am I, Vincent? And what the hell am I doing here?' Helen was having doubts about leaving the kids with her brother's wife and jetting off to the south of France, and now, alone with her brother in their private, luxurious cabin of a superyacht she could release some of the tension that had been bottled up inside her.

On board the *Rara Avis*, she was surrounded by wealth and privilege, notions that she had railed against all her life. When her own newfound wealth had come so suddenly, she didn't feel at all comfortable about it. She understood why her late husband had felt so conflicted.

'I'll tell you what you're doing here,' said Vincent calmly. 'You're trying to find out what happened to David. You're trying to find out what's behind all this Rara Avis bullshit. And you're doing good. If anyone can get to the bottom of all this, it's you, little sis. And even though all the other black people on this ship left with their friends, the Rolling Stones, and we are probably the only ones left on board, you look like you were born into this life. I don't know where you get it from.'

It was true. Helen had always exuded a quiet confidence. Vincent knew that this was often a front, and that she was as nervous as hell inside, but still he felt jealous of her ability to project such a calm facade.

'I must admit, though,' Vincent continued. 'It's a bit mind-blowing. This place out-does the Kardashians. We've just seen the Rolling Stones, man! I never thought I'd see them. I mean, I don't even like them much, but they were pretty good, weren't they?'

'Yeah, I guess,' said Helen, in a tired voice. 'To be honest, my mind wasn't really on it. I was trying to suss out the people here. I wouldn't trust any of them farther than I could throw them. And there's a lot of fat old bastards that I couldn't throw very far.'

'Oh, come on, sis. That couple, Jason and Sarah, they seem okay?'

'He's alright. She asks a lot of questions.'

'Not like you then,' Vincent grinned. He was one of the few people in the world who could get away with pointing out any tiny trace of hypocrisy that his sister might be exhibiting.

'You may have a point,' Helen admitted in a playfully stern voice. 'Let's get some sleep. I feel I haven't slept for seventy-two hours.'

Vincent switched on the TV while Helen changed in the en-suite bathroom.

'I'm going to complain,' he said. 'I don't think much of the entertainment system. There's only French and Italian stations. And Sky news channel. And the cabin phone doesn't work. I was going to check in with home.'

'Vincent,' his sister said. 'You've just been to a private concert by the Rolling Stones. It's nearly three in the morning. No one wants a phone call from you just now. Shut up and go to sleep.'

6

Three young men were not quite ready for sleep for various reasons. Jason, Stuart and Sultan sat on the top deck around a small table sipping ice-cold Czech lagers while roadies efficiently dismantled the stage and equipment after the performance of the Counterfeit Counterfeit Stones.

'You can't really call them "roadies", Jason,' said Sultan. 'Not on the sea. No roads'

'What then?' asked Jason.

'Boaties?' suggested Stuart.

'So, come on then,' said Jason. 'What are you two idiots doing here? Can't you leave me alone for a couple of days, even?'

'It's our new job, isn't it?' replied Stuart. 'They've hired us to fly drones over the ship. Boss wants some promotional footage, apparently, but he's also said we should try to get pictures of any boats that get close by.'

'The boss being...?' asked Jason.

'Some guy called Richards,' said Sultan. 'Bit of a weirdo, if you ask me. Amazing hair! But what about you, millionaire playboy? Decide to jet down to the South of France and catch a private gig with the Rolling Stones, did you? You and Sarah, eh? What are you doing tomorrow, then? Afternoon tea with the Prince of Monaco?'

'I couldn't tell you, mate. My life is now officially out of control. I haven't got a clue, but...' Jason burped for dramatic effect. '... I can confirm that the millionaire lifestyle is all very pleasant. Pity you two will have to work tomorrow, ha-ha!'

'Oh man! More than you know,' replied Stuart. 'We picked up some extra work tonight, didn't we, bro?'

Sultan just rolled his eyes up to the star-filled sky while Stuart explained what had happened.

'So we were watching the gig,' he said. 'Now we probably shouldn't have been there because it was meant to be for guests like you, not humble crew like us. But we'd only just got here, nobody knows who we are and we haven't got the regulation crew black tee-shirts. Sultan figured we could always plead ignorance if they challenged us, so we crashed the party. I kept expecting to be thrown out, so we was clocking everyone and keeping a low profile at the back. And then I noticed this guy with two phones. This was before the Stones took to the stage, before Jagger asked everyone to switch phones off. You know: "We are the Counterfeit Counterfeit Stones, and there must be no evidence of this gig, because if they ever find out, the real Counterfeit Stones will probably sue us". Very amusing. Well, I could tell this guy, one of the crew, was preparing to film the gig. He's got one phone taped to the lighting rig at the back and he's speaking to someone on the other phone, and adjusting the angle of the phone while he's talking. And I'm explaining to Sultan that something clever is going on here because there is no coverage out here, so they must have some IP connection and a relay service or something.'

'You are truly the prince of nerds, Stuart,' groaned Sultan. 'But it's probably just as well. Because we're one song into the gig and I've got a touch on the shoulder from the boss man, Mr Richards, asking what the hell we're doing at the concert.

To be fair, he was more polite than that, but I could tell he was pretty pissed off. So, straight off, I just say "This is clearly a security-sensitive situation, and although we weren't given any instructions, we thought we'd better take the initiative, and give the place the once over." He didn't seem to be buying it until I dropped the bombshell. "For instance," I said, "We were just about to report that someone appears to be livestreaming the concert." Richards is sceptical. "I doubt that very much," he says, all high and mighty. "The comms on this ship are locked down. All traffic is routed via the comms room. When we're out at sea, no connections are made with the outside world without them being routed through the comms team." So Stuart points out the guy with the phones and it turns out he is the communications officer. Richards goes over, has a brief word with him and ten minutes later the muscle arrives and they escort our friend off the ship, on a speedboat bound for the shore. Unless they pushed overboard and fed him to the sharks, I'm not sure. Anyway, the important thing is suddenly Richards is telling us how brilliant we are and asking if we can fill the temporary vacancy in the comms room, given our obvious expertise. Ha! Don't tell him I'm only a maths teacher.'

'What can I say?' answered Jason, beaming. 'You are an esteemed employee of Tranter Diall Electronic Surveillance

Services. Naturally, you can adapt to almost any role thrown at you. But speaking as the Chief Executive Officer of that organisation, I'd like to know what the bloody hell you're doing still awake at three in the morning? What time are you supposed to be reporting for duty tomorrow... I mean this morning?'

'Yeah, yeah. Alright boss. What about you, though? Hadn't you better turn in? Sarah will wonder where you've got to.'

Jason's smile vanished, and the tips of his ears reddened. It bothered him that there was now a taboo topic of conversation for his closest friends, but his friendship with Sarah was definitely off limits. He didn't even allow himself to think about it much, always pushing it to the back of his mind. He didn't know what sort of relationship he had with Sarah, and he didn't even know what kind of relationship he wanted. What he did know was that the cabin that they had been given contained a double bed. They hadn't spoken about it when they briefly checked in and changed for the concert, each discreetly using the en-suite. Then, after the concert, Sarah had said that she was beaten, and that she was going back to the cabin. Jason had said that he had wanted to catch up with Stuart and Sultan, and that he'd be back shortly. And that was over an hour ago.

He said his goodbyes to the lads and, after a few wrong turns, made his way to the cabin. He briefly considered the option of finding somewhere else to crash out for the night — he could remember seeing a sun lounger on an upper deck — but after a moment's pause, he gingerly opened the door. A bedside light was on, and Jason could see that someone had somehow re-configured the double bed into two singles, and Sarah was fast asleep in one of them.

Ten minutes later he was stretched out in the other, trying to work out whether he felt disappointed, excited, or both.

7

Helen woke at eight o'clock with a start. Sunlight leaked into the cabin from the curtained portholes. The same questions were back in her mind. Where the hell was she? And what the hell was she doing here? These questions were joined by several others. How long were they going to be on this boat? Was it going anywhere? What if they wanted to leave? Was this some sort of high-class prison ship? She decided she needed answers more than she needed sleep. Within twenty minutes, she was up and dressed, and left her sleeping brother to go looking for breakfast and some answers.

The morning sunshine seemed impossibly bright, and although there was a light breeze, it already felt warm. The ship was at anchor and the French coast looked a long way away, but Helen guessed they hadn't moved while she had slept, which reassured her a little. A few crew in black t-shirts were clearing the debris from last night's festivities, but otherwise the decks were deserted. For a while she stared at a buoy bobbing in the blue-green sea. Small fish were nibbling around a rope that descended from the buoy and faded out of view. 'I guess that sums it up,' she thought. 'Out at sea, and out of my depth.' She pulled herself together and found her way down to the lower stern deck, where she saw Richards and Jane Fortune breakfasting together.

'Mind if I join you?' Helen asked, taking hold of the spare chair at their table. Richards looked up, frowning, as if ready to complain about the interruption, but Jane Fortune stood up and hugged Helen, bestowing air-kisses and saying 'Of course not, Mrs Yarnley. Wow! You're an early riser!'

Helen decided she might as well go in head first. 'I couldn't sleep. This has all happened too quickly for me. I only found out about this Rara Avis thing a few weeks ago. Perhaps I'm a fool, but I've come out here without knowing what it's all about. I had no idea we'd be on a boat. Forgive me for asking, but what happens next? What if I decide I don't want to stay?'

'Jane, was Mrs Yarnley given all the details?' Richards didn't seem to acknowledge Helen at all. He fixed his stare on Jane Fortune.

'Of course, but it's a lot to take in. Mrs Yarnley has a lot on her mind.' She wrung her hands in an awkward gesture of sympathy as she added softly, 'Mrs Yarnley is David Yarnley's widow, you remember? She's only recently become aware of his involvement in Rara Avis.'

'I understand that. I don't see why that stops her being briefed on what's going on. It seems to me...'

Jane cut in. 'Helen... you don't mind if I call you Helen?' She leaned forward, grabbed Helen's hand and held it in both of hers.

A bit over-the-top, thought Helen, and she stared confidently back.

'I'm sorry things haven't been explained better,' Jane continued. 'Normally, we would have had a meeting last night, but with the concert and the fireworks, we've had to shift things around. It must seem all very mysterious, but it isn't, really. Rara Avis is just a private club for individuals of high net worth. All we do is help people part with their money... in the nicest possible way, of course! We arrange great experiences in spectacular locations, so that our members and their guests can have wonderful times, while still being discreet, out of the public gaze.'

A waiter approached the table, pushing a heated trolley.

'Ah, here comes Pip,' Jane purred. 'Richards and I have ordered a cooked breakfast. Would you like to join us? I'm having the full English. I know it sounds mad in the middle of the Mediterranean, but I'm a firm believer that it sets you up for the day. Can we tempt you?'

This morning, Pip Nelson was the model of an unobtrusive, efficient waiter. He pressed a button and the heated trolley opened like a Chinese puzzle box, displaying all kinds of breakfast items in separate secret containers that slid out automatically with a satisfying pneumatic hiss. Jane Fortune's eyes widened at the array of food on offer.

'I bet you like pressing that button,' she chuckled. 'What about you, Helen? What can we tempt you with?'

Helen looked up at the Pip's cheerful, accommodating face, and she frowned.

'Just coffee and toast, for me, please.'

Breakfast was served. Helen's toast was crisp and warm, the coffee was excellent. Richards had croissants that smelled freshly baked, and a plate was laid out with sausages, bacon, mushrooms and a perfectly fried egg for Jane Fortune.

'Perhaps an extra sausage for me, Pip,' she said.

It was quite a big breakfast for a small woman, Helen thought. But Fortune looked like one of those women who was always full of energy — perhaps the calories didn't stick to her.

Richards looked directly at Helen for the first time.

'Ms Fortune makes Rara Avis sound like an upmarket version of Thomson Holidays,' he said. 'There's a more important side to the organisation that she hasn't mentioned yet. I set up this whole thing back in 1990 as a way of introducing wealthy people to good causes. You see, my day job at a London bank involves me helping wealthy people invest their money wisely. But early in my career, I realised two things. Firstly, although most wealthy people love to flaunt how wealthy they are, there are some rich people that, for one reason or another, prefer to keep it quiet. Secondly, although, in my experience a lot of these private wealthy people, are eager to keep a tight hold of their money, there are a few rare birds who want to do good, spread their wealth and support good causes, but they want to do it anonymously.'

Helen was interested. This was exactly what she wanted to hear about. Her husband was one of these 'rare birds' who wanted to do some good with the money that his father had given him.

Richards continued, 'So I started setting up events where charities would pitch to a group of potential donors at discrete private meetings. Then I noticed something else that was very interesting. I had assumed that these shy, retiring philanthropists would prefer to attend events held in modest, nondescript locations — rented meeting rooms in hotels, that sort of thing. But it turned out that the more upmarket the location, the more generous the benefactors were. And they started telling me how much they enjoyed the events, and how much they appreciated the fact that I kept everything out of the public spotlight, and eventually, the entertainments side took off, so that today we have this current jamboree, where I have to wonder whether the primary aim of the organisation has been lost, somewhat.'

By the end of his sentence, Richards sounded very irritated, and there was a short, awkward silence.

Jane Fortune shifted on her seat.'Forgive him, Helen. Richards is such a misery. Although I saw him tapping his feet to the Rolling Stones last night. Weren't they wonderful?'

'But isn't this all a bit dodgy?' Helen didn't want to allow the conversation to drift now that she was getting a better understanding of how Rara Avis operated. 'I mean, secret millionaires in hideaway locations, making anonymous donations? Forgive me, but it sounds like a perfect breeding ground for corruption; money laundering, that sort of thing.

I'm not accusing anyone, of course, but you know what I mean. How do you keep it all "above board"?'

Richards looked at Jane Fortune, but she had a mouthful of sausage, so he spoke for her. 'That's where Ms Fortune comes into her own. My background is in banking and finance, Jane's is in law. She and her team check that all our members are bona fide and that all transactions are "strictly legal in the appropriate countries of jurisdiction". Is that the correct wording, Jane?'

'Something like that, yes,' Jane replied. 'It's all very tedious. There are the non-disclosure agreements, especially with charities, who have to respect our members' privacy. And then there is the daunting task of understanding all the various tax regimes around the world.'

'And how to evade them?' suggested Helen with an air of casual reproach.

She was pleased with herself for keeping her cool and not appearing intimidated by this alien world of high-fliers. Inwardly, her heart was beating quickly and her stomach wouldn't let her do more than nibble her toast.

'And how to tread that fine line between tax evasion and tax efficiency,' returned Jane quickly, with a hint of a frown. 'Paying every penny of tax that is due, and not a penny more.' She had the manner of a schoolteacher, reprimanding a cheeky pupil, and wagged her fork, loaded with sausage, in Helen's direction to emphasise how serious she was.

'The last thing anyone here wants is a tax fraud scandal,' she said. 'Rara Avis is a rare example of a set-up where everyone wins. It's a unique and delicate balance that we work hard to protect. Our members get to have a great time, put their money to good use and stay anonymous. The charities get access to some of the richest benefactors they are ever going to find.'

'And you?' asked Helen.

'Richards and I get to use our talents to help all of this happen. And we get to do it with working breakfasts on luxury superyachts in the sunny Mediterranean.' Jane Fortune waved her fork in a long arc to point out the magnificent view of the Riviera coastline, which gleamed expensively in the sunlight. 'The salary we draw from Rara Avis is negligible, believe me. But we live like millionaires!'

With this, she flung her arms out in a wide, celebratory gesture.

It was all too much for a seagull that was perched on the deck rail, keenly regarding the progress of this last remaining piece of sausage. It saw its chance and took off on a flight path that beautifully intercepted the trajectory of Jane Fortune's fork, gaining the tasty morsel.

8

A short, bearded man, dressed in the same white tuxedo and black open-necked shirt that Helen had seen him dancing in the night before, clumsily descended the stairs to the lower deck. He had a glass in one hand and a bottle of vodka in the other, and he clinked the two together in a gesture of appreciation.

'Bravo! Bravo, Boris!' he called. 'Did you ever see such a talented seagull?'

Jane looked furious, presumably more concerned by the close encounter with a sharp-beaked, sharp-clawed scavenger than the loss of sausage.

'Are you okay?' asked Helen.

'That blasted bird! I'm fine, thank you,' said Jane. 'Allow me to introduce Anatoly Morozov, who I swear has been training that bird to be a nuisance for the last week.'

'Boris needs no training,' said Morozov. 'He has natural talent. Now, who do I have the pleasure of...?'

'This is Mrs Helen Yarnley,' Jane said. 'I think you knew her late husband, David.'

'Mrs Yarnley,' said the man, looking suddenly very serious. He pulled up a chair, sat down and focussed his bleary blue eyes on Helen. 'Yes. I had the pleasure to know your husband.

He was very fine man. May I give you my... great, great, sorrow. His death was a sad, sad....'

'Yes, quite,' interrupted Richards, and suddenly various meaningful glances were traded across the breakfast table. Anatoly Morozov, showed his resentment at being interrupted by leaning back on his chair and raising his hands as if to say 'What have I said?'. Richards and Jane Fortune both leaned forward, looking embarrassed and concerned that the drunken Russian might be about to tread on Helen's feelings. And for a moment, Helen dropped her guard and looked backwards and forwards at Richards and Fortune with wounded surprise. How did this stranger know David?

Richards spoke up. 'I'm sure Mr Morozov won't mind my mentioning that he was a joint donor to the fund that your husband, David, was involved with. A school in Africa, wasn't it?'

Morozov slumped back down in his chair and closed his eyes, perhaps to signal his agreement, but possibly because he could hardly keep them open.

'Ah! Okay then.' Helen regained her cool. 'I really want to find out more about the charity. I want to be sure that David's help has reached the children he was trying to support. My solicitor is looking into the matter, but I haven't heard anything yet.'

'That's a.... Mr Jarrold, isn't it?' Richards frowned as he tried to remember the name. 'He contacted me several weeks ago. I'm afraid we don't track all the projects of the charities we introduce our members to, but I asked Jane to pass on the query to the charity manager. I would have thought he would have responded by now, surely, Jane?'

'Yes, I would expect so,' Jane replied. 'It's a Monsieur Bertrand, if I remember correctly. He's based in Belgium himself, but he's in contact with the charity workers. He'll be able to report back to your solicitor, but it sometimes takes quite a while.'

'Ksshhh!' Anatoly Morozov sat up and was alert again. 'I doubt he will get a report.' He locked his eyes on Helen with an intimidating stare.

'Why ever would you say that, Anatoly?' asked Jane, trying to calm him.

The Russian slowly turned towards Jane and said, 'Say what?'

'That you doubt Ms Yarnley's solicitor would ever get details of the African school project?'

Anatoly Morozov shrugged and his mouth twisted in a leery half-smile. 'I too have tried. Is difficult to get any information out of that country. Is difficult to get any reliable information.'

His speech was slowing, and words competed with hiccups. 'So much trouble in that country. Democratic Republic of Congo. So much trouble. Lawlessness everywhere. Danger. Everywhere.... '

Richards interrupted. 'Mr Morozov, you're looking very tired. Perhaps Jane could show you safely to your room? I'm sure there'll be a chance to talk with Mrs Yarnley later.'

Morozov made a noisy protestation, but whether it was his lack of ease with the English language or an alcohol-induced problem with language in general, he was unintelligible. Jane Fortune rose and steadied him with a supportive arm. Pip Nelson appeared from behind the bar, and taking Morozov's other arm, somehow the three of them ascended the stairs.

'I'm so sorry, Mrs Yarnley,' said Richards. 'Perhaps Mr Morozov will benefit from a little rest. I like to think the members of Rara Avis are a self-selecting group who prefer the quiet life, but we do still find the odd larger-than-life character amongst our party. And perhaps that's no bad thing. Anatoly Morozov has been a member for a good many years, practically lives on board the *Rara Avis*, and has supported many of our good causes. But I think you may get a more reliable account of the African project via your solicitor.'

Helen looked impassively at Richards, weighing him up. A banker. She couldn't count the number of times she and her friends had verbally slung mud at all bankers and their kind. She knew it wasn't really fair to stereotype all members of a profession, but such was her hatred and distrust of that profession, she felt justified in making an exception. And he didn't seem to make any effort to break out of the stereotype. He was aloof, detached, emotionally repressed. Or at least that was how he came across.

'Thank you, Mr Richards,' she said coolly. 'I'd call Mr Jarrold, but my phone has no signal here, and the phone in my cabin isn't working. Is there any way–?'

'You should be able to make calls from the phone in your cabin.' The note of irritation had returned to Richards' voice. 'If you prefer to use your mobile, take it to the tech team on the forward deck. Any of the Black Tees will show you the way. The tech team will sort it for you somehow. In fact, here are the two newest members of that team now. I'm afraid they only arrived last night, so they won't be much immediate assistance, but I'm sure if you give them an hour or two, they will be up to speed and able to help. Gentlemen! This is Mrs Yarnley. She'll need some help with her phone. Can you speak to Mr Smethwick and get him to show you around the comms room? I appreciate you'll have a steep learning curve, but I'm sure you'll manage. And I'm keen that you get started on your drone work as well. And now, I must get ready for the members' meeting, if you'll excuse me. It's been a pleasure, Mrs Yarnley.'

Sultan and Stuart, dressed in new black tee-shirts, and trying to look like alert and presentable members of 'the team' after less than three hours' sleep, nodded to Richards as he left. Stuart told Helen they'd fix up her cabin phone as soon as he'd worked out how.

Rather than heading straight for the comms room, as soon as Richards had left the deck, the pair went to the bar and asked for coffee to take with them.

'Sorry lads, guests only,' the barman said. 'Staff galley is forward on this deck. But do us a favour first, will you? Pip is supposed to be here with me, but he's had to help Ms Fortune take a Russian guest who was a little the worse for wear back to his cabin. Now I can tell exactly what is going to happen next. The gentlemen will start demanding his *selyodka*. He comes here every morning for it. He claims it's a perfect hangover cure. It's Russian pickled herring and we get it in especially for him and serve it on black rye bread. I was just about to serve him, but now he's back in his room. Can you take it, please? Pip will probably still be there — you can give it to him if you like.'

Stuart and Sultan watched the barman quickly prepare the breakfast and then followed his directions from the lower deck, up to the main deck and to Anatoly Morozov's cabin. As they approached, they could hear raised voices and the door was slightly ajar. Sultan raised his hand, indicating that they should hang back for a moment. They could hear two voices, one a clearly distressed man with a slurred Russian accent and the other a woman's voice, evidently trying to placate him.

'Best to get some rest now, Mr Morozov,' said the woman. 'You'll feel better if you can sleep.'

'Very kind lady,' mumbled the Russian. 'Yes, put Anatoly to bed. Put him out of the way. There, there. You make everything right. No trouble on the *Rara Avis*. All quiet on the *Rara Avis*. But I still have this! Ha! Yes, I still have this.'

Stuart couldn't resist peering through the gap in the door to see what it was that Anatoly Morozov still had. He was lying on the bed, but triumphantly holding up a small hip flask. Jane Fortune reached over the bed to take the flask off him, but Morozov pulled her down onto the bed on top of him. He had one arm across her back, the other still holding the hip-flask aloft, and the two were rolling from side to side. Pip Nelson joined in, trying to release Jane Fortune from Morozov's clasp, but the Russian swung the hip-flask round, catching Pip just above the eye and he fell to the floor. Jane Fortune continued to struggle, but her muffled screams were drowned out by what were presumably Russian obscenities.

Stuart and Sultan felt they had to intervene and entered the cabin. Sultan was an easy match for the surprising strength of Morozov, and he quickly freed Jane Fortune. Stuart picked Pip off the floor. Morozov fell quiet and closed his eyes.

Jane Fortune didn't seem particularly grateful for the intervention. Rather, she seemed annoyed. She grabbed the flask from Morozov, saying 'Yes, well, that's enough of that.' She turned to Sultan and Stuart and, frowning at them, said, 'I don't think it needs four of us in here, thank you.'

Stuart said by way of explanation, 'The barman at the Stern Bar asked us to bring this up for the gentleman. It's his usual breakfast. Apparently.'

'Well, I don't suppose he's going to want that now. Just leave it on the side there. Then you can leave us.'

Morozov was already snoring lightly. The pair retreated and closed the cabin door behind them. They retraced their steps to the lower deck without speaking and found the crew galley, by some sort of instinct, drawn by a primal need for coffee and calories. As they opened the door, however, Mr Smethwick greeted them.

'Ah, good. I've been looking for you. You'll be wanting me to show you around the comms room.'

9

As a teacher, Helen hoped that the lecture theatre aboard the *Rara Avis* would offer a refuge of familiarity, in what otherwise was the very alien world of a superyacht. This room doubled as a small cinema, so the seats were more comfortable than the lecture theatre seats that Helen was used to. Helen and Vincent were the first to arrive, and the gnome-like Smethwick greeted them. Vincent made for the back row, but Helen insisted on sitting near the front. The other new members to Rara Avis started to arrive and Helen mentally checked them over, the way she always liked to check over her students when they arrived for the first class of term. First were the couple, Spencer and Drew, both dressed in Hawaiian shirts and cargo shorts. They had tried to drag her onto the dance floor at one point last night, but she had resisted. She admired their spirit, though. They were determined to bring a touch of Village Soho to the stuffy, respectable millionaire clientele of Rara Avis. Today, they were more subdued. They had switched to being an earnest pair of students, who were going to hang on to teacher's every word.

The couple from the Midlands, Jason and Sarah, came in next and made their way to sit next to Helen and Vincent. Helen wasn't sure about these two. He looked a bit of a poser with his hipster beard and pointy shoes and Sarah was so nosey — always asking questions. Vincent was pleased to see them though, and he wasn't a bad judge usually. Then came the young couple, the reality show star, Debbie, or rather, Rita, and her bloke, Travis. The pair made for the back row; the boy walking with a laboured, 'too-cool-for-school' swagger. He looked ridiculous, but Helen guessed he wasn't at all bothered.

Finally, Richards and Fortune entered along with the young man, who had served her breakfast; Pip, wasn't it? She hadn't really noticed his face then, but observing him now, he looked oddly familiar. He was young enough that he could have been a recent pupil at her school. Now and then, back in Bedford, strangers would greet her outside of school and she'd not have a clue who they were. An occupational hazard. But that was unlikely to be the reason for recognising someone all the way out here, surely? She guessed she had just seen him the night before, perhaps.

Helen realised several minutes into the talk that she was going to be disappointed by the event. She was here on a mission. She wanted to find answers to the questions she had about how her husband David had come to be shot in the head on a dusty track in the Democratic Republic of the Congo. Somehow she had thought that this introduction to Rara Avis was going to lead her to these answers, but Richards and

Fortune were telling her nothing she hadn't heard already. The organisation existed to provide private settings in which wealthy people could combine philanthropy with luxury. As well as this superyacht, the organisation owned a mountain retreat in the Swiss Alps, a country estate in Wiltshire, and a private island off the coast of Italy, with its own huge luxury resort hotel, complete with pools, secluded beaches and its own car-racing track. As well as the properties they owned, the organisation also had access to many elite destinations in the Caribbean, South America, Africa and Asia. Jane Fortune described these while photos were projected onto the screen behind her.

Richards' portion of the talk was concerned with the philanthropic side of the ventures. He gave examples of the charities and causes that they had contacts with. Some of it was emergency relief work, other projects tackled longer-term problems. He explained that many members wanted to use their wealth to help address the climate crisis, for example, and that they had hosted successful fundraisers for conservation pressure groups. This would have normally interested Helen, as she could easily see how this could stray into political territory, and already had deep suspicions about which direction the politics of a club like Rara Avis might lean, but she was distracted. She couldn't take her eyes off the young man sitting at the front with Jane Fortune, and she still struggled to place him. Was he an ex-pupil? He caught her staring a couple of times and flashed a grin at her. Something about his smile unnerved her even more, and she began to feel dizzy. Eventually, Richards introduced him to the audience.

'I'm sure you all have many things you are uncertain about and in a minute I'll open the session up for questions, but first I'd like to introduce Philip Nelson, if you haven't met him already. Stand up, Pip. Philip, or Pip as he likes to be called, is a promising young chap, and I've made him responsible for making sure that you all enjoy your trip on the *Rara Avis* — and so please feel free to ask him for anything you need or desire.'

Pip started his prepared speech about his role on the ship, albeit a little hesitantly at first.

Helen listened, but couldn't concentrate on what he was saying. Something about his mannerisms and voice was unsettling her. By the time it came for questions at the end of the session, she was desperate to get outside into the fresh air. For a moment, it looked like no-one had any questions, but unexpectedly Travis, the reality star's boyfriend, spoke up.

'Er... yeah. Can anyone, like, bring a charity along... y'know... like suggest a charity that people can give to?'

Richards looked confused by the question and angry at the inarticulacy.

Jane Fortune replied. 'Well, yes, I'm sure we could accommodate that.'

Travis grinned proudly. 'Alright then, I suggest the "Build Travis a Fuckin' Mansion" charity. Sweet!' and collapsed into his chair, laughing.

'Ignore him' said his girlfriend and punched him as he sat down. 'He's a dickhead.'

As they left the meeting, Jason Tranter invited Helen and Vincent to join him and Sarah for a cup of tea at a bar he'd found on an upper deck. Vincent agreed at once, and Helen liked the sound of an upper deck.

As well as sets of sun loungers, this open-air bar included a games area, including a ping-pong table and a computer game console, with virtual reality headsets. It was these that attracted the attention of the two men. A Black Tee was on hand to get them started and soon they were standing on special mats a few feet apart with headsets that resembled elongated motorcycle helmets covering their heads. For a moment they stood still with their heads turning from side to side and looking up and down and just making appreciative noises. 'Wow!', 'Oh man!', 'Yeah!'. Then suddenly, presumably, the game began, and they started waving hand controls about in the air, ducking and weaving and looking generally ridiculous.

'They have literally zero shame, don't they?' said Sarah, reclining on a lounger next to Helen. 'I mean, what on earth are they doing?'

'I guess it makes as much sense as anything else around here,' said Helen, almost to herself.

Sarah looked hard at Helen before saying, 'So you've got your reservations about all this as well, have you?'

Helen blinked her eyes and gave a half smile as confirmation.

'It's all a bit too easy, isn't it?' Sarah continued, 'I've been telling Jason he's got to be careful. All this money, all this wealth all on one boat, I keep thinking we're going to find it's a great big kidnap plot. Maybe I'm paranoid, I haven't had half enough sleep lately, but I'm really not sure about that Richards character. What do you think?'

'He's interesting,' said Helen guardedly. 'He seems very uptight. I hadn't thought about kidnap plots, but you're right. It does all seem a bit too good to be true. The combination of obscene wealth and secrecy has never sounded like a good idea to me. And yes, I think we should all be on the look-out.'

They looked around. A man at a nearby sun lounger lay on his back, with a copy of the *Financial Times* over his face. Over by the bar, with virtual-reality helmets securely strapped on, Jason and Vincent flailed about in the Mediterranean sunshine like blindfolded men fighting wasps.

Helen asked, 'But, tell me, what did you make of Philip Nelson? There's something about him I can't put my finger on, but it was bugging me throughout that meeting.'

'Oh, Pip, you mean,' Sarah laughed. 'Well, Jason can't stand him. I think he's okay. He's very young, but quite sweet. A lot more fun than most of the old guys here. Harmless, though, I would have thought. But you say you never liked the sound of a secret society of rich people... so why are you here? If you don't mind me asking? Tell me if I'm being nosey.'

Helen decided it was time to drop her guard. She thought Sarah was being very nosey, but nevertheless, it was reassuring to find a fellow woman who was also curious about this strange situation. She told the whole story about how her late husband had secretly received a fortune from his estranged father, how he'd joined Rara Avis and become a donor to the Yepi-Kasai School Foundation charity. Sarah listened attentively, asking questions now and again. When Helen spoke of David's trip to the DRC and his murder, Sarah placed a reassuring hand on Helen's arm. She was interested in all the details of the Congolese Police report that Helen's solicitor, Jarrold, had managed to obtain. Helen felt relieved that someone else was thinking along the same lines as her.

'I don't see his death as just a random act of violence in a violent country,' Helen insisted. 'There's something more to this than that. And that's why I had to come here, to trace David's steps almost, to work out what went on. I met a man at breakfast this morning who was also sponsoring the same school in the DRC. A Russian guy. He was drunk...'

Helen suddenly became aware of someone blocking her sunlight. It was a Black Tee carrying a tray holding two gin and tonics, and a small bowl of nuts. Helen squinted up at him crossly.

'I don't remember us ordering these...' but the clinking of the ice cubes in the tall stemmed balloon glasses was too much temptation. Her eyes rolled, and she gave the boy a grateful smile, '... but they're very welcome, thank you. Oh, it's you! Pip, isn't it? How did you know we needed these?'

'Just a lucky guess. I hope I haven't intruded and I hope you like the drinks.' He flashed a smile and was gone.

Sarah remarked she could get used to this life, where drinks were served before you'd even realised you wanted one. She grinned, but Helen looked perplexed. She was still trying to work out why that boy made her feel so uneasy.

Sarah said, 'I think you need to phone your solicitor and find out what he's unearthed about the charity. And I think we need to speak to your Russian friend and find out what he knows. Let's take a stroll.'

Helen noticed how Sarah had somehow invited herself in on her quest, but she didn't object. She suddenly felt stronger and more prepared to ask questions again, and thought how often it was the case that the support of a sisterly woman had this effect. Or perhaps it was just the gin and tonic. They finished their drinks and got up from the comfortable loungers. Jason and Vincent were still engrossed in their virtual reality game.

'I wonder when they'll miss us,' said Helen.

As they left the deck, the corpulent man who had been reclining beneath a copy of the *Financial Times* removed the paper, stared after the two women and tutted.

10

The Communications Room of the *Rara Avis* was just aft of the Bridge. Stuart and Sultan were being shown the equipment by Mr Smethwick.

'I don't pretend to be an expert by any means, gentlemen, but as you can see, we have a hybrid set-up that keeps the ship's systems running and allows crew and passengers to connect with the outside world. When we're out on the open sea, as we are now, all the traffic is sent and received via VSAT, the satellite dish on the upper deck. When we're closer to land, we can pick up a 4g signal, so the system automatically switches to that. The ship's LAN has ethernet connectivity to all the cabins and there are four Wi-Fi hotspots. It's enough bandwidth for most needs, but I gather the latency leaves something to be desired. But as I say, I'm no expert in these matters.'

Stuart and Sultan exchanged guilty looks, wondering, not for the first time, whether they were soon to be exposed as tech imposters. But Stuart had learnt along with Jason back at PKR Aerospace that to be the tech guru, you only had to sound like you understood more than those around you. Perhaps Smethwick was trying the same trick.

'Well, I guess, latency only becomes an issue for any critical real-time control systems,' said Stuart, earning a look of appreciation from Sultan. '... and gaming, of course.'

'Exactly sir,' said Smethwick with a beaming smile. 'Which is why we run our own local gaming server.' He jerked a computer mouse on one of the workstations and a screen burst into life.

'This is currently running the virtual reality game on the sports deck.'

The screen showed a scene from a fantasy game, set in a castle's battlements on a misty mountain-side. Two animated figures waved swords at a multi-headed dragon. Stuart recognised the game as '*Slayer 6*'. It was a game that he was very familiar with, having played it himself. He'd even run a version of it on his own server at home. Sultan recognised the name tag that floated next to one of the characters, 'trantermaster'.

'I don't believe it! Stu, it's Jason. He's playing the game right now.'

Stuart's eyes widened, and he smiled and said to Smethwick, 'Do you mind...?'

Smethwick gave a knowing smile. 'Sorry gentlemen,' he said. 'I've just remembered I'm wanted elsewhere. You'll find everything you need here and I'm sure I can rely on you to take greatest care of all the equipment.' With that, he left the room.

'I think that means he doesn't mind,' said Sultan. Stuart had already sat down and was quickly tapping away at the keyboard. As system administrator for the game, he could set various parameters of the virtual world in which the action took place, such as whether it was day or night, the density of the mist, and the frequency of monsters that needed to be fought. He also had access to a vast library of characters or 'skins' that the players could choose as their avatars in this virtual world, and a vast range of weapons that could be made available to fight them with.

Within moments, Stuart had substituted Jason's character's top-of-the-range mega-sword for a bottom-of-the-range wooden stick. The character looked down at the transformed weapon in disbelief, presumably mirroring Jason's own real-life reaction on the sports deck. The dragon was making short work of its opponent while Stuart and Sultan high-fived in recognition of a job well done.

There was a knock at the door and once again Stuart and Sultan looked guilty, in case someone wasn't happy with the way they had just interfered with a guest's game. But when Stuart opened the door, he was greeted by the familiar face of Sarah.

'Hello guys! How's it going?' she asked 'Jason told me you two were now cabin boys or something. My friend Helen needs to make a call to the UK and there's no signal on her phone, and her cabin phone is dead. Can you sort something for her?'

Stuart explained that in theory it should be no problem to reconnect the phone in Helen's cabin, but at the moment they were still learning the ropes and they'd have to plough through the manuals, which would take a while. If it was urgent, Helen could maybe use the phone here in the Comms Room?

'Yeah, it's urgent,' said Sarah.

Helen was surprised that Sarah was answering for her, but agreed that she wanted to make the call now.

'And it's private, so if you don't mind...,' Sarah added.

Sultan and Stuart said something about needing to launch a drone, and grabbed some equipment and left. Sarah stayed behind, despite this being a 'private' phone call, but Helen was grateful that Sarah had at least managed the two men away.

'Thanks, Sarah,' she said. 'I'm not normally paranoid, but I feel like everyone's watching me or listening to me at the moment. Did you check that guy snoozing under the newspaper on the sun deck? I could have sworn he was listening to our conversation. I don't know why.'

Helen got Jarrold's number from her mobile and dialled it on the Comms Room handset. There was a delay and then a voice announced: 'Sorry, the number you have reached is not in service or has been disconnected. Sorry, the number you have reached is not in service or...'.

'What the hell does that mean?' Helen asked, passing the phone to Sarah so she could hear the message for herself.

'Umm, could be a fault on the line, or he hasn't paid his bill..., or maybe switched provider?' Sarah offered. 'Is there anyone else you could contact, a partner, secretary?'

'No, he's recently retired and closed his business down,' Helen replied. 'He was just doing this as a favour for me. As far as I know, he lives alone, no family. But I could get Brett, my son, to drop in on his house on the way home from school. That's what I'll do.'

She made a call and was visibly disappointed to find that Brett's mobile was switched off, but she left him a message.

'It would have been nice to hear his voice,' she complained to Sarah, looking uncharacteristically vulnerable.

'Well, so much for phone calls,' Sarah said breezily. 'Let's see if we can find anything from this Russian bloke.'

11

Stuart and Sultan stepped out of the comms room, still pleased with their stunt of hacking into Jason's virtual reality game.

'Nice work, Stuart,' said Sultan. 'I think we're going to have fun with that one.'

'Yep. But I guess we ought to get the drone flying,' said Stuart. 'Better check with Richards that now's a good time.'

They approached the little office on the upper deck where Richards had told them they could usually find him, but he was already seeing someone; a stout man in a pink polo shirt and white shorts, mirrored sunglasses and a sun hat. He was complaining loudly.

'It's disgraceful, Richards. You should have told me. I'm a dead man if she finds out I'm here.'

'Now look, all you need to do is keep a low profile until we get into port. It's a big ship. It shouldn't be difficult,' Richards said condescendingly. 'I'm afraid it goes with the territory. People here all have their secrets, but the trouble with secrets is that they can make life very awkward. Sometimes even... Hello? What can I do for you?' Richards became aware of Sultan and Stuart lurking by the door. The stout man in shorts took a moment to glare at them through his mirrored sunglasses and then pushed past them and hurried away.

Richards watched as the man disappeared from view and then turned to his two new recruits with a smile and said, 'Now, what fresh problem do you have for me, then?'

Stuart explained that there was no problem, and that they were just checking that it was okay to fly the drone.

'I need you to do something first,' said Richards. 'A passenger by the name of Helen Yarnley needs to make a call home. Can you sort her phone?'

'Already taken care of, Mr Richards. She's making the call now,' said Stuart.

'That's excellent. Well done. Let's get that drone airborne, then. Excellent.'

Stuart and Sultan carried the equipment to the open deck, but their progress was suddenly blocked by Anatoly Morozov leaving his cabin. The Russian was still wearing the white dinner suit and black shirt he had worn at breakfast, and indeed the night before.

'Hey!' he called to them, holding up the palm of his hand unsteadily. 'You can take this back to kitchen, please.'

He shuffled round back into his cabin and brought back the same tray with its silver serving cloche they had delivered to his room earlier that morning.

'Certainly, sir,' said Sultan professionally. 'I hope you enjoyed your fish.'

'Eh?' Morozov looked confused and then stared at Sultan's face with an accusatory look. 'I haven't touched it. It stinks! The smell woke me up. Take it away, now!'

He pushed the tray into Sultan's hands and stomped off up the corridor ahead of them.

'Well, frankly, given the state of him, I'm surprised he could smell the fish,' muttered Stuart quietly. 'You take it back to the galley. I'll go up and get the drone ready to launch. See you up there.'

'No,hang on,' said Sultan. 'I've had an idea.'

12

Helen and Sarah left the Comms Room a few minutes later and rejoined Vincent and Jason on the upper deck. The men were still on a high after their virtual reality quest.

'You've got to try it, Sarah! It's bostin'! It really feels like you're there fighting a humongous bloody dragon.'

'With a stick!' added Vince, with eyebrows raised.

'Yeah, what happened there? Was it a glitch or something?' admitted Jason. 'Fancy trying again, Vincent mate? Come and watch, Sarah. You'll love it.'

Vincent readily agreed, but Sarah wasn't impressed with the idea of watching video games.

'Another of Pip's gin and tonics then, Helen?' she said, gesturing towards the sun loungers.

'Actually, do you mind if we get something to eat?' Helen replied. 'I haven't eaten since breakfast.'

The two went back down to the Stern Bar on the water level deck, where Helen had breakfasted that morning. Several other guests had also had the same idea of afternoon tea, including the hairdressers, Spencer and Drew. Helen went to the bar to see what food was being served while Sarah looked around for somewhere they could sit and approached a table at the open stern edge of the deck, where a lone gentleman in a sun hat was reading his paper.

'Excuse me, mind if we share your table?'

The man looked up through dark glasses, made a sort of snorting noise, stood up and walked away from the table.

Helen arrived from the bar clutching laminated menus, and Sarah told her what had happened. 'It's the same guy you thought was eavesdropping on us earlier, Helen,' said Sarah, as they watched him walk over to a vacant seat in an alcove well away from their table.

'Oh, I can't stand this!' Helen slumped into her chair. 'What is his goddamn problem? Last time he was all for listening in on our conversation, and now he can't bear to be on the same deck. Was it something we said? What is it with these people? It winds me up... so much! It's ironic, isn't it? You'd think that a luxury yacht on the Mediterranean would be a place to relax, wouldn't you? But every time I start to feel the least bit calm, some jerk winds me right back up again.'

She looked down at her menu. 'Agh! I couldn't eat a thing! My insides are knotted up.'

Helen's tirade wasn't loud, but the slightest display of discontent drew attention on this floating paradise.

The ubiquitous Pip appeared from nowhere.'Hey! Sorry, very rude of me, I know, but I couldn't help overhearing a bit of that. Just a suggestion, but we do a fantastic pina colada that usually has the effect of "smoothing things out". Shall I bring you a couple?'

'You'd know all about smooth, I suppose,' Sarah grinned. 'Sounds great. I thought you worked upstairs, though?'

'I try to be wherever I'm needed most. Two pina coladas then?'

'Just a glass of sparkling water for me.' Helen was having none of this boy's precocious charm.

He left them and took an order from the man behind the newspaper. Sarah judged it was probably better not to speak for a while, and tilted her chair back and closed her eyes. The sun was dropping in the sky, but it was still deliciously warm. The noise of little waves lapping at the edge of the ship was soothing. Helen picked up a section of the Sunday newspaper that the disagreeable man had left on the table when he had stormed off. It was the puzzle section. She found a pen in her bag and tried for a while to make sense of the cryptic crossword clues, something she usually enjoyed, but today she found the clues irritatingly opaque. She gave up and stared out to sea. A seagull made a couple of lazy passes across the stern of the boat before wheeling around and landing on the railing near them. Helen stared at it.

In a low voice, she said, 'I swear I know that gull...'

'Boris! My friend!' A voice boomed across the deck and a man in a white tuxedo approached Helen and Sarah.

'Ladies, may I please join you?' he said in a low, soft, husky voice. 'I would very much like to make apology to Mrs Yarnley.'

He turned to Sarah, though. 'Allow me to introduce. My name is Anatoly Morozov. I'm afraid I was rude to your friend this morning. It was unforgivable. Mrs Yarnley, please to accept apology.'

'Thank you,' said Helen. 'I think perhaps you were very...' The most appropriate word didn't seem friendly, and Helen was keen to keep this man on good terms so she could find out more about his connection with her husband.. '... tired.'

'Aha! Tired, yes. My lady, you would not believe how tired.' He slumped down in the chair recently vacated by the man in dark glasses. He had evidently assumed that his presence at their table was a welcome one. In a similar way, Boris, the seagull, decided that this was a safe party to join, and hopped down from the railing and stood near the Russian's feet, looking up at him.

'Perhaps we are all tired, eh?' he said. 'Perhaps the sea bird is tired? Perhaps the sea is tired? Listen to those lazy little waves. Perhaps it is tired now. Tired of all the back and forth, tired of storms and calms, tired of summers and winters, tired of plastics and chemicals. Tired of it all. Perhaps the sea will give up soon?'

Sarah and Helen exchanged apprehensive glances. This was a strange opening to a conversation. They said nothing and Morozov picked up the section of newspaper and stared at the puzzles.

'Someone has given up with this too, I see. And why not? Why should we try to find the answer to all life's puzzles, eh? Why can't we just let them be puzzles? Every day, the newspaper prints a new puzzle, and every day a man completes the puzzle, and he has won. But the next day there is a fresh puzzle, and he has to start again. He gets tired. And then eventually the day comes when he will not complete the puzzle. I think that day is coming soon.'

He leant back in his chair, looking at the afternoon sky, which was just picking up a yellowish hue over the western horizon. He seemed to sense Helen's and Sarah's discomfort.

'Perhaps you disagree. You are young. The party has only just started, and here we are on a beautiful ship, with beautiful people. Heh! Some of them not so beautiful, eh? Haha! ... but rich! And that is the next best thing to beautiful, correct? And so we sail on, aboard this party boat, the rich and the beautiful, and we are all very happy.'

'You don't seem very happy,' interrupted Sarah.

'Hey! Well done. You got me! It's true. I am unhappy,' Morozov admitted. 'I have all the money I could ever need, but still I look around for something else. I am like this sea bird, Boris. He has all the fish in the sea, but he hangs around for scraps from this boat. But are the scraps worth having? Are they good for his health? Are they good for his soul? Or is he a sad hanger-on, dependent upon the easy pleasures on the *Rara Avis* and no longer able to look after himself?'

'If you are so unhappy on this boat, why do you stay here?' asked Helen.

Just then, Pip arrived with the pina coladas and Morozov stared hard at him, as if he thought it was the height of rudeness to bring drinks for the ladies and nothing for him. Pip was unfazed by the Russian's hostility and simply grinned in a childlike way, narrowing his eyes to slits and wrinkling his nose, and asked if he could fetch anything 'for the gentleman'. A vodka was ordered.

Before he left, Sarah asked, 'Do you know the man who was sitting here, just before us? A rude, fat man with a newspaper?'

Pip laughed. 'I'm sure I couldn't possibly identify any of our guests from that description!'

'Well, he's sitting round the corner now,' Sarah said. 'Could you take this section from his newspaper to him? He left it here when he stalked off a minute ago. Please say it's from the two young ladies sitting at the back of the boat. With our compliments.' Pip bowed and left with the newspaper.

Helen reminded Morozov that she'd asked him why he stayed on the *Rara Avis* if he was so unhappy.

'Ladies, you ask the right questions,' Morozov said, pulling on his earlobe with his thumb and forefinger. 'You are very clever. Rara Avis is many things to many people. For some, it is a holiday. For some it is a school, for others a business meeting place. For me, it is a place to hide.'

'From what?' asked Helen. She figured that if this rude old man just wanted an audience for his ramblings, she might as well dig a little and get some background from him.

'I need to hide from the world. A lot of dangerous people would like to find me. I know such a lot of things, you see. I have heard people say, "a little knowledge is a dangerous thing". Well, I know a lot. And let me tell you, that is dangerous.'

'Go on then,' said Sarah. 'What do you know?'

'If I told you, then you would know. And you would be in danger. I will be kind. I will not tell you what I know. My lips are sealed.' He pretended to zip them, and closed his eyes. There was a brief silence.

'I will tell you how I know what I know. You are young ladies. You listen to music on your phones, yes? Headphones on, Kanye West, Michael Jackson, yeah, yeah, yeah! When I was boy, I listen to music on record player, Beatles, Rolling Stones. In Soviet Union, when I was boy, Rolling Stones were forbidden. Western decadence. Last night I am at their concert, on a boat! Crazy! Crazy! Back in old Soviet Union, we manage to smuggle some forty-fives in and listen to them in secret. Later, a guy showed me how to make copies of the discs. We didn't have vinyl, so we pressed them onto old plastic x-ray photographs. Ha! You could still see the x-ray image sometimes, so we called them "bones". Soon I am making good money selling these "bones". This is how it begins. Later, came cassette tapes and suddenly everyone is doing it. Not so much money for Anatoly. But always there is a way. A new technology comes along, you stay ahead of the curve. So I am copying films; VHS, Betamax. No money, really, but I am making connections. People want what I have to sell and they don't want anyone to know they are buying it. Am I a bad man for making money on black market? You tell me. In West they call it free enterprise. Anyhow, as Soviet Union collapses, everyone is doing it. People are getting rich doing it. Are they bad men?

'Then comes computers and MP3. You want Dire Straits song? I get you complete catalogue on a mini-disc. Then the internet. I get some clever boys from Finland, we make file-sharing service. Music, films, photos. Then it becomes interesting. Tough guy from police says he is going to take my service down and put me in prison. Then he changes his mind. Says I can keep service going but I must supply certain type of film. Kinky stuff, you know.'

He paused, scanning their faces, as if he was wondering whether to elaborate on what he meant by 'kinky stuff', but seemed to decide it wasn't necessary.

'Tough guy from police wants list of people who download this kinky stuff sent to him, privately. I wonder why? Ha! One day, same tough guy from police is found dead in Moscow sauna. Then I think "Shit! This is dangerous. Anatoly, you must be careful". So I am very careful, I stay one step ahead and I become very rich. But always I am looking over my shoulder, you understand. Always wondering who is standing in the shadows. Maybe I was a bad man. Maybe.

'So I get out. Like many others, I come to London. What happened in Moscow, stays in Moscow, yes? But still there is danger. Sometimes I think there are more Russians in London than in Moscow! I am getting tired of running. So Rara Avis is an escape for me. I can relax. Cruise around the Mediterranean, enjoy best caviar, vodka, *selyodka*. Find peace in my old age. But there is no peace. There is danger, even on this ship!'

Apparently, someone else on the ship agreed because just at that moment there was a loud and drawn out scream.

13

Sultan was on the sports deck, concentrating hard, trying to control a drone that was hovering just above. A small screen on the remote-control handset relayed pictures from the drone's video camera. He could see Jason and Vincent as they played round two of their virtual reality battle with the dragons of *Uth R'dar*. With their headsets covering their eyes, they looked like they were playing a two-man version of blind man's buff where the other participants had wandered off, leaving the blindfolded pair flailing wildly.

Sultan set a lock function on the handset that kept the drone hovering automatically in the same spot with its camera locked on Jason and Vincent. Sultan's walkie-talkie beeped. A voice in his earphone said, 'Okay, I'm in the comms room. I'm ready to make the switch, over.'

Sultan pressed the talk button and spoke softly. 'Nice one, Stuart. Okay, I'm approaching the target now. Standby, over.'

Sultan put down the remote, checking that the drone remained motionless above the deck. He picked up the tray that he had taken from Anatoly Morozov's room earlier. He walked towards Jason and Vincent. Again softly into the walkie-talkie, 'Okay, Five, four, three, two, one... Replace!'. He put the tray onto the warm deck floor by the players and removed the serving cloche.

14

The mountains of *Uth R'dar* turned blood red as the sun set behind the castle. An evening mist rolled in off the ocean as the two warriors cautiously crossed the bridge into the town and up the main thoroughfare. The streets seemed empty; the townsfolk were probably cowering in their houses and shops, too frightened even to look out of their windows. Well might they be afraid. The two warriors themselves looked fearsome enough. Tall and swarthy, with thick muscular arms protected by armour plating that glinted in the dying rays of the sun, they held razor-sharp broadswords aloft as they patrolled the streets and alleyways, searching for adversaries even more fearsome, more terrifying. Good elvish broadswords, these. They had already proven to be worthy, slicing through flesh and bone on the battlefields of *Kr'nar*, and they had not suddenly and magically dissolved into willow staves, like the dwarf-forged steel blades of a previous adventure. Limbs had been lost that day.

Warrior Trantermaster saw his companion turn into one of the side alleys and decided to follow. Ominous drums warning of impending danger beat in his ears. And then, suddenly, as the alley joined the market square, there it was: a dragon twice as tall as anything they had so far encountered. Five heads on five writhing necks looked down on them, hissing, with steam coming from their nostrils. Then the heads swooped down towards them, one after another, and vicious jaws with silver teeth snapped at them. Trantermaster prepared to slash the dragon-flesh but was forced to duck out of the way to avoid losing his arm. He could see that Vincentio was also being attacked, with two separate dragon heads looming over him. Trantermaster saw a third neck and head sneakily moving low across the ground, approaching Vincentio's feet. Trantermaster saw his chance, and raised his weapon high so that he could bring it powerfully down, saving his companion and scoring valuable kill points for a full decapitation.

Alas, once again, there was sorcery at work. The weapon that he held aloft was no longer a trusty broadsword, but was now a silvery fish, a salmon by the look of it.

'Oh man! I can even smell the pigging thing!' said Trantermaster, not in Middle English.

And then suddenly, from another world, he heard a blood-curdling scream.

15

Helen was growing increasingly uncomfortable while Anatoly Morozov was giving his drawn-out warning of danger, and when it was interrupted by a woman's screaming somewhere on an upper deck, she jumped to her feet. Sarah was even quicker. She was already making for the stairs, to find out what the disturbance was.

Helen turned to Morozov and told him she'd be back to carry on their conversation and then followed her companion. The Russian looked more puzzled than concerned, and a bit annoyed at having been interrupted whilst in mid-flow. He summoned a waiter and ordered a vodka.

Meanwhile, on the sports deck, Jason saw that Vincent had dropped out of the game, immediately following the scream, and took off his own virtual reality headset. He saw Vincent call out, 'Helen!' They both looked at the faces of the other passengers and determined that the scream had come from the deck immediately below the sports deck, and made their way down the stairs to see what was happening. They met Sarah, followed by Helen, coming up from the lower deck.

'What's going on?' they asked in more or less one voice.

'Nothing to worry about, ladies and gentlemen.' The authoritative voice of Richards cut through the hubbub.

He was standing under an awning at the stern of the upper deck, with Debbie Angelinie and her boyfriend, Travis Smak.

'Maybe not for you, pal. But I came here to get away from this!' It was obvious from Debbie's stressed voice that it was her scream they had all heard. She held out an iPad displaying her picture.

She read from the caption. ' "Debbie Ditches the Doldrums in a Dash for the Cote D'Azur. Seen here with on-off boyfriend, Travis, on a hideaway holiday yacht, it looks like once more, she is 'Back with Smak'. Sparks always fly when these two are together — looks like the fireworks have already started!" Who took this picture, I wanna know? And how did it get to *Buzzfeed*?'

'Those are excellent questions,' said Richards, 'and I wish I knew the answers. Everyone on this boat should understand the need for privacy and discretion. I will have this investigated, and we will get to the bottom of it. And when I find out who is responsible...' He looked round accusingly at the passengers and staff who had gathered following Debbie's outburst. '... whoever it is will be removed from the *Rara Avis*. In the meantime, please accept my apologies, Miss Angelinie.'

'Miss Peru, to you,' said the young woman, who was regaining her composure.

Travis reinforced the comment by popping his eyes, curling his lip in a mock snarl, and rocking his head from side to side.

The people who had gathered to find out where the scream had come from now became aware of an approaching speedboat. Until just now, it had been such a quiet day, moored in the middle of the Med, that the noise of the approaching vessel attracted attention and everyone turned to look. The boat slowed down as it approached and a man stood up and pointed a camera with a telephoto lens at the *Rara Avis*. He remained standing and holding up the camera with one hand as the speedboat glided alongside.

Waving with his other hand, he called out, 'Cheers, Debbie. Give us a wave!'

'Shit, Babes!' said Travis. 'It's the Paps again.'

16

Jason, Sarah, Helen, and Vincent left the scene and went down to the Stern Bar on the lower deck.

'I want to finish talking to Anatoly,' said Helen. But Anatoly Morozov was no longer there.

'You should have heard him, Jason,' said Sarah. 'It was dramatic stuff. "There is danger on this ship."' She did a passable Russian accent. 'And then Debbie's screaming came just at the right moment. Oh, my days! Turned out to be a bit of an anticlimax, though. I thought someone had died or something, but it turns out it's just Debbie Angelinie's hissy fit over a photograph on a website. Big deal. So, what are we drinking?'

She waved to attract the attention of Pip, the waiter.

'Well, it's a relief that no-one is physically hurt or anything,' said Vincent, 'but I guess I'd be pissed off if I'd been promised seclusion and privacy, and then found out that someone had photographed me and published my picture. Did you see it? Someone must have taken it during the concert last night, when the fireworks started. And it looks like we're going to get more media attention. I've never been photographed by the paparazzi before.'

Pip arrived at their table. 'No prizes for guessing what you're talking about. What can I get for you?'

They ordered four Pina Coladas, on Sarah's recommendation, but Helen said, 'Listen, if I start drinking now I'll be all over the place. I need something to eat. Can you do me something really plain and simple?'

'I can bring you a menu.'

'Can I just have a cheese sandwich, vegan, if you've got it, but never mind if you haven't? Just a plain cheese sandwich? Cheddar, preferably.'

'Of course,' Pip said, and then in a low conspiratorial voice added, 'It may take a bit longer than it usually would. Mr Morozov is currently in the galley giving our chef a lesson in preparing the perfect vodka Martini. Bit of a car crash, but I'll try to get your cheese sarnie as quick as.'

He left them and the four looked over to the galley, where Morozov was gesticulating in his flamboyant style.

Vincent said, 'Cheese sandwich, eh? Living the high life then, Sis?'

'I'm just trying to cling on to normality,' she said. 'Everything here is just a bit weird for me.'

Jason said that if she wanted to try weird, then she should have a go on the virtual reality game that Vincent and he had been playing, where swords turned into fish and it was so realistic you could even smell them.

As he spoke, Stuart, in his black t-shirt, came to their table carrying a phone handset. He winked at Jason, but spoke to Helen.

'I have a call for you, Mrs Yarnley. It's your son.'

Helen's heart leapt. She took the phone and walked to a corner of the deck, where she could be a little more private.

'Alright, lad?' Jason asked Stuart. 'How's it going?'

'Yeah, busy thanks. It's getting a bit mad, actually. Mr Richards wants us to get the drones to film any other vessels approaching us. Sultan's up on the sports deck at the moment. You might have seen him?'

Jason said he hadn't and explained that he'd had a headset on most of the time that afternoon. He wondered how Stuart knew that he'd been on the sports deck, and somewhere in his mind, he pieced together that he may have been pranked.

'I'd better go up and help him anyhow,' Stuart said. 'Can you get Mrs Yarnley to hand the phone back to any member of staff when she's finished? Or if you want to bring it to the comms room, you can see what we get up to.'

He grinned, winked at Jason, and left. Jason explained to Vincent that he was buddies with a couple of the staff and that he was sort of responsible for them being employed here.

When Helen rejoined them, her eyes were edged with tears, and her voice was shaky.

'He's dead! The poor man is dead.'

She sat next to her brother and buried her face on his shoulder for a few seconds. It was all she needed to regain some composure so that she could recount what she had heard.

'I spoke to Brett. He'd dropped round at Mr Jarrold's house on his way back from school. He couldn't get an answer at the door, but a neighbour saw him and asked who he was. Brett explained, and the neighbour said she wanted to speak to me as soon as possible. So that was Brett calling me back, just now.

He handed the phone to the neighbour, who explained to me that Mr Jarrold had been found dead in his home a couple of weeks ago. The saddest thing was that they had no idea how long he'd been dead. He was a very private man, with no family. He kept himself to himself. She said that Brett and I were the first people to have taken an interest in the man since he had died. Can you believe that?'

'Did they say how he died?' Sarah asked.

'She said that he just died in his armchair,' answered Helen, wiping her eyes. 'It looked like he'd been doing his gardening, and then he'd come inside and died in his armchair. She supposed it was a heart attack or a stroke or something. Oh, it's just too sad. He's such a kind and lovely man.'

Vincent put his arm around his sister and no-one spoke for a while. Above the sound of lapping waves and the polite deck chatter, they heard the drone being launched from an upper deck. They looked up and saw the black machine hovering a little way to the stern of the ship, looking distinctly out of place amidst two or three white gulls that wheeled around it inquisitively.

Pip Nelson returned to their table with Helen's cheese sandwich and four pina coladas. He sensed a mood change.

'Hey Guys! Did someone die, or something?' He winked at Jason.

'Mate, just piss off, will you? Thanks,' said Jason.

Sarah looked shocked at Jason's rudeness, but Helen gave him a grateful smile.

Pip said 'Well... enjoy your drinks... er, and your sandwich. So... let me know if I can get anything else for you, yeah?' and walked off with a slight swagger.

As he left, Boris the seagull appeared on the railing and eyed the plate of food.

'You can have this,' said Helen, throwing half the sandwich towards the bird. 'I just don't feel hungry anymore'.

The bird caught its beak and demolished it in two gulps. The four laughed and clapped, and Helen threw the other half, higher this time. Boris launched from the railing, caught the sandwich in midair, and flew out over the sea, where it devoured the rest. It returned to the railing to receive more applause.

As if he was playing to the crowd, Boris jumped down onto the deck, spread its wings and hopped around in a circle. It reminded Jason of a native North American war dance.

Other people on the deck also took notice and joined in the clapping, beating out a rhythm for the seagull's dance. But then the dance stopped, and Boris the seagull fell limp and motionless on the deck.

The applause stopped, a few people laughed nervously but were hushed when it became clear that the seagull was dead.

'Are you sure that cheese was cheddar?' said Jason by way of a joke, but Helen frowned at him.

'That cheese sandwich was poisoned,' she said. 'Someone is trying to kill me.'

17

Vincent and Jason tried to convince Helen that she was overreacting.

'Perhaps seagulls just aren't supposed to eat cheese, y'know... like dogs and chocolate,' suggested Vincent.

'Perhaps it was just his time,' Jason offered, and Sarah elbowed him in the ribs.

Helen was having none of it.

'The Russian, Mr Morozov, said there was danger. He was right. I want to get off this boat. I want to call the police. There is something not right here.' She was shivering with fear, her eyes gleamed with determination.

Sarah put an arm around her. 'C'mon. Let's go and see Richards. We'll get this sorted. I can't imagine anyone would want to poison you. There must be another explanation, but this needs looking into. Jason, make sure no-one gets rid of that seagull. Find a plastic bag or something for it. It should probably be examined by an expert.'

'Hang on!' thought Jason. 'I'm the millionaire; you're supposed to be the personal assistant — and yet you're the one giving out the orders! Still, impressive to take control of the situation like that. Respect.' He nodded silently and went off in search of a plastic bag.

Helen and Sarah found Richards on the main deck, but he was already occupied by a different emergency. Jane Fortune was arguing with him and she was clearly angry.

'This is unacceptable, Richards,' she said. 'They should never have been taken on. We expect high standards of the Black Tees and this pair haven't got a clue.'

'I employed them for their expertise in electronic surveillance and security, Jane, and so far, I am more than happy with their work. They've already exposed a security breach by our Communications Officer, and Smethwick tells me they've made a good start in covering his role, now that he's been removed from the ship. They're going to be needed more than ever if we're going to have paparazzi hanging around again. If they've made a less than satisfactory job of clearing away a plate of fish...' Richards stressed these words to emphasise their absurdity and his frustration. '... then all I can say is that is not what I employed them for, and the fault lies with whoever delegated that job to them.'

Jane bristled. 'No-one delegated the job, they took it upon themselves. And then they left a plate of stinking fish just lying there in full sun near where guests were relaxing. It just shows a lack of thought and a lack of common sense. Our guests expect more.'

'I will speak to them about confining their activities to those for which they are being paid. Now, if you'll excuse me, I think I am wanted by the ladies here.'

Jane snorted and walked off.

Without looking back, she said, 'By the way, I have cleared up the fish myself, in case you are interested.'

Richards turned to Helen and Sarah with a faint smile on his lips, suggesting that no matter what sort of problem they were bringing to him, nothing was about to ruffle his feathers, still less his luxuriant black hair.

'I want to leave this ship immediately,' said Helen. 'Someone is trying to poison me.'

Richards raised his eyebrows as Helen launched into how Boris the seagull had died immediately after eating a cheese sandwich that was meant for her.

'Morozov was right,' she said. 'He told me that there was danger on this ship. I don't know now whether he was warning me or threatening me, but I know I want to leave. I have two boys. Their father was killed. I shouldn't be here.'

'It's really shaken her,' added Sarah. 'She's also just heard this afternoon that her solicitor has also recently died. He'd been looking into the African charity that Helen's husband was helping – so you can't blame her for thinking there may be a connection.'

Helen turned to Sarah, looking more shocked than ever. 'Oh no! I hadn't even made that link! It was me that asked him to investigate the Yepi Kasai charity. What have I done? What is going on?'

She paused as tears welled up in her eyes. Then, a little more calmly, she said, 'Look, Mr Richards, I'm sure you think I'm just a silly, neurotic woman, but I demand that you take this seriously.'

'You're quite right,' said Richards and quickly added, '...to demand that this is taken seriously. I don't think you are silly or neurotic at all. I can see how disturbing this incident must be. As a matter of fact, Mr Smethwick has already informed me about what happened at the Stern Bar and I've already contacted the police. They have asked me to return the *Rara Avis* to the port of registration where officers will investigate the incident. Now, I'm sure that there is a perfectly sensible reason why the bird died, but for safety's sake, we will get the matter investigated. I'll ask the Captain to up-anchor shortly. The police would like to talk to you, of course, so I'm afraid I can't allow you to go back to Cap Sainte Marie. It will be the Italian police who will investigate, you see, even though we are currently in French waters. It will take five or six hours to reach our home port of Isola Gallinara, on the Ligurian coast. That will make it the middle of the night when we arrive, but if you still wish to leave the ship, we have comfortable accommodation near the harbour, and I imagine the police will wish to interview you first thing in the morning.'

It surprised Helen and Sarah to see how helpful Richards was being. They had expected him to play down their concerns, but he seemed to take them seriously.

Sarah said, 'Let us have a quick private chat about this, please.' but Helen said, 'No, it's okay, I'm prepared to stay for a day longer... but I want that young man locked up. The one who served me that sandwich... Pip... Who is he?'

'Pip Nelson?' said Richards. 'I sincerely doubt that he is any threat to anyone. As I say, I'm sure there's a perfectly innocent explanation. I happen to know Mr Nelson reasonably well. He's young, but no more feckless than any of his generation. I can't think of any reason he'd wish you harm. Can you?'

'I have no idea. But I feel I have met him before, somewhere. I can't think where, but he unsettles me,' said Helen.

'That's interesting,' said Richards.

Sarah added, 'He unsettles Jason, too. Perhaps it's just his way. He is rather cocky for a crew member, don't you think?'

'Hmm, perhaps so,' Richards agreed. 'There is a reason for that. I wouldn't normally disclose this, but as well as being one of the crew, young Pip will also one day be a member of Rara Avis. He's an orphan, but his mother has left him extremely well provided for. His money is held in trust with me until he is twenty-five. I offered him the chance to work onboard until he comes into his inheritance. It's a chance for him to sample the life he will one day lead, make some connections, and decide what to do with his life. I can't see that someone in a position like that would be likely to get involved in poisoning passengers, can you?' he asked Helen.

'I'm a parent and a teacher,' answered Helen. 'I'd say there's no way of accounting for anything any young person does. Isn't that why his money is held in trust? Young people do strange things. And I'm afraid that the fact that he will one day be a member of this secret millionaires' club makes me even more suspicious. This combination of money and secrecy creates a toxic environment where all kinds of mischief might happen. Maybe that's the danger Mr Morozov has been trying to warn me about.'

Richards paused for a moment, his blue eyes fixed on Helen, before he responded. 'Hmm. I can understand why you would think that. We have to be very careful about membership. Ms Fortune spends a lot of time looking into the backgrounds of the potential members, examining where their money has come from and so on.'

'In Anatoly Morozov's case, I gather it was a mixture of copyright piracy and blackmail,' interrupted Sarah pointedly.

Richards looked pained. 'Is that how Mr Morozov has described it to you? I think business practices in the former Soviet Union are... different to what we are used to. But I'm assured that Mr Morozov, like all our members, has a clean bill of health with all police agencies in Russia, Europe and the United States. That doesn't mean, of course, that there aren't people that might like to catch up with him. Seclusion and privacy are the chief benefits that Mr Morozov seeks from Rara Avis. If I were you, I'd be inclined to put any warnings of danger down to alcohol-fuelled paranoia. Now, if you don't mind, I think I should help get everyone ready to push on to Isola Gallinara. I hope I have given you some reassurance. Let me know if I can be of any other assistance.'

'You can,' said Helen. 'You can lock Pip Nelson up. I don't want him roaming around this ship while I'm on board. I hear all your assurances, and maybe you're right, but I still don't feel comfortable. And as a paying passenger on this floating gin palace, I think my feelings deserve to be taken into consideration. Even if they, too, are "alcohol-fuelled paranoia".'

'Very well then, Mrs Yarnley. I'll see that Mr Nelson is confined to his quarters until we reach port.'

'Until the Police have interviewed him,' corrected Helen.

'Just so, Mrs Yarnley. Just so.'

18

Message: 26 July 2019 18:05

Jenny,

Unexplained seagull death. Local police are investigating. You might want to liaise. Also does the name Arthur Jarrold mean anything to you? Recently deceased. Will call later.

Robin

Message: 26 July 2019 18:26

Robin,

A bit confused... actual seagull? Do call ASAP. We need to talk re: Jarrold.

Jenny.

19

Detective Superintendent Liz Sharpe of the West Midlands Counter Terrorism Unit looked out of a window onto a quiet Birmingham backstreet as she sipped her plastic cup of water and wished it was time to go home. She'd spent a long day reviewing incident protocols for Birmingham Airport, and that had left her feeling hot and tense. It all felt so... vulnerable. It had to be the likeliest target on her patch and no matter how many protocols, or how many leads she had her team follow up, she never felt comfortable that they were doing enough to address the possibility of an attack.

She thought about the walk to her car that she'd soon be making and hoped the streets had cooled down. Her uniform, although it was ultra smart, was prone to being hot, tight and itchy, and the logistics of moving between the comfort of the air-conditioned building and the luxury of her Range Rover, some ten minutes' walk away, were foremost in her mind. The few pedestrians down below moved lazily along the pavement. An open-topped car stopped at traffic lights and the driver fanned himself. Still too warm. Ah well, one more appointment left in the diary to go.

'Ah, Jerry. How can I help you?' she said, as Detective Inspector Wren entered, but she knew what Wren wanted just from the way he carried himself. It was all to do with the shoulders. They always held them raised by an inch or so in a submissive sort of shrug. Only men, though. Not women, for some reason. He wanted approval for something. She didn't know what for, but she knew she was going to grant it, because she liked Jeremy Wren. A short, stubby man, bald on top, but with a wide, generous face and a winning smile. He was a skilled detective, with a lot of experience and a lot of common sense.

'Oh, afternoon Ma'am,' he said 'It's a request for overseas travel, if you wouldn't mind.'

'Another one, Jerry? You're already running an officer overseas, aren't you? You haven't forgotten we're supposed to be a domestic organisation, have you? We're not Interpol, you know. Who's it for this time?'

'It's for myself, actually, Ma'am and no, it's alright, I hadn't forgotten. It's just that the overseas officer has uncovered something, and it needs a bit of intervention. The officer doesn't want to blow their cover just yet, so has requested a bit of support.'

'In the French Riviera, in July? Are you pulling a fast one, DI Wren?' but she was already signing the request form.

Wren's shoulders dropped to their normal position.

'Don't worry, I'll declare any Casino winnings, in full, upon my return,' he grinned, but then looked serious. 'To be absolutely honest, Ma'am, I'm not sure where this operation is going. It may end up in SO15 territory, in which case we'll hand it over, of course. But we know how busy those boys and girls are, fighting ISIS and everything, and until recently we didn't even have any confirmed evidence that our target was a genuine threat. But things are heating up. We've uncovered a link to the Jarrold murder, so we'll stick with it.'

'Okay Jerry,' said DSI Sharpe. 'Good work. Don't forget to pack your Speedos. The French don't allow Bermuda shorts around the pool.'

20

Jason was freshly showered and in his boxer shorts when Sarah returned to the cabin.

'Whoa! Do you want me to give you a minute?' she offered, backing out of the door.

'It's okay,' replied Jason, pulling on his evening suit trousers. 'I'm decent.'

'No arguing with that.' Sarah looked him up and down and gave a playful wink. 'Anyway, you'll be happy to know that your friend Pip Nelson has been confined to his cabin. In fact,

I've just seen Stuart, and he's told me that Sultan's been told to sit outside to keep guard.'

'Blimey, do they really think he tried to poison Helen, then?'

'Well,' said Sarah, 'Richards has informed the police about the dead seagull business, apparently, and we are about to set sail for Isola Gallinara, in Italy where it's all going to be investigated. I don't think he really suspects Pip, though, no. I think Richards just wants to make Helen feel they're taking her seriously. The poor woman's in a right state, understandably, I guess. But I don't really believe that Pip Nelson could have tried to poison her. It's just too random. He seems a sweet lad; apparently he's an orphan. Poor feller, being locked up in his cabin.'

'Serves him right. They should lock him up just for being a pratt,' said Jason. 'Still, at least it means that I'll have a decent meal tonight, without that grinning idiot interfering all the time.'

'Enough of that, you grumpy bastard,' said Sarah, throwing a sock at him. 'Anyway, Richards has asked us to keep quiet about the whole incident. He doesn't want us to alarm the passengers. He's going to explain to everyone that we're heading to Italy, to give the paparazzi the slip. Now, get dressed, will you, and clear out while I make myself beautiful? I want to try every one of those expensive-looking bottles of smelly stuff in the bathroom.'

The *Rara Avis* was making good passage through the evening Mediterranean waters by the time Jason made it to the dining room. The gentle rocking of the ship while they were at anchor was okay, but the pitching and rolling, now that they were in motion, took some getting used to. He didn't feel nauseous, though, as he had feared he would. He'd once been told, on a channel ferry crossing, that it was a good idea to drink a couple of fizzy lagers to avoid seasickness. The theory was that your brain would attribute any queasy feeling to the gas in your stomach, and so you wouldn't worry about the motion of the ship. He wondered if the bubbles of premier cru champagne would work in the same way. He ordered a glass at the bar, feeling rather pleased with himself.

He'd felt flattered by the flirtatious remarks that Sarah had made in the cabin earlier. He felt cool and sophisticated in his smart, comfortable suit, with a shirt that had been laundered and ironed for him by a Black Tee, earlier, and perhaps most of all, he felt pleased that he'd got one up on the man-boy, Pip Nelson.

He went over to sit at the long table of the dining room, next to Debbie and Travis, who, although smart, weren't looking quite as spick and span as the previous evening. They looked bored and as if they'd rather be somewhere else.

'Ahoy there... Rita,' he said as he sat down.

The young lady perked up, smiled, and laughed. 'Cheers Jason, thanks for remembering. I thought I'd left Debbie Angelinie behind me, but it seems like she's followed me here. Friggin' *Buzzfeed* and their friggin' photographers. Still, perhaps I'll be able to shake them off at the next place. A private island, innit? That's what they said at the presentation this morning. Luxury villa, pools, beaches, and a racetrack or something. Sick. Sick, wasn't it, Travis?'

'What? Yeah, sick.' Travis looked as though he had the more traditional meaning of the word on his mind. His face was pale, his mouth turned down at the corners.

'Alright there, pal?' said Jason, in a friendly tone. 'Bit seasick, mate?'

He told him about the idea of fooling your brain with fizzy drinks. Travis said he was always ready to give lager cures a try.

Sarah joined them just as they were ordering their drinks. 'Evening, all! Can I get an Espresso Martini added to that order, please? I need coffee and I need alcohol. Quite a day! Are you feeling any better now, Debbie? That must have been very upsetting to realise that the press are still hounding you.'

She sounded just a little patronising, though it was hard to tell whether it was intentional.

'I'm getting there, thanks. And I'm sticking to "Rita", if you don't mind.' She tilted her head back, looked at the ceiling, and sighed. 'I bet it seems petty, doesn't it? Someone who's made their name by chasing publicity, doing God knows how many stunts to get more likes, more magazine spreads and then suddenly she doesn't want it anymore. What right have I got to privacy, eh?'

'No, I don't think that at all,' said Sarah.

She lies well, thought Jason.

Rita obviously thought the same. 'Don't worry, I get it. I don't really expect any sympathy. People like me only get sympathy after they're found slumped on the loo with a needle sticking out their arm, or swinging from a light fitting in a Kensington flat. Then it's suddenly a blame game; "How did the people around her let this happen?", "Fifteen warning signs we all missed" and all that bollocks. So what this is, right, it's not me playing some cat-and-mouse game with the media, and it's not me getting all precious now that I've made my stash. It's plain, bloody survival instinct. I've lost friends, good friends, and I don't want the same happening to me, so I'm getting out. I thought this...' she swept her arm around indicating that she meant the *Rara Avis*, '... would be my ticket out, but some jerk with a phone has already ballsed that up. If I could get my hands on them! Anyway, Richards thinks that sailing to this private island by night should shake the bastards off. I bleedin' hope so.'

The drinks arrived, and the waiter took their food order. There were a couple of options on the printed menus, but Travis decided that what he really needed was a burger and fries.

Rita rolled her eyes at him, and Sarah couldn't suppress a smirk, but the waiter assured him it would be no trouble at all. Jason would dearly have liked to follow suit and order the same, but he felt pressure to differentiate himself from Travis and ordered the Filet Mignon, and even made a fair job of pronouncing it properly. He was rewarded by the waiter saying, 'Excellent choice, Monsieur.'

'Ooh, "Excellent choice", Jason. How about that? Bit of a connoisseur, are you?' asked Rita.

Jason was about to deny it but Sarah jumped in with, 'He's got great taste, this one.'

This is new, thought Jason. She's usually teasing me, not paying me compliments.

When their meals arrived, Jason found that his Filet Mignon wasn't the beefsteak he'd expected, but was in fact a pork tenderloin steak, covered in a creamy, mustardy sauce. He tried not to look disappointed, which was made easier by Rita saying how jealous of his dinner she was and how she wished she'd ordered it herself instead of the grilled octopus that spread its alien tentacles over her plate. If it had been something more palatable, Jason would have offered to swap with her, but there was no way he'd have been able to swallow a mouthful of anything that actually had suckers still clearly visible.

Again, Sarah saw the dilemma and chipped in with, 'Yeah, Jason adores his Filet Mignon. It's probably his favourite — your lucky night, eh Jason?'.

Was that a wink from Sarah? Whatever it was, he couldn't let her down now, and so he bravely tried a mouthful of the pork in cream and mustard sauce and found to his surprise that it tasted fine. 'As my old Great Aunt used to say, "tender as a maiden's heart",' he said.

It was only worth a polite laugh, but Sarah and Rita both seemed to think it was hilarious. Travis just looked puzzled and increasingly bored.

Spencer and Drew Simon made a flamboyant entrance. They were dressed like the caricature sailors in the Jean Paul Gaultier perfume adverts; white culottes, striped shirts and white hats at a jaunty angle. In the adverts, the shirts showed off the muscular trim bodies of the models, and the hats highlighted their lean, square-jawed faces. The effect on Spencer and Drew was to make them both look like they had come to a fancy dress event as Popeye, but it was obvious from their big grins and infectious laughter that they were under no illusions and were just enjoying making a spectacle of themselves. They saw that there were spaces on the table next to Sarah and Jason, and made a beeline for them.

'Bonsoir mes petits choux-fleurs!' called out Spencer. 'Mind if we join you? Everyone enjoying themselves? What about the latest goss, then? That junior member of the crew, Pip Nelson, confined to his cabin! What's all that about, then?'

Jason and Sarah exchanged glances; after the warnings from Richards, neither was about to explain that Pip had been accused of trying to poison Helen Yarnley.

Spencer Simon didn't give time for anyone to reply, anyway. ' Mind you, I'm not surprised. We're not surprised, are we Drew? He's not as sweet as he likes to make out. We overheard him, didn't we? Last night, talking to Richards. That's the great thing about all being squeezed together on a boat like this. You get to hear so many juicy conversations! We were just by the office and old Richards was laying down the law to poor young Pip. He was saying, "You mustn't let your personal feelings get in the way. Any member of the Rara Avis is entitled to be on board, and your job is to look after them and make sure that they have an exceptional time." And then Pip goes, all sullen-like "Yeah, but it doesn't stop me wanting to kill them, though does it?" Richards went ballistic — gave him a right telling off. But who was Pip talking about? That's what I want to know. It sounded like he really had it in for someone.'

Jason thought he could imagine who it was. It sounded like his own animosity for Pip was reciprocated. Sarah was very interested in finding out more from Drew and Spencer, but Jason didn't want to think about the man-boy any more. He turned back to Rita and asked her about her decision to change her life. He was really interested in how she planned to spend her time if she was going to opt out of the celebrity circuit.

'I haven't thought it through that far,' she admitted. 'I just want to get away from it all, for now. Don't laugh, but I'm going to read a book. You know, just sit down a read a whole book from one end to the other. Which book? I dunno. I haven't even got any books. Have you got any? Can you lend me a book to read, Jason?'

Travis pulled a face. 'Give it a rest, babe. Book? What am I supposed to do while you're reading a book?'

It was evident that Rita and Travis had a fair bit of life planning to do. They had no idea what a world of fortune without fame might entail. Their life truly had been one long succession of parties. There were genuine parties, hosted by themselves or their celebrity friends. There were 'publicity events' which were organised by media companies, fashion houses, or record labels. These felt the same as genuine parties, except there was usually a boring bit when someone made a speech or something. And then there was work, which for them meant reality TV. This was basically like a party, but with more cameras and microphones everywhere. The spaces in between these parties were downtime spent binge-watching Netflix series or rival reality TV shows. Travis also had football to watch.

When it came to ordering dessert, Jason wanted to keep up his debonair cool, so was determined not to follow Rita and Travis's lead of 'just a bowl of ice cream, please'. Sarah ordered crepe suzette, and Jason raised an eyebrow and gave a pleading look.

'Orange pancakes,' she quickly whispered, and Jason said he'd have the same. When they arrived, smothered in blue brandy flames, Rita made an appreciative cooing noise, but Travis said that it reminded him of a mate of his who was fond of lighting his own farts.

'Travis Smak, you are an uncultured dickhead! I'm sorry, Jason and Sarah. I'm going to bed. Sober up before you come back to the cabin, babe, or you'll be sleeping on the toilet.' But they both left together, squabbling, with Travis putting on his puppy dog face, trying to get Rita to laugh.

'What a pair! What are they like? Never a dull moment with them,' said Spencer Simon.

'Never a *quiet* moment, you mean,' his partner, Drew, added. 'Their cabin is next door to ours and the noise they make! Arguing and fighting all the time. And then they make up — and that's just as noisy, believe me, if you know what I mean.'

'Well, perhaps the noise of the engines will drown them out tonight,' suggested Sarah, pushing the last bit of crepe through the sticky, sweet orange sauce. 'Jesus! That was bloody fantastic... excuse my language. That's not very ladylike, is it? I think the Martinis may have gone to my head. I believe I'm a teensy weensy little bit tipsy. We should get back to the cabin as well, Jason, before I regret something I haven't done.'

Jason's mind raced again as they left and walked back to the cabin. It was all said so carelessly, but there was surely no doubt that she was giving him a green light this time. It had been months since Jason's lottery win. He had somehow, for some reason, suppressed the aphrodisiac effect of all that money for all that time. He guessed it was because he was terrified of the consequences of getting into a relationship while he was still struggling to get a sense of direction in his life. Tonight though, with two attractive women both competing to compliment him, he decided he didn't really give a stuff about the consequences, and if Sarah was going to give him the come-on, it would be rude not to accept.

But what if it was really just the drink talking? She'd made it pretty clear on previous occasions that they were just mates. Suddenly she was squiffier than he'd ever seen her before, and she appeared to have changed all the rules of the game. Taking advantage of this situation felt just too creepy. She needed time to sober up a bit, and they needed to talk.

'Look, I hope you don't mind, Sarah, but I promised the boys I'd look in on them before I turned in tonight. I won't be long.'

They were outside their cabin door. Sarah turned to him and looked into his eyes. She gave an appreciative smile, leaned in, and kissed him. 'Don't be,' she said.

21

Helen Yarnley's determination not to eat another morsel on board the *Rara Avis* was rock solid, but that had no dampening effect on her hunger, which was driving her to distraction. She'd successfully persuaded her brother, Vincent, not to go to dinner or order cabin service, and they'd confined themselves to their cabin until they docked and could leave the boat for good. Vincent's way to cope with the boredom of this confinement was to sleep through it. He'd tried to stay awake for Helen's sake because he knew how upset she was, and how much she needed to talk the whole business through. But during the pauses in conversation, while Helen tried to make sense of such an unusual day, the comfortable mattress, the smell of the freshly laundered sheets, and the drone of the ship's engines proved irresistible to him, and he gave way to a deep sleep.

Helen watched him for a while, jealous that he could find that peace so easily. Gradually, she found that watching Vincent lying there was helping her to calm down more effectively than sitting talking to him.

There wasn't really anything that either of them could say to each other that would help. Nothing was going to alter the fact that a seagull had died moments after eating a cheese sandwich that she was meant to eat. Nothing was going to change the shocking news that Mr Jarrold — kind old Arthur Jarrold — was dead. Nothing was going to ease the pain she felt, even sharper than her hunger. A horrible, familiar feeling had gripped her, a feeling she hadn't felt for several weeks, but which now, suddenly, was back. It wasn't just that her stomach felt empty, her whole body felt hollow, like someone had stolen half of her internal organs, and now there was a gaping void. It was the feeling of missing David, her soul-mate, her husband, her beautiful, murdered husband.

The cabin seemed unbearably warm and stuffy. The cream-coloured walls, the dark mahogany furniture and the shiny brass fittings were overpoweringly ornate; too much 'not like home' and she had a powerful urge to get outside. She didn't want to see anyone, but if she could just get some fresh air on the deck, she felt she might think more clearly. It would be cool on deck; she put on her scruffy, warm, grey, padded coat and grabbed her red scarf and quietly left the cabin.

Thankfully, there was nobody about. For some reason, she imagined herself bumping into that fat old man who seemed to be avoiding her. That was another weird thing that had happened today. Who was he and did he know her? Or did he just object to there being a black guest on board? It couldn't be that, could it? Really?

Without really thinking about where she was going, she wandered along the starboard edge of the main deck and towards the steps that led to the Stern Bar on the lower deck, where she had eaten breakfast with Richards and Jane Fortune earlier that day. The steps were chained off; a notice declared 'Danger! No Access to the lower deck while the ship is in motion'. But it felt to Helen like the perfect place to hide away from passengers and crew for half an hour, so she carefully climbed over the chain. If it looked dangerous down there, she could turn back.

She took the steps slowly. There were no lights, and it was difficult to place her feet in the dark. She froze. Above the increasingly loud roar of the engines, she could just make out a voice, singing plaintively.

It was a voice she recognised. It was Anatoly Morozov. What was he doing down here? There was just enough ambient light to make out his figure, slumped down on the deck in his white tuxedo, his back resting against a lifebuoy stowed in the ship's bulwark. He had a bottle of vodka in his hand and was oblivious to Helen's presence. Helen didn't want to talk to anyone at the moment, but this was the man that had warned of danger. Did he know what had happened this afternoon? She continued down the steps and sat beside him.

'Hello, Mr Morozov.'

'Please, call me Anatoly.' He seemed unfazed by her sudden appearance at this out-of-bounds part of the *Rara Avis*. 'So, you want to hide too, eh? I think this is good place. Good as anywhere. Drink? You drink with Anatoly. We sing the night away.' He started up again, some lilting Russian song.

'No, thank you. I wanted to ask you, did you hear what happened this afternoon? To me, and to that seagull, the one you called Boris?'

Morozov didn't answer her question, but stopped his singing. Helen reckoned she had gained his attention and told him the story of the poisoned cheese sandwich.

'So you were right to warn me about danger on this boat.'

He took a swig of vodka, then raised the bottle and pointed with his index finger over the stern of the boat. 'Look over there. See those lights? Watch them. They are following us. Are they coming for me? Are they coming for you? I cannot say, but I think they are coming for me. I think the world is coming for me. There is no safety anywhere. No safety for me, no safety for you, no safety for Boris, my seagull. Poor Boris, he shouldn't have to die. They are getting closer. But they will not find me in my cabin. They will not find Anatoly Morozov. There are plenty of places to hide on *Rara Avis*. I will stay out all night. How do you call it when you stay up all night for a dead friend? A vigil? A wake? We will do that for Boris. We will stay, and drink, and I will teach you Russian song.'

Helen remembered how Richards had talked of Morozov's 'alcohol-fuelled paranoia'. It sounded like he had a point. The Russian was completely uninterested in the fact she had escaped a close encounter with death, preferring to imagine that twinkling lights out at sea were the ghosts of his past, coming for him. And then she wondered: was his paranoia contagious? Perhaps her brother, and Sarah and Jason were right, and there was a more rational explanation for the day's events. She stood up.

'I'm going back to my cabin, Anatoly, and I think you should go back to yours and get some sleep. It's freezing out here. You'll make yourself ill.'

'Lady, I am not going back to my cabin. I stay here. I'm safer here.'

'Well, have this then,' said Helen firmly, and handed him her scarf. 'You can give it back to me tomorrow.'

She walked towards the steps to the lower deck, passing the little alcove that the rude man had retreated to earlier that afternoon. Sticking out of the wastepaper basket was the puzzle section of his paper that they had returned as a peace offering. He'd obviously just thrown it away. Ah well, if she couldn't sleep that night, she could always do the crossword. She took it and proceeded carefully up the stairs. As she was crossing over the chain that hung over the top stair, she saw Richards walking towards her.

'Mrs Yarnley, the Stern Bar is closed. Passengers are not allowed on the stern deck when the ship is in motion. It can be very dangerous.'

'I'm sorry,' said Helen, being careful that her voice didn't betray any guilt for being caught where she shouldn't have been. 'I thought I had lost an earring there this afternoon, and I thought I could look for it, but I can see it's too dark down there, so I didn't go any further. It's okay, I'll check in the morning. Thanks, Mr Richards.'

'I'll mention it to the staff in the morning,' said Richards. 'We should arrive at Isola Gallinara at about five in the morning, but we won't be disembarking people until between seven and eight. I hope that is acceptable to you. I know you're anxious to leave.'

'Yes, thank you. I'll go back to my cabin and try to get some sleep then. Good night.'

22

Jason's heart wasn't really in meeting his friends after Sarah had kissed him at their cabin door, but he went back upstairs to the comms room, anyway. The room was dark, warm and stuffy, and only Stuart was there, lit by the glow of a computer screen.

'Sultan's been told to sit outside Pip Nelson's room,' Stuart said. 'He's confined to quarters. No idea why.'

Jason told him about the poisoned seagull and its strange dance of death that they had witnessed on the Stern Bar. 'Sounds cool,' said Stuart, without taking his eyes off the coloured shapes moving around his screen. Jason guessed he hadn't really listened to his story.

'What are you doing, Stu?'

'Trying to get my head round the ship's systems. Look at this. I've tapped into the pilot's multifunctional display.'

'Sounds a bit pervy, mate.'

'No. It's the radar and sonar displays overlaid on a map. It's cool.' It looked complicated, a jumble of brightly coloured shapes and lines, as far as Jason could make out. Stuart explained: 'Basically, the pale blue is the sea, the brown shapes are obstacles below the water, the green and red shapes are obstacles above the water. And what's super-cool is the system detects Doppler shift. So the green shapes are objects that are moving away from us, the red shapes are objects that are moving towards us. The dark blue objects are stationary in the water, I think, like moored boats or something. Richards has asked us to keep an eye on these two boats here, the red ones. They seem to be following us, but it might just be a coincidence — this is a pretty busy route along the coast, apparently. But look, I can toggle between the radar, above water, and the sonar below water. This picks up shoals of fish even. I reckon it would pick up sharks and stuff... Whoah!' Stuart pointed his finger at a small green blob drifting away from the stern of the boat. 'Ha! Tut, tut. I reckon someone's just dumped some rubbish overboard. Or perhaps someone's throwing up. You feeling seasick, Jason?'

'I'm good, thanks,' said Jason. 'Just had a brilliant meal, and I'm feeling tip-top, as it happens. We've been chatting with Debbie Angelinie, or Rita Peru, as she likes to be called now. These are the elevated circles I move in nowadays, man. It will be pictures of me in the magazines soon. "Who is Debbie's new nautical friend? The don't-wannabe celebrity is pictured here with a mystery man onboard a luxury superyacht. We don't know who he is, but that beard is certainly ship-shape." Maybe not. Actually, I feel quite sorry for her. It's bad news if she can't step out of the limelight if she wants to. Especially here. I was wondering, do you reckon there's any way of tracing who aboard the ship could be responsible for that *Buzzfeed* photo?'

Stuart considered. 'I could scan the IP logs from the ship's router, I guess. I might find a trace of when the photo was transmitted to the *Buzzfeed* server IP address. Might be able to work out which device made the connection. I could write a little programme to trawl through the logs, shouldn't be impossible.'

Jason's technical background was nowhere near the level of Stuart's, but was good enough for him to see that his pal was not likely to succeed on this tack.

'Mate,' said Jason, 'you need to get some sleep, I think. The photo probably wasn't sent to *Buzzfeed* directly. Whoever it was probably posted the photo on Instagram or some other photo sharing, social media sites. *Buzzfeed* could have lifted it from anywhere. You'd be better loading a photo up to a few of those platforms, capturing the logs of that and then trying to match patterns with traffic from last night.'

'Good idea. I'll give it a try. Jason Tranter, you are on fire!'

'You're not the only one who thinks so tonight.' But the comment was lost on Stuart, who was a sudden storm of keyboard activity. Jason slipped out of the comms room and made his way to find Sultan, intrigued and amused by the idea that he was now Pip Nelson's gaoler. He didn't know where Pip Nelson's cabin was exactly, but guessed it must be two decks below the comms room, on the lower deck, with the other crew cabins. There was no-one about now on the upper deck. He could see that inside the dining room all the guests had gone and a couple of Black Tees were preparing the room for tomorrow's breakfast. He went down to the main deck where his and Sarah's cabin was. Why wasn't he in there already? What was he thinking? What was she thinking right now? The same round of thoughts led to the same conclusion. Let her have a little more time. He found another small stairwell leading down to the main part of the lower deck, where the crew's quarters were.

Sultan was sitting on a small stool in the corridor. As soon as he saw Jason, he raised his finger to his lips. 'Shhh! You shouldn't be here, Jason. Crew only!' he whispered.

'Your laws don't apply to me, sunshine. And don't be rude to me or I'll have you reported,' Jason joked, but in a whisper.

'Not funny, rich boy. I've just had an earful from that Jane Fortune.' Sultan pointed at the next door cabin. 'She just came back a minute ago and gave me a bollocking for not clearing up the fish we pranked you with earlier. I didn't run away to sea to be verbally abused by the likes of her. There's a headteacher and a bunch of kids back in Dudley I can get that from. What you doing wandering about, anyway? Sarah kicked you out of the cabin? What have you done now, you depraved animal?'

'Nothing. What about Pip-squeak, anyway? Prisoner given you much trouble?'

'Not heard a thing from him,' said Sultan. 'How do you know about this, anyway? What's he done to deserve being put in the slammer? They've not incarcerated him just because you took a personal dislike to him, has he? I had no idea your opinion carried so much power round here!'

Jason quickly filled him in on the details. Sultan was much more interested than Stuart had been.

'Crazy! They could have at least told me I was guarding a sadistic, homicidal maniac. I'd have paid more attention. I dozed off earlier. It was only Madam Fortune that woke me. Hey, but perhaps the sandwich wasn't meant for Helen, man. Have you thought about that? Stu and I heard this bloke earlier on today, talking to Richards. He was in a right state. He was saying "I'm a dead man if they find out I'm on here". Perhaps "they" *did* find out he was here, and hired the services of the deadly assassin from the order of "*Le Sandwich Fromage*". That's the sort of shtick that goes down on these superyachts, you know. All day long. Do you think I'd better look in on the deadly assassin? He might have tunnelled his way out.'

'From a cabin on the lower deck?' said Jason. 'I think we'd know about it, mate.'

23

Jason paused briefly outside his cabin door, and thinking that there was no harm in looking his best before entering, wiped the perspiration from his forehead with his handkerchief and flicked his hair back. A shriek from the next cabin, Helen and Vince's, distracted him.

'What the..? Is this your idea of a joke, Vince?' Helen's voice sounded angry and upset. Jason couldn't make out Vince's words of reply, but he could tell from the tone that he was trying to calm down his sister, who started sobbing.

Jason waited. He didn't want the romantic reunion with Sarah he was anticipating to be spoilt by the sound of a domestic row next door. He didn't particularly want to be standing there listening to whatever was going on next door either, but the sobs eventually subsided and finally he knocked softly on his own cabin door. There was no reply. He opened the door quietly and called in a soft voice, 'It's me. Sorry, I've been a bit longer than I thought.' There was a muffled murmur from beneath the duvet that Sarah had buried herself under. He undressed and washed quickly in the en suite, and returning to the cabin, he whispered, 'Sarah?'

'Night, Jason,' came the sleepy reply.

24

The *Rara Avis* sailed on steadily through the night, following the Ligurian coast past the towns of Sanremo and Imperia, whose lights twinkled on the port side horizon. The captain knew he couldn't dock at the small harbour on Isola Gallinara until daybreak, so there was no rush. A cruising speed kept the engine noise low, and that would help the guests and most of the crew get some sleep. A handful of the crew were about, quietly making preparations for breakfast and disembarkation. At about four in the morning, the enormous vessel slowed to a halt and dropped anchor about half a mile from the island.

Two small motor launches had been following the superyacht's progress. When the *Rara Avis* hove to, the launches followed suit, killed their engines, and drifted in the dark. After twenty minutes, two men in wetsuits lowered themselves off the boats into the water and swam quietly towards the stern of the ship, where ladders allowed them easy access onto the lowest deck. Cautiously, they stepped onto the deck, looking around and removing their diving masks.

Suddenly there was the sharp noise of a switch being thrown and the intruders were caught in the glare of the deck lights of the Stern Bar.

'Can I help you, gentlemen?' asked Smethwick, politely.

Part Three

1

For a while, Martin was the only person on the island, which suited him fine. He needed solitude and time to sort his head out.

The trouble had begun during his time in the army, a couple of years before. He'd never really fitted in, and even the smallest things about him seemed to jar with the other soldiers. He remembered one incident when he was on patrol in winter, and he came across a poor civilian who looked like he was about to die of cold. All he'd done was lend the guy his overcoat, but he'd never heard the last of it. His comrades mocked him, and told him that the army was there to maintain order, not to care for the poor. Didn't he understand the army needed to keep an arm's length distance from the population, or else they would never be respected? Martin thought that was a load of bollocks, but he kept quiet and just sat by himself in the canteen and in the barrack room. The more time he spent alone, thinking about his life in the army, the more he realised it had been a mistake. Things came to a head the night before his division were due to engage in what looked like it would be a significant battle. He approached his commanding officer and said that in all conscience, he couldn't fight in the morning. He was no longer prepared to kill. The officer told him he was a coward and threatened to have him court-martialled. Martin said it wasn't that he was afraid. In fact, he was quite prepared to go into the battle; he just wouldn't carry a weapon. The officer angrily told him that was exactly what would happen then. The enemy could save him the trouble of having to execute Martin for cowardice. As it happened, in the morning, the enemy had sent an envoy requesting a truce, and the battle had never happened. But Martin's time in the army was now effectively over and he bought his way out of his commission.

He had returned home at first, so that he could think again about which direction his life should take him. His mother was pleased to see him, of course, but his father refused to speak to him; being an ex-military man himself, he saw Martin's departure from the army as bringing shame upon the family. Martin left his family home and wandered from town to town, but couldn't settle. He would visit the churches to connect with the people there. After all, it was his faith that had led him to quit the army; surely he would find sympathy amongst the congregations? But somehow he'd always end up getting into religious rows — he wondered whether he was just the kind of person who was always at odds with authority. Then the rows got violent and people made threats to his life. That was when he fled to the island.

From the shore, the island looked like a giant turtle swimming in the sea; a tall dome with a lower, flattened 'head' at its northern end. A kind old sailor had ferried Martin over to the island, which was just over a mile from the mainland. As he set Martin ashore on a small, rocky natural harbour at the 'head' end, he looked sceptically at Martin's meagre possessions. He told Martin he'd call back in a couple of weeks to see how he was getting on, then pushed off his boat. Martin surveyed the island, which was rich with vegetation. Wild chickens roamed amongst the trees and shrubs. He found a cave that offered shelter from the elements, although at the moment, the blue skies and warm breeze suggested to him he wouldn't need it. He had found a hermit's paradise island.

All that had been over seventeen hundred years ago. After a couple of years on the island, Martin the Hermit had attracted a small following of like-minded people who admired his constancy to his Christian faith. He had then left the island and been successful in converting many people in what is now Northern Italy and Southern France. He'd eventually been made Bishop of Tours and later canonised as Saint Martin. A monastery was founded on the island where Saint Martin had taken refuge.

The island was called Isola Gallinara after the wild chickens that lived there, although that population, unsurprisingly, had not lasted. These days, herring gulls had replaced the chickens. The monastery had fallen into disrepair in the nineteenth century, but a fortified tower had been built to keep watch for pirates. The island had some military uses, right up to the Second World War, when the Germans used it to house prisoners of war. After a succession of private owners who had failed to do much with the island's natural resources, Isola Gallinara was now in the hands of the Rara Avis organisation, who had transformed the old monastery into luxury accommodation and developed the island.

This morning, the organisation's superyacht was moored peacefully in the island's small harbour.

2

Jason woke up from a deep sleep and it took him a few moments to work out where he was. Noticing there was no longer any noise from the ship's engines, he looked across at Sarah's empty bed. He called out for her, but there was no reply from the en suite bathroom. He checked his watch, nearly eight o'clock. She must have crept out of the cabin and left him sleeping. So where did they stand, then? She had definitely given him the come-on last night, hadn't she? And he had foolishly, stupidly, messed things up completely. He'd thought he was being a gentleman by letting her have time to sober up, but now he thought he'd just been an idiot. Spending time with his mates when he could have been... He had to find her and apologise.

He showered and dressed quickly and left the cabin. The decks were already busy. Black Tees were carrying suitcases. He went to the main deck dining room, where Smethwick was waiting by the door.

'Good morning, Sir. I hope you slept well?'

'Yeah, thanks. Are people leaving the boat already?'

'We have started disembarking, sir, yes. There's no rush though, if you'd like to take breakfast first?' Then Smethwick lowered his voice and said, more discreetly, 'The police were waiting on the quayside when we docked this morning. They would like to talk to some of the passengers and crew in relation to yesterday's incident. They would like to talk to you, I'm afraid. I'm sure it's just a formality and I don't expect it will take very long.'

'Oh, okay,' said Jason. 'Well, I'll just grab a coffee and some toast and then I'll pack up our cabin and go down to meet them, of course. I don't suppose you've seen Sarah... Miss Headly, this morning, have you?'

'I have, sir. She was one of the first to leave the boat this morning.'

'Right, yes, early bird. Good.'

'I hope you don't mind me saying, sir,' said Smethwick. 'I think you'd want to know. Miss Headly looked a bit upset, sir. Please do let me know if there's anything I can do to assist, sir. And there's no need to worry about packing up your cabin, sir. If you are happy, I can arrange for everything to be moved to your room in the Villa.'

'Yes, okay. Look, I'm going to skip the coffee and toast and go find Sarah, then. Thanks, Mr Smethwick.'

Jason went back to the cabin, figuring he'd need his passport and perhaps a jacket. He looked round at the cabin. Both of their things lying about, like a couple. But they weren't a couple. Still, it was strange that she had left the boat without telling him, and he wondered what it was that had upset her.

3

As Jason descended the gangway onto the small dockside, he saw Jane Fortune standing with what he assumed was an Italian policeman. Jane held her clipboard and traced her finger over a list of names as Jason approached.

'Good morning, Jason. Welcome to Isola Gallinara. This isn't quite the welcome we normally give our members. I'm sorry. We weren't expecting to be here so soon, and it looks like we are going to need to accommodate all our guests... which isn't a problem. It's just all been a bit of a rush, getting the Villa prepared and everything. On top of that, as you are aware, there was a minor incident yesterday afternoon, and it turns out that the police are keen to talk to witnesses, including yourself. Now the police are seeing someone at the moment, but they'd like to speak to you before you go up to the Villa, so if you don't mind waiting over there, I'm sure we'll get it sorted very quickly. In the meantime, I can arrange for your things to be transferred from your cabin to the suite I've arranged for you in the Villa, if that's okay?'

'I've already told Mr Smethwick that's fine, thanks. Does Sarah know? I gather she's already on the island. Do you know where she is?'

'Yes, that's right. She was the first off this morning. She's already had her chat with the police and I think she's gone to her room. I see you are having separate rooms on the island? I've put you side by side. I hope that's okay?'

'Of course. That's fine,' said Jason, trying to look like he meant it.

She directed Jason to a bench outside a low, white building on the dockside. He sat in the morning sunshine, watching tiny lizards dart over an old concrete wall. He felt lost. Clearly, he had messed up things with Sarah last night. He needed to see her and apologise. He didn't like the idea of being interviewed by the police before he had spoken to her, either. Not that they needed to get their story straight, of course. They had nothing to hide, but he would have liked her help in remembering what they had seen.

'*Buongiorno signore. Per favore...*' Jason was shown into a little office that the police had commandeered for their interviews. There were two uniformed Italian officers, and a plainclothes man who he quickly discovered was English.

'Good morning, Mr Tranter. I am Detective Inspector Jeremy Wren. The local *carabinieri* have kindly allowed me to lead these witness interviews, so that we can just establish what happened yesterday afternoon, when a lady believes that someone tried to poison her. I just want to take your statement for the record. Actually, would you like a coffee? I could do with one. It'll be my third this morning, but I have been travelling all night, so you'll forgive me.'

Jason welcomed the idea of caffeine too, and DI Wren looked pleadingly at the more junior Italian officer, who took the hint and went and arranged the coffee with Jane Fortune. Jason described the afternoon's events from when he and Sarah, Helen, and Vincent had ordered four Pina Coladas and a cheese sandwich at the Stern Bar. He explained how Helen had changed her mind about the sandwich and fed it to the seagull, which had then had an apparent fit, or something, and died. DI Wren took notes, but let Jason tell his story without interruption.

When he had finished, he said, 'That's great. About what time did this happen, sir?'

Jason had no idea. Again, he wished Sarah was there. She would have known, or at least, they'd have been able to work it out together.

'I'm not really sure. Five-ish?' he said. 'I've been losing track of time on board the *Rara Avis*.'

'That's fine, Jason,' said Wren. 'It's okay if I call you Jason? I understand this is your first trip with Rara Avis — do you mind my asking, how did you end up joining this organisation?

You're rather young for its clientele, I imagine. It must seem a bit... crusty?'

'Not particularly. There are a few younger people. There's one young lad...,' Jason paused, not sure if he should talk about Pip Nelson, who presumably was in custody as the prime suspect.

He felt so unprepared for this interview. He wasn't sure how much information about Rara Avis he was at liberty to tell Detective Inspector Wren. It was the Secret Millionaires' Club, after all. On the other hand, he was the Police, and there was something about Wren's friendly, round face and his faintly noticeable West Midlands twang that appealed to Jason. He felt like he was on home ground with the policeman and felt inclined to open up to him.

'I suppose I joined out of curiosity. You see, Inspector, I'm pretty new to this lifestyle. Nouveau rich, you could say. I won the lottery back in April. I didn't want any publicity, and to be honest, I hadn't a clue what to do with my money. Rara Avis seemed like a good way of learning about what might be possible.'

'I see,' said Wren. 'When you say you didn't want any publicity, I guess you just told your friends and family, work colleagues and so on?'

'Just friends,' Jason said. 'Three in total. I mean, I've got more than three friends, you understand, but I've only told three. And I haven't got a big family, there's just my Mum and Dad, and they would be worried to bits if they knew... And no work colleagues, either. I was laid off the day before I won my money. One door closes, and another door opens, I suppose.' Jason watched the Inspector's face to see whether he appreciated the understatement.

Wren's lip curled fractionally. 'Quite. And these three friends have joined you on the *Rara Avis*, I understand?'

Of course, he's spoken to Sarah already, thought Jason. Interesting though, that details about his friends, two of whom weren't present when the incident happened, were deemed worthy of interest to the police. Surely, all they needed to know was that his story coincided with everyone else's? As a witness, his background wasn't important, was it? Surely, Pip's background and Helen's background, the suspect and the victim, were more important? Jason suddenly felt less inclined to open up to DI Wren quite so freely.

'Umm, sorry. Yes, that's correct. Sort of. Sarah Headly is here as my guest, the other two are actually employed on the boat.'

Wren raised an eyebrow. 'Quite a coincidence?'

'They got the jobs through me. They run an electronic surveillance and security consultancy that I've started up. Camera drones and stuff. Mr Richards was interested in hiring them,' said Jason, and as he said it, he noticed how suspicious it all sounded.

'Yes, I've heard about the drones. And Miss Headly is a close friend then, is she?' asked Wren.

'Just a friend,' said Jason firmly and tried not to make it sound too poignant. 'Look, I didn't realise that you were going to be asking personal questions about me. I haven't done anything wrong. I was just a witness to the death of a bloody seagull. Hasn't all this gone a bit far?'

Wren offered a conciliatory smile. 'Well, it might sound a bit OTT, but I'm only trying to understand a bit of the background so that I can make sense of this all, Jason. I'm sorry if the questions seem intrusive. They're not meant to be. And you may well be right. The forensic report on the dead bird may reveal that it died of natural causes, in which case this will have turned out to be a waste of your time and mine. Although, personally, I can think of worse places to waste it.'

The view from the window of the little harbour office, with the majestic *Rara Avis* set against the sparkling blue Mediterranean, reinforced the Detective Inspector's point. Could it be, thought Jason, that this policeman was making the most of a possibly futile call-out to a rather exotic location? Jason smiled to himself and relaxed again. That was it. He knew a fellow West Midlands slacker when he met one.

The interview continued, with Wren asking more questions about what Jason knew about Helen and Vincent, which wasn't much, and about the incident itself. He was interested in what had made Helen change her mind about the sandwich she had ordered. Jason explained that she had received bad news on the phone about her solicitor. Wren nodded quietly for a moment and then returned to the subject of Sultan and Stuart. He wanted to know more about them, and the surveillance work. Did Tranter Electronic Surveillance Services have a licence for surveillance activities? This caught Jason on the back foot.

'Er, no. I don't think we have one... yet. We are applying...'

'It's okay,' said Wren. 'It's not mandatory to have a Private Investigator's licence in the United Kingdom, yet. In France, it's a different matter. I believe you do need a licence there, and here in Italy too. You might want to look into that fairly soon, Jason.' Wren's friendly tone was reassuring. 'No. I just have a professional interest in that line of work. My retirement from the force isn't too far away, and it's something I've been thinking about. Your colleagues, are they from a security background, then?'

Jason explained about his friends, Stuart and Sultan, but became increasingly impatient about the questions Wren was posing. Jason just wanted to get out and find Sarah and straighten things out with her. His saviour came in the form of Jane Fortune. She popped her head round the office door.

'Excuse me, Inspector. Just wanted to check whether you've finished with Jason yet? We've got his things off the boat and we're about to take them up to the Villa. Obviously, if you need more time...?'

'No, that's fine, Miss Fortune. Thank you,' answered Wren amiably. 'I have got rather a lot of people to talk to. It's good to be kept on schedule. I'm sure that if I need to ask any further questions, I'll be able to find Jason. Nobody's going anywhere, after all.' His geniality gave way to a hint of menace for those final words.

4

Outside the office, Jane Fortune led Jason to a golf cart that held all of Jason's and Sarah's possessions from the cabin. Jason jumped in and sat next to a young woman in a black tee-shirt, who drove the cart up a wide and well-tarmacked road. She flashed an empty smile and Jason thought that he probably wasn't the only person she'd ferried from the harbour this morning.

'Your first time at the Villa?' she asked.

'I saw the Wolves there, last season,' replied Jason, by way of a clumsy joke. The young woman looked confused, but didn't ask for any clarification.

'Impressive roads for a little island,' said Jason, thinking he should remember to avoid wisecracks with strangers in future.

'They double as a racetrack.'

'You race golf carts?'

'We have some better cars than these,' said the young woman in a tired voice.

They continued in silence on the twisting road through lemon and tangerine groves until, as they approached a collection of buildings, she spoke again, this time with the air of an unenthusiastic tour guide.

'What we call the Villa was actually a monastery, founded here around 300 AD. The main building and tower were built in the sixteenth century. Monks finally left the island in the eighteen hundreds and buildings were left to ruin. The tower was used as a lookout and in the Second World War, the old monastery was used to house prisoners of war. Rara Avis bought the island in 2005, and have refurbished the entire complex. It can now accommodate sixty guests, as well as a staff of forty. The dining hall, lounge bar and meeting rooms are located in the main building. Your room is on the west side, with sea views. Sunsets are spectacular.'

Jason wondered whether 'postcards and souvenirs were available from the gift shop', but left the quip unsaid. The white stone tower looked picturesque when seen poking above the trees, but when the cluster of buildings beneath came into view, they revealed a hotch-potch of architectural styles from all stages in the island's history. Jason could make out the guests' accommodation, which looked to be original out-houses or stables that had been completely gutted with one wall replaced with tinted glass. As they pulled up to a small courtyard that sat in front of three of these conversions, Sarah stepped out from behind a glass door, her face flushed. She looked agitated.

'Hiya!' she said without looking at either of them. And then 'Oh, thanks. You've brought the luggage.'

'Hi. I see you are in separate rooms,' said the Black Tee, checking her notes.

'Yes.'

'But you were in one cabin on the boat, yes?'

'That's right.'

'I see. No problem. Can I leave you to sort out whose things are whose?'

'Sure. As you say, no problem.'

Jason and Sarah stood awkwardly until the Black Tee drove the golf cart away.

'Look, I'm sorry Jason, I was flirting with you last night and it was wrong of me. Put it down to a long day and too much alcohol. I'm really, really sorry. You won't mention it to anyone, will you? Stuart and Sultan, I mean.'

'It's okay. I didn't mind... I mean, I thought that might be it. Of course, I won't mention it.'

'Have the police interviewed you yet?'

Jason described his interview as they sorted through their belongings, while still avoiding eye contact. They had just about sorted everything into two piles when a new golf cart arrived in the courtyard. It was Rita and a supine Travis.

'Hiya!' called Rita 'Oh, brilliant! Wake up, babes. They've put us next to Jason and... his friend. Who's in the other one, do you know?'

'That's me,' replied Sarah.

'Oh right. I see. I thought... Damn! Wish I'd known there was an option for separate apartments. This one's getting on my tits.'

Travis contorted his face into an idiot scowl and started carrying the bags into the apartment.

Half an hour later, Jason was alone in his apartment, lying on a sofa, staring at his view of the blue Mediterranean sea. The accommodation surpassed even the room he'd had in the Hotel Majestic in Cap Sainte Marie. Just inside the entrance to the property, the walls were of natural stone and gave a cosy, rustic feel. The double bedroom and bathroom were spacious and furnished with plain wooden furniture and tasteful cream-white fabrics. There was a small kitchen area complete with the same model of coffee machine that Jason had back in Hambourne. Further inside, the stone walls gave way to a brilliant white lounge, where Jason now reclined, nursing a demitasse of a fine Sumatran espresso. A full glass wall framed the stunning view. Just outside was a decked area, including a small private infinity pool, just the right size for two to share while watching the sunset. It was as if he'd been transported to somewhere he'd previously only glimpsed in the photos of a style magazine.

The combination of the peace and quiet and the gentle kick of the caffeine acted as a catalyst that crystallised Jason's thoughts. It suddenly became clearer than ever to him that his money meant that locations such as this could be his lifestyle from now on. All sorts of comforts and luxuries were possible. The world was indeed his lobster, as Sultan had once told him.

But the thing was, no matter how fine the surroundings, his happiness would always come from people, from his family and his friends. And his mood would always be affected by the emotional turmoil that people always bring along with them. Just at this moment, he was dealing with the feeling of humiliation that he'd been left with after last night. He'd thought... he'd hoped that he was going to find happiness with Sarah, but it turned out that she wasn't interested in him. He wasn't at all angry. He just felt a bit daft. A bit like how he felt when Stuart and Sultan had played that prank on him with the fish in the VR game. Which reminded him that Stuart had passed him a copy of some film footage of that event. If he was feeling like a chump already, he thought, he might as well get it all done in one go. He scanned through his phone for the video clip.

5

Sarah pressed the buzzer by the door of Helen's and Vincent's apartment. Helen's face appeared on a small video screen by the buzzer.

'Oh, hi! Fancy a walk around the island?' asked Sarah. 'Just thought I'd...'

'Yes, give me a second to find my shoes,' interrupted Helen, sounding eager to accept the invitation.

A minute later, they were strolling along a path leading away from the cluster of apartments through a grove of olive trees. Sarah said, 'I wasn't sure whether you would still be here. I know you wanted to get home.'

'I'm not allowed to leave,' sighed Helen. 'The Police have said no-one can leave the island until they have finished their investigations. At least they're treating it seriously. Did you know they've flown a Detective Inspector out from England? I've had a long interview with him, first thing this morning. Actually, it's a real relief. I think I would have gone mad. Sarah, I received a death threat last night! Well, a threat anyway. I was in the cabin. I couldn't sleep, so I thought I'd do a crossword, but someone had already filled in some of the answers. But when I looked at what was written in the squares, I saw they weren't answers at all. It was a message; it read, "*I will never forgive*

you for what you did".'

'You're joking! No, sorry, that's batshit. Of course you're not joking. How awful!' Sarah instinctively grabbed Helen's hand to comfort her. 'That must have been a shock.'

'It was,' Helen said. 'I screamed. It's a wonder you didn't hear me. Sorry if I disturbed you and Jason.'

'Oh, I'm afraid I was well out of it last night,' said Sarah. 'If I'd heard a scream, I would have checked you were okay.'

'I blamed Vincent at first,' said Helen, 'which was a bit stupid. But I couldn't imagine how someone could have got into our cabin and written that message, yet alone why!'

'But what does it mean?' said Sarah. '*"I will never forgive you..."* What are they on about?'

'Well,' said Helen, 'the Detective Inspector thinks it maybe nothing to worry about. He thinks there may be an innocent explanation. He asked me a lot of questions about the newspaper and where it had come from. I'd actually picked it out of a bin on the stern deck. So anyone could have written the message, for anyone to read. It could be a bit of harmless banter between a husband and wife or anything, really. But given it ended up in my cabin... and given that very possibly someone tried to poison me yesterday... DI Wren has promised me he's taking it all seriously. He's actually quite reassuring. He's admitted that he thinks I've probably just got a bit paranoid, which he said was understandable in the circumstances, but he said that since he's flown out all the way here, he's going to do a thorough job, anyway. They've sent the dead seagull to a toxicology lab in Turin and they're interviewing all the kitchen staff and everyone who saw the incident. It's good to see that I'm being taken seriously. Despite last night's upset, I feel a little better, less jumpy. Perhaps he's right, perhaps I have been leaping to conclusions. If so, I'm afraid I've caused a lot of trouble for everyone. Have they interviewed you yet?'

'Yes,' said Sarah. 'I've spoken to them. Couldn't tell them much, obviously. Hopefully, it will all get cleared up quickly, anyway, and we can all get back home.'

'Oh! Have you had enough too? I thought you and Jason would be enjoying yourselves. Is your apartment as good as ours? Vincent was blown away by the view from the room, the fancy bathroom and everything. I think he's hoping we're here for a few more days, at least. He said that there's quite a lot on the island to enjoy... a gym and everything. Having said that, I've left him sparked out on his bed. Typical! Jason the same?'

'I'm not sure,' Sarah replied hesitatingly. 'We're in separate apartments, actually.'

The comment was left hanging as they arrived at the gym. Once again, a traditionally built building had been updated with a glass front wall that showcased rows of sleek-looking exercise bikes, rowing machines, and treadmills, all equipped with touch-screens. They had been designed to give the impression that working out on them would be a pleasure, that they would do the work for you; all gain with no pain. Seductive though those machines were, it was the pool beside the gym that attracted the attention of Helen and Sarah. It was a straightforward, rectangular pool, in a classical style courtyard, decorated with palms and ferns planted in ornate urns. Comfortable white loungers were arranged in pairs along one side of the pool, angled to take in a dramatic, sweeping view of the island's rugged coastline. The pool was empty. They wondered if it was available for use, or whether they needed to book a slot, so they enquired at a reception desk inside the gym building. It was free to use now, and there were correctly sized swimsuits and towels available behind the desk, so there was no need to go back to the apartments. It was too good an opportunity to miss.

After a few vigorous lengths of the pool, they rested at one end while the water regained its mirror-calm. Helen said, 'Okay, so forgive me for being rude, but I'm confused. Are you and Jason an item or not?'

'We're not,' said Sarah, quickly. 'Just friends. I mean, we are... just friends. Oh, Helen, I've messed things up! I overdid the alcohol yesterday and I may have led him on a bit last night. It was so stupid of me. But nothing happened, and it's all sorted this morning. So it's okay. We're just friends.'

'But if you led him on yesterday, you must fancy him a bit?' insisted Helen.

'It's complicated.' Sarah smiled conspiratorially at Helen.

'Isn't everything these days?' sighed Helen, and unusually for her, gave a broad grin. She pushed off from the side and the two friends swam a few more lengths.

'Sarah, can I ask for your advice?' Helen looked very serious again.

'Me? Of course, Babe, anytime.'

Their friendship was really too new for terms of endearment, but Helen let it pass. 'I'm worried. This morning at the interview, I didn't tell the Police everything. Police officers make me nervous; it's just an instinctive thing with me. Straight away at that interview, even though they were investigating an attempt to kill me, I felt like I was the suspect, like they didn't believe what I was telling them. It's ridiculous! I know it's all in my head. They were fine, really, but still I couldn't help clamming up. I just told them the bare minimum. I answered all their questions. But there was something I didn't tell them. They didn't ask me about it and I didn't mention it. And now I'm wondering whether I should have told them?'

'That kind of depends on what it is?' said Sarah, patiently.

'Yeah, well, after the whole thing with the seagull yesterday,' said Helen, 'and after you and I had spoken to Richards, I went back to the cabin to sit out the voyage to the island with Vincent. It just felt the safest thing to do. But in the middle of the night, Vincent was asleep, and I just got restless, I suppose. I went out and walked the decks for a bit, for some fresh air. I didn't mention any of this to the police. As far as they know, I stayed in my cabin all night. The thing is, I met our Russian friend, Morozov, down at the Stern Bar. It was all sealed off. Neither of us should have been there, but for me, it was a place to be alone. Him too, I guess. He was hanging out with just a bottle of vodka for company. It was a continuation of our chat with him in the afternoon, really. Except that he was even more pissed and even more paranoid. He'd worked himself into a real state, convinced that there were people following the boat who were going to kill him. His paranoia was so over the top that it made me think that perhaps I'd got too worked up myself. I went back to the cabin a lot calmer... until the thing with the crossword and the message.

'I should have told the police about meeting Morozov though, shouldn't I? I mean, he may tell them himself — if he remembers anything about it — and then they'll wonder why I didn't mention it. I must tell them. The thing is, I feel kind of sorry for him. I don't want to get him into any trouble.'

'Why should you get him into any trouble?' asked Sarah. 'Hiding away on a sealed-off part of the boat with a bottle of vodka isn't a crime, is it?'

'No,' Helen admitted, 'but as Morozov told us himself, he had a dodgy past with pirate music services and all that stuff. Richards said they'd checked that he wasn't wanted by the police, but I got the idea that he was living on the *Rara Avis* to stay under the radar. I have no idea why I should care, but I don't really want to be the one that directs a searchlight at him.'

'I think you should tell them,' Sarah said. 'Just tell them you saw him and he was drunk. You don't have to go into all the details if you don't want to, but just let them know you saw him. You never know, it may help them. Come on. A couple more lengths and we'll both go and find DI Wren.'

While they were swimming, a figure emerged from a sauna room and went to stand under a poolside shower. He stood motionless, with eyes closed, as cool water cascaded over his head and shoulders and washed the sweat from the creases of his considerable belly. When the shower timed out, he remained still for a few more seconds before taking a few steps to the edge of the pool and making an ungraceful dive into the water. Helen and Sarah were just approaching the opposite end when they heard the loud smack of his body hitting the water. They clung to the edge of the pool and watched the swimmer approach, his head face down in the water, with regular turns to the side to take in air.

He stopped swimming a couple of metres from them and found his feet. Wiping the water from his eyes, he looked at them both.

'Oh my God!' he exclaimed and turned and swam back to the stairs at the other end of the pool. He was out of the water surprisingly fast and headed straight for the changing rooms without looking back.

Sarah watched all this open-mouthed and then, with a slight laugh, said, 'What the hell is that man's problem?'

'It's alright,' said Helen. 'I know who he is, now.'

6

Jason met Sultan just outside the main building of the Villa. It must have been the main quarters of the monastery once, but like most of the rest of the buildings on the island had been totally refurbished. Jason checked his friend had brought his laptop, as instructed.

'Ah, Mr Tranter. Settling in, I trust?' The ubiquitous Smethwick greeted Jason and Sultan as they entered the main front door and added a nodding acknowledgement to Sultan or 'Mr Ahmed', as he knew him. Jason still found the use of the word 'Mister' quaintly formal.

'Yes, thank you Mr Smethwick. We've come to speak to DI Wren. Richards said he would be here?' Jason looked around the impressive entrance hall, which was dominated by a marble mosaic floor and a grand imperial staircase.

'Yes, they're finishing off a discussion with the Italian Police, just now,' said Smethwick. 'They won't be a moment. I'm just putting up a notice about some activities we've laid on for our guests over the next couple of days. It's been a bit of a rush as we weren't expecting to be here so soon, but we should be able to entertain you. There are a few seminars this afternoon. Two good causes, one investment opportunity. It's all optional, of course, and the same seminars will run tomorrow, so there's no pressure if you just want to relax today. Then this evening, we've got a concert, not The Rolling Stones this time, but something a little more cultured, perhaps, if I may say so. I won't try to pronounce the programme but you can see it on the board. I would definitely recommend it. Whether or not you like classical music, the setting is quite remarkable. Then tomorrow we have some motor racing on the island. I don't pretend to be an expert, but we have some superb roads around the island and the short course we have is very popular with our younger members. I've been known to take a spin myself, sir. '

'Thanks, Mr Smethwick, that sounds... um.. interesting. I'll have a think about it. I'm quite keen to see the Detective Inspector now though.'

At that moment, Richards appeared on the half-landing and called down. 'Mr Tranter, do come and join the Inspector and I, upstairs.'

He led them to a gallery on the first floor, a long room with paintings of various styles and periods on its inside walls. On the opposite wall, elegant leadlight windows on the outer-facing wall of the gallery overlooked an ornate formal garden which, in turn, overlooked the sea. Through the windows, Jason could see Black Tees erecting a stage and arranging seats on the lawn for tonight's concert.

'Hello, you've got something to show us, I gather?' said DI Wren, wiping his mouth. He was sitting at a small table at the end of the gallery, nursing another cup of coffee and tucking into a plate of sandwiches.

'That's right,' said Jason. 'We've got some video footage taken from drones flying above the *Rara Avis* yesterday.' Richards gave a puzzled looked towards Jason and then towards Sultan.

Jason continued, 'My friend played a bit of a joke on me yesterday whilst I was playing a virtual reality game on the sports deck. I was fighting dragons in *Uth R'dar*... but that's not important right now. It involved fish. The thing is, he filmed me playing this game and let me have the clip. But the clip goes on longer than the prank that he played on me, and that's what I want to show you.'

Sultan positioned his laptop on the coffee-table so that Wren could see it. Richards stood behind Wren, so he also had a view.

'Yeah, hello everyone,' said Sultan, 'So here you can see Jason... Mr Tranter and his friend on the sports deck, playing the game *Slayer 6*. That's them flailing about with the virtual reality headsets gleaming in the sunshine. The white circle you can see at their feet is a plate of disgusting smelling fish I'd put there myself, for a joke. Don't ask; you had to be there. Now see how they abandon the game — this is the moment when Debbie Angelinie screamed on the lower deck. She'd had just found out that someone had leaked a photograph of her to the press. It causes a bit of consternation, as you can see. Now I'm going to move the video forward about forty minutes. You can see that there are no people on the sports deck now. The plate of fish is still there, though. Now watch carefully what happens next. At precisely 4:45 you can see a seabird flies in from the starboard side and settles by the fish.'

'Watch the bird carefully,' Jason cut in. 'See, it's not much more than a white blob on the screen, but it takes the fish, and here, it flies off around the boat, out over the sea, and then comes in here at the Stern Bar. And you can see here a group of us, Helen, her brother, Sarah and I, sitting at a table and the bird lands on the railing just close by. And here it is, taking the cheese sandwich that Helen throws to it. It's here that the bird starts behaving oddly on the deck. You can't really see it. You can stop the video, thanks, Sultan. But you see what this means, don't you? What I'm saying is, it could be a reaction to the fish — that kills the bird, I mean. I can tell you myself it stank pretty strong, that fish, didn't it Sultan?'

'That's right, Jason,' agreed Sultan. 'It's some sort of pickled fish that the Russian bloke has every day for breakfast. I took it to his cabin in the morning, but I know he didn't touch it, 'cos he gave it back to me about three o'clock in the afternoon. Even he said that it smelled off, and then I used it to play the joke on Jason. I'd say it's probably a bit rank in the first place, but after sitting in his cabin all day and then sitting out on the deck in the sunshine, then maybe it's no surprise that the seagull croaks after eating some, innit?'

While Sultan was speaking, Jason looked for a reaction in Wren's face and saw him give a knowing look to Richards when the Russian was mentioned.

After Sultan had finished, there was an awkward pause before Wren said, 'You may as well know. Mr Morozov is unaccounted for at this time. He didn't appear to be on the *Rara Avis* this morning when the crew checked all the cabins, but he didn't appear on Ms Fortune's disembarkation lists either. It's possible that he slipped off the boat before anyone else and is hiding somewhere on the island. Mr Richards here tells me he is rather prone to paranoia. In any case, we would dearly like to talk to him. This was useful information, thank you. Could I have a copy of that video, please?'

'Of course,' said Richards. 'Please arrange that, Mr Ahmed. And could you and your colleague get the drones flying again, please? They may be able to help the police in their search for Mr Morozov and the sooner he is found, the better. In the meantime, Detective Inspector Wren, I take it that there is no longer any reason for me to keep Pip Nelson locked in his cabin? And there are several members who would like to make onward journeys from the island and return home. I take it that is alright? After all, it doesn't even look like there has been any crime at all, does there? Just an unfortunate incident with a piece of rancid fish. Hardly worth your flying all the way out here, I'm afraid.'

For a moment, Wren lost his characteristic, pleasant demeanour. 'A seagull has died. A man is missing. You can release Mr Nelson, but until I get a toxicology report from the lab and until we find Morozov, no-one leaves this island.'

7

The sound of stiletto heels on the wooden floor of the gallery broke the moment. Jane Fortune approached, clipboard in hand. 'Richards, are you ready for the welcome briefing, please? The guests are assembling. Mr Tranter, if you'd like to make your way downstairs when you are ready?'

They all made their way down to the library on the ground floor. Bookcases filled with antique volumes lined the walls, and there was a range of comfortable seating and desks. As Jason entered the room flanked by Jane Fortune, Richards, and Wren, he barely received acknowledgement from Sarah, who was already seated next to Helen at one of the desks, their heads bowed in together as if they were plotting something. When he sat down beside her, however, she did smile and wink at him, showing that she was excited about something, before turning back to Helen. Jason surveyed the room. It was the same group of people that had met in the lecture theatre on the *Rara Avis* just the day before, but Jason noticed a change in them. Whereas yesterday all the new members had mostly been excited to learn about the society they had joined and were unsure of the etiquette, today everyone seemed much more nonchalant, as if they'd rather find their own way around the island themselves than sit here and be told about it.

Helen, in particular, looked like she had something else that she'd rather be doing. Her knee was bouncing up and down impatiently. Her brother, Vincent, just looked tired. Perhaps chaperoning his sister, even in these most glamorous of surroundings, was losing its appeal. Or perhaps he was feeling his presence was unnecessary. Sarah now appeared to be a constant companion for Helen. Travis was definitely there under sufferance; Rita had virtually had to push him through the doorway. There was now a tension between these two that Jason found uncomfortable. After the goings on of last night, he felt involved in it.

Spencer and Drew, just entering the room, also seemed to be arguing. They were dressed in tennis gear, but weren't carrying rackets.

'I told you we were late,' snapped Spencer.

Drew replied with, 'It was you that wouldn't get out of the pool, you lazy cow,' a point which Spencer had to agree with, and they both laughed loudly and sat down.

Jane Fortune moved to stand in front of her audience with her arms spread in an open, welcoming gesture and a beaming smile. Jason wondered how she kept her energy levels so high. She must have been working late into the night and he knew she had started early in the morning, but still she projected an air of enthusiasm that any package holiday tour guide would be proud of. She stood at the top end of the room, in front of a wall of neatly arranged bookshelves. After she had welcomed everyone to the meeting, she squeezed a remote control device that she held in her right hand. Instantly, the wall of books faded and gave way to a picture of Isola Gallinara taken from the air. The whole back wall of the library was, in fact, a high resolution LED screen.

'Now, I know you are probably all itching to get out and explore the island,' she began, 'but I like to give this short talk first to all new visitors, because otherwise I can guarantee that you'll be seeking me out to ask questions later. And let me tell you, after this meeting, I intend to be lying sparked out by the pool for the rest of the afternoon, with just a bottle and an ice bucket for company, so better to get the information to you now.' She gave a fruity, infectious laugh that made Richards scowl.

She continued with a brief, illustrated history of the island and quickly went on to its present day amenities.

'I know some of you have already found our world-class gym and spa. I'd recommend this place even to the most gym-o-phobic of you. The delicious Tré and Simone can show you exercises and equipment that are just perfect for you. You can try everything out and if you like, they can advise on getting them installed at your personal gym in your own homes. They also do personal one-to-one video training sessions to help you stay in trim at home, which you might want to subscribe to, even if it's just so you can have your choice of Tré or Simone saying encouraging things to you in the comfort of your own home.' Again, the fruity laugh.

'If cycling or motor sports are your thing, Isola Gallinara boasts its own short race track. Its twists and turns and ups and downs through the woods make for some thrilling driving and riding and we've arranged for some test drives tomorrow, so do come along if you are interested in that. Now you may have noticed that the members of Rara Avis, particularly the men, tend to be on the older side. Our "silver foxes" as I like to call them. Well, I'm very pleased that this year our new intake is younger than usual.' At this point, Spencer and Drew, who were in their late fifties, preened themselves. If you youngsters are craving an adrenaline rush, then we have facilities for paintballing in the woods. It's all high tech, we have remote control paintball guns and drones chasing you around and stuff, and it sounds dreadful to me, but I'm told it's "well dope" by some of the Black Tees, who won't take much persuading to join in if you are interested.

'You'll find more traditional fun on the island's many beaches. Those on the west of the island are the sandier ones with sunbeds and an excellent tiki bar. From the little harbour where you landed this morning there are speedboats and racing dinghies for those of you that sail, or would like to learn. The beaches on the east are more rugged and secluded. In fact, there is a bird sanctuary on the southeast of the island, so we ask you to stick to the marked paths and bird hides here. Ask Richards if you want to know about that.' Richards stared impassively into space.

'Finally, I want to tell you about the excellent concerts we put on here. With this location and the top-rate facilities we have to offer, we have no trouble persuading internationally renowned musicians to perform for you in exclusive, intimate settings. Tonight, for example, you have the choice of jazz music in our cellar bar or a classical concert in the Italian Garden. Now, just so that we can get the seating right, could I just ask you all individually whether you prefer jazz or classical?'

Jane Fortune looked to Helen and Vincent first of all. Helen said 'Classical' and Vincent looked slightly disappointed, but nodded. Jane noted down the choice on her clipboard and then turned to Jason and Sarah. Both replied simultaneously.

'Jazz,' said Jason, but Sarah followed Helen's lead with 'Classical'.

'That's fine!' said Jane. 'I'm sure you won't mind being split up for an hour or two and you can compare notes afterwards.'

She continued round the room. Rita and Travis chose jazz, Spencer and Drew chose classical.

'Right,' said Jane 'Now, I'm going to be cheeky and perform a bit of a switcheroo. I'm going to ask those of you that chose "jazz" to go to the classical concert, and those who chose "classical" to go to see the jazz. The thing is, at Rara Avis, we see it as part of our mission to broaden your horizons and get you involved in things that you might not always naturally choose to do. Believe me, we've had many people thank us for doing this sort of thing in the past, so please do go with our suggestion. Of course, you are the guests, so ultimately it's all up to you. If you would like to stick with your original choice, you can appeal to Richards' kinder nature.'

Richards was frowning, as he usually was anyway, which helped reinforce Jane Fortune's joke.

'Thank you, Jane,' he said drily. 'Before you all leave us, there is one last thing we need to cover. As you all know, we have representatives from the Italian *Carabinieri* and from the UK police force on the island. Most of you will have been questioned this morning. I just want to keep you informed. Detective Inspector Wren, would you like to say a few words?'

Detective Inspector Wren looked like he wasn't that keen, but stood up anyway. 'Hello, again ladies and gentlemen. I won't keep you. Well, that's not *quite* true actually.'

Helen looked up and paid attention for the first time in the meeting.

Wren continued. 'I just want to explain that we were originally called in to investigate a potential case of deliberate poisoning on board the *Rara Avis*. I'm pleased to say that we have discounted the original suspect we were holding, Mr Philip Nelson. He has now been released.'

Helen's eyes widened.

'In fact, we no longer think the poison attack, if indeed there was one, was directed at Mrs Yarnley. The focus of our investigation has now shifted and we would very much like to know the whereabouts of Mr Anatoly Morozov. My Italian colleagues are searching the island and I ask you to give them your full co-operation. We expect to conclude the search in the next twenty-four hours, but until then, we ask that no-one leaves the island. Thank you.'

'Excuse me,' Helen objected. 'Do you have any authority to detain us? I want... I need to return to my family.'

Wren smiled. 'I don't have authority, you're right. But I am asking for your patience. If you wish, you can move on, as long as you give details so that we can contact you, but what I would say is that it would help us get to the bottom of all this if everyone could stay put in this very pleasant place for another day or so.'

While he was saying this, Smethwick brought Pip Nelson in. His arrival distracted everyone from what Wren was saying. A serious frown had replaced Nelson's normal cheerful 'how-can-I-help-you' smile, and he walked purposefully towards Richards. Jason imagined him saying, 'They tried to lock me up for a crime I never did, but their bars could never hold me.'

Richards brought the meeting to a close. 'Thank you, Detective Inspector. Thank you everyone. If you have any questions, please approach me or Jane, or indeed Mr Pip Nelson, who will resume his duties of ensuring that you have everything you need to enjoy your stay here. However long.'

Everyone stood to leave, and Pip Nelson walked towards Jason, Sarah, Helen and Vincent. As he approached, his serious frown dissolved and was replaced by his fatuous, 'hello guys' smile.

'Hello, guys!' he said. 'I just wanted to say that there are no hard feelings. About me being locked in my cabin, I mean. I understand it's just been a misunderstanding. So... we cool?'

Helen stared at him, unable to speak. It may well be that he was no longer an official suspect, but this boy was acting like he was forgiving her. She still felt that she was the victim here.

Sarah felt she'd have to be the first to break the silence. She couldn't bear to see Pip's puppy dog eyes pleading for favour.

'Well, I suppose being confined to quarters does seem a bit harsh for making a crap cheese sandwich.'

Jason was watching Helen's face, however, and disregarded Sarah's clumsy attempt to diffuse the tension.

'No, mate. We're not cool. This lady has suffered several shocks and, as she thought anyway, an attempt on her life. The last thing she needs is any of your smarmy bullshit. So, do us a favour, will you? Just fuck off!'

Pip looked surprised and, not knowing what else to do, decided the best thing he could do was to treat Jason's request as a joke, and screwed his face into an ingratiating smirk.

8

Jason decided he needed to cool off. Shouting at Pip Nelson wasn't as satisfying as it should have been. He never liked it when he lost his temper and he thought he'd embarrassed himself in front of Helen, Vincent, and Sarah. He made his apologies and took off for a walk. The island offered several trails, all marked with different coloured posts along the way. He chose the indigo route, the longest one, which headed south through the forest. There was a pleasant background aroma of pine by the Villa and its surrounding cluster of buildings, but now, as he crunched along paths strewn with needles, the smell became more intense and helped clear his head.

He found it was nice to be doing something on his own, for himself. He started noticing the sounds he could hear: the noise the breeze made through the pines, the sound of waves washing against the island shore. The forest became less dense, and here and there were clearings that offered splendid views of the dark blue sea.

The well-kept path was wide enough for two to walk side-by-side, but now he came to a junction with a narrower, more intriguing path that ran off to the left, up, over a small hill. It looked like a path with a purpose, not a walk for walking's sake, and he took it. After the hill, the path descended and Jason could hear that he was getting closer to the sea.

Two or three more minutes later, the path levelled out to a marshy little valley and he could see that the path led to an old wooden shed with a rusty corrugated iron roof. As he approached the back of the shed, he could hear a quiet voice from inside.

'Yes... yes... So where are you from, eh? You've come a long way, haven't you? All the way from Africa, I think. Is that right? How did you know to come here? Come on then, are you going to sing for me?'

It was Richards's voice, but it didn't carry its usual menacing tone. It was softer, as if he was coaxing answers out of whoever he was questioning. Jason was intrigued and tiptoed around the shed to the front, but despite his careful movements, he disturbed a bird from a nearby tree, and it flew off with a flash of blue wings, cawing noisily.

The shed was a bird watcher's hide, with a short, wide glassless window across its front. Richards followed the bird with his binoculars as it flew off and then turned to Jason.

'Hello, Mr Tranter,' he said with unusual geniality. 'European Roller. *Coracias garrulus.* Quite a common bird, but we're lucky to see one on the island here.' He passed him a book through the viewing window, open at the page that showed the bird. It looked strikingly blue.

'I'm sorry I disturbed it. Are you a bird-watcher, then?' asked Jason.

'I grab a few minutes when I can.'

He paused briefly and then said, 'I find it very calming. I'll tell you something, Mr Tranter. The Rara Avis organisation affords me many pleasures. While I'm arranging outstanding experiences for our clients, I get to travel the world, do wonderful things and see spectacular sights. There have been cruises through fjords, helicopter rides over thundering waterfalls. I've had ringside seats at the most exciting sporting occasions, private viewings of the world's finest art collections, concerts, parties... the list goes on. But do you know the thing I've enjoyed most during all my excursions? Watching birds. Watching birds in places like this. Off-piste skiing in the Rockies was thrilling, but seeing bald eagles fishing in a Colorado lake is breathtaking. People get excited to see the "big five" on an African safari, and it's true that seeing elephants at a water-hole is a remarkable thing to see. But your first slender-billed curlew is something you never forget, Mr Tranter.'

'Call me Jason. They're good, are they? Slender-billed curlews?'

'Exquisite. It's not for everyone, of course, bird-watching. Thank God!'

'What is it you like about watching birds?' Jason was genuinely interested.

'So many types, although less every year, I'm afraid. But even the commonest birds are fascinating if you watch them closely. Their behaviours, their songs. As rich and as complex as any human activity. Of course, just like humans, it all boils down to getting the best food and breeding with the best mate, but let's face it, that *is* endlessly fascinating, isn't it?'

9

As evening fell, a gentle breeze picked up over Isola Gallinara, but the sandstone buildings released the heat they had stored during the day's constant sunshine, and the atmosphere around the Villa was stifling.

Helen, Vincent and Sarah descended the brick staircase lined with black-and-white photos of the jazz greats and entered a moodily lit cellar with a low ceiling. This was a cool room in both senses of the word. Intimate booths lined two of the walls. There was a bar at one end, and a low, spot-lit, empty stage at the other. There was no smoking in the cellar, but the pictures on the wall evoked an era when night club lights were softened by a cigarette haze. The three were wearing the same evening wear they had worn for three nights now, but Helen and Sarah had taken advantage of a rapid laundry service that freshened up their clothes and Vincent had applied an expensive-smelling cologne that masked any staleness. Helen scanned the room, looking carefully at every dark corner.

'He's got to be here. I checked with Jane Fortune. He's definitely on her list,' she said. 'Over there!'

She walked purposefully over towards a booth where the disagreeable, portly man who had been snubbing her for the last couple of days was sitting by himself.

'Hello, Brian!' said Helen as she sat down opposite him, uninvited. Vincent sat by his sister, which left Sarah to sit by the man, who had leant forward, elbows on the table and face buried in his hands.

'Hello, Helen,' he said in a resigned, muffled voice.

Sarah and Vincent both looked quizzically at Helen.

'Sarah, Vincent, this is Brian Yarnley,' Helen explained. 'My father-in-law. I guess you'll be asking two questions. First, why didn't I recognise him before? To be honest, today at the swimming pool was the first time I'd seen his face properly, the other times he'd had his mirrored glasses or a newspaper over his face. And the last time I'd seen him before this week was about fifteen years ago. You haven't aged well, Brian. The second question you may ask is why has he been so rudely avoiding me these last few days? I'm afraid I can't answer that. Over to you, Brian.'

'Helen,' said Brian Yarnley, slowly, resignedly. 'I don't seem to be able to avoid you, do I? Ah, well. I suppose this was always going to happen. Can I get you and your friends drinks? If we're going to have this conversation, we might as well be civilised about it.'

Vincent knew little about Helen's in-laws, except that they had cut themselves off from her and David soon after they married. He saw Helen was only just managing to keep a lid on her anger and instinctively knew that it would be better if he ordered the drinks, rather than letting her father-in-law occupy the role of genial host and benefactor. He went to the bar, proud of his sensitivity to the situation, and pleased to be out of the way in case his sister went thermonuclear.

'Believe me, Helen,' Brian said earnestly. 'I've tried to keep my distance. It was a shock to see you on the *Rara Avis* and at first, I wasn't sure it was you, but I overheard you talking about David. I hoped you wouldn't recognise me. I just felt it would be easier for you if we didn't meet.'

'Easier for me? What is that supposed to mean?' The PA system started playing a song by Billie Holiday at a volume that meant Helen needed to raise her voice anyway, but perhaps she overdid it because it caused Vincent to look round from the bar.

'I didn't want to cause you any pain... about David, I mean.' Brian Yarnley stumbled over his words.

'Pain? About David? Your son? My husband? No, it wouldn't do to feel any pain, would it? It wouldn't do to show any emotion. Heaven forbid that we should share any natural sympathy! That would be embarrassing, wouldn't it? What is wrong with you, Brian?' Helen paused. 'Where is your wife, by the way? Where's Norma?'

'Now, don't go bringing her into this. She's at home.'

'Oh yes, I forgot. Norma doesn't come to these little Rara Avis holidays, does she? She doesn't even know about them, does she, Brian? You see, Sarah, Brian prefers not to tell his wife about his massive fortune.'

Brian Yarnley's face clouded. His eyes looked close to tears. 'So, David told you about that, did he? I thought he'd agreed to keep my secret. Oh, dear God! I suppose that's the end of it then. You don't understand, though. I'm sure it all seems very mean to you, but believe me, I'm not a mean man. Norma has everything she wants. We have a very happy life. We have our friends, the club, a lovely house, garden, two or three holidays a year. If I thought she'd be any happier with more money, I'd give it to her. But she wouldn't be... I know she wouldn't.'

Helen thought about saying something about a man 'knowing' what his wife did or didn't want and how, perhaps, it might be better to ask her. A knowing look from Sarah showed she was thinking something similar, but Helen decided that now wasn't the time to tackle this man on the subject of his entrenched sexism. He seemed to have settled himself into some sort of confession and she didn't want to interrupt it.

'I remember when we first moved into Cheverny Gardens,' Brian continued, 'just after David was born. It was a big move up in the world for us. Before that we'd had a two-up two-down semi in Reading, and this was the first time that we had a house in a nice neighbourhood, and we started mixing with the posher set. It was a big upheaval for Norma. She lost touch with all her old friends and had a job settling in and making new ones. She's very status conscious, is Norma, and she's not happy until she's at the top of the pile. If she knew about the money, she'd want an even bigger house, which we don't need, in a posher neighbourhood, where we'd have no friends. She'd want to be mixing with the people she reads about in magazines.'

Sarah couldn't help herself. 'Yes, and she might want to go on the occasional cruise on a superyacht or stay on an exclusive millionaires' island.'

Brian stared at her for a moment, as if trying to work out who she was and why she was part of this conversation, but then smiled weakly and continued. 'She gets sea sickness, she'd hate it. Besides, in a way, it was Norma who suggested I came on these trips. I remember coming home from a Golf Club dinner in the early days. She was furious that one of our friends, Nigel, had been bragging about the business trips he'd been making to Silicon Valley. "You could go on business trips, just as well as him, Brian," she said to me. "You actually own your business. You're not some British Telecom middle manager. You could go all over the world on business trips. You should do it. That would show Nigel and Katie." To tell the truth, there was no genuine need at the time for overseas travel in the cardboard box business, but this was about the same time that Richards was trying to get me to join Rara Avis, so it just seemed to make sense. At first I was just interested in the chance to hear about investment opportunities, diversifying my portfolio and so on. But actually, I made some contacts with other members that helped the business.'

'And you didn't mind making these trips alone?' asked Helen, knowing full well that he'd actually been making the trips with his lover, Ingrid.

'Norma encouraged me to take my secretary with me. "A manager shouldn't have to sort his own travel arrangements," she said. So that was how it was for a few years, but it didn't really work very well. These days I prefer to come by myself.'

So this isn't a complete confession then, thought Helen. But that was fine. What she really wanted to know was how her husband, David, was involved. 'Did you meet with David on these trips?' Her voice was quieter now.

Brian Yarnley looked directly into his daughter-in-law's eyes, perhaps for the first time ever. 'No, David never came on any overseas trips. Surely you know that? He became a member of Rara Avis, but he only went to a couple of meetings in London as far as I know. Charity presentations, I remember.' He paused for a moment, still looking into Helen's eyes, searching for some clue to how she was feeling. 'It made quite an impression on me. You see, that had never been how I did things. Giving money away, I mean. I built my business by being careful with every penny — I had to be. There's a lot of risk in business, Helen. If the factory hadn't been a success, it would all come down on me. And my family. The house, the car, everything. There were times in the early years when it nearly came to that, as well. But through hard work and careful management, things got easier, and I started to make a profit. Still, I was careful. I invested all that spare cash, building security for the future. Building something that my son could take over when he was ready. But it turned out that he had other plans. No, don't worry. I'm not going to go over all that old ground again. He chose a different life, and that's fine. I know we didn't handle it well at the time. Norma and I, I mean. I'm sorry about that now, of course I am. Anyway, the investments did well. Better than anyone could have expected, and eventually I was sitting on a tidy pile. I had to pass some of it on to David. He's the only.... he was the only one I could... and you and the boys, of course.'

There were tears in both Brian's and Helen's eyes now, and Sarah felt she was intruding on their privacy by sitting there. She saw Vincent at the bar, talking with Pip Nelson. 'I'll just see if Vincent needs a hand,' she said and left father- and daughter-in-law.

'But you didn't pass it on to me and the boys, did you?' Helen spoke calmly and without malice, despite the tears on her face. She just wanted to understand. 'The money was made over to David, and it was kept secret from me and the boys. Can you imagine how that makes me feel?' Brian looked helpless. 'I'll give you a clue. It doesn't make me feel welcome in the Yarnley family. Although that's hardly a surprise.'

'I know. I'm sorry,' said Brian. 'It's too late now, but I did try, Helen. I've tried to heal this divide many times, but Norma... she's very set in her ways; old-fashioned. Maybe she feels threatened, I don't know. I can't excuse it, or explain it in any way that wouldn't make you more angry, I expect. The money had to be a secret just between me and David. If anyone else knew, it would get back to Norma and I couldn't let that happen. That's why I reacted the way I did when I first recognised you on the *Rara Avis*. I thought my secret had been exposed. I thought it was all going to come out. Actually, I thought Richards was behind it. I said to him, "My wife will kill me if she finds out I'm here on a cruise with Helen" but he just told me to avoid you — which wasn't really that successful, was it? He's a shifty bloke, is Richards. I mean, I trust him. The whole Rara Avis thing is built on trust, isn't it? And I've been coming here now for so many years and seen it grow into what it is. I know I'm not being ripped off. In fact, the connections and investment advice I get from coming more than pay for the cost of coming here, so I'm quids in. But... at the same time, I don't trust him. I always feel there's something else going on with Richards. Do you know what I mean?'

Helen thought it was time she spoke. The Billie Holiday ballads playing in the background had acted to calm her, and she spoke softly and without hostility 'Yes, I know what you mean, sort of. I've been worried that "something else is going on". That's why I'm here, trying to make sense of it. Look, you need to know David kept your secret, about all your money, and about Rara Avis and the trips, and the affair with Ingrid, your secretary...'

Brain Yarnley looked pained.

'...and how that ended up. I didn't know any of it while he was alive. He left a couple of letters for me, to be read in the event of his death, which told the whole story. He had to. What the hell would I have thought if he hadn't tried to explain it to me? I'd have probably thought that the letter announcing how many millions I'd inherited was a scam and ignored it. It was a lot to take in, Brian. A lot of money, and a lot of information. I first saw the letters six months after David was killed, and all my shock and anger about what happened to him came back.

And something about the whole thing makes me suspicious, which is why I'm here.'

'Suspicious? Of what?' Brian asked. 'The money is all legitimate, Helen. As long as you count the whole business of private stocks and equities, as legitimate... which perhaps you don't?'

'Suspicious about David's death,' said Helen, ignoring the sarcasm. 'Look, Brian, I know that the Democratic Republic of Congo is a war-torn, desperate place. That's why David and I, and the school, wanted to raise money to help. But, you know, not every doctor, nurse, pastor or schoolteacher that goes out there to help gets murdered. So when it turns out that the lowly paid schoolteacher travelling in Africa for the first time is actually a multi-millionaire, then the fact that his car gets ambushed by bandits takes on an extra significance, doesn't it? I think it does. You see, Brian, it all keeps piling on, one thing after another. My solicitor, Arthur Jarrold, was investigating the DRC school charity that David was helping, but he has died suddenly. The Russian man, Mr Morozov, was also giving money to the same charity — he's gone missing. Someone tried to poison me yesterday... well, maybe anyway. Maybe they were trying to poison Morozov. Look, it might all be coincidence, but it doesn't smell right to me. I had no idea that you were here, Brian, and I can't say I was pleased to see you, given our history. But I will say this. Be careful, Brian. Just be careful.'

When Sarah joined Vincent and Pip by the bar, she found they were talking about Jason.

'He's a good guy,' said Vincent. 'I don't know why you've got a problem with him.'

'He's the one with the problem, man,' said Pip. 'He's abusive to me every time he sees me. Hey, Sarah, what's the deal with your guy, Jason? He doesn't seem to like me.'

'I can't think why,' said Sarah, smiling. Any irony in her voice was lost on Pip.

'Exactly! I mean, what's not to like? Perhaps he's just aggressive towards young unattached males, eh? You know what I'm talking about. Where is he, anyway? I'm getting nervous, in case he catches us talking together,' Pip laughed. 'Oh, here we go...'

The room darkened and the Billy Holiday song faded.

'He's taking Rita to the classical concert, actually. Travis refused to go, apparently. And listen, for the record, Jason and I are just good friends, okay?' Sarah had to raise her voice and lean close to make herself heard as the band took to the stage and started playing.

'I hear you, Sarah!' responded Pip, loudly in her ear, and he started dancing happily by her side.

10

The moon shone over the sea the way it always should on summer nights. The roses in the terraced garden let off their heady scents into the evening air. But tonight, the moon's sparkling reflections in the water had fierce competition from the glittering diamonds and pearls that adorned the gathering audience for the outdoor classical concert held in the terraced garden of the Villa. The scent of roses was barely detectable under the cocktail of expensive perfumes and colognes. The members of Rara Avis and their guests liked to dress up for an evening occasion such as this.

The programme, the details of which Smethwick couldn't pronounce, indicated that the Sacconi Quartet were going to play Dvorak's *Fifth Quartet in F Major*. Rita and Jason took their seats in the terraced garden and looked down at the stage, set with four chairs.

'It's not a very big orchestra,' Rita commented.

Jason explained the nature of string quartets using the little knowledge he had himself. Rita listened politely.

'I don't think I'm going to like it, Jason. It's boring, isn't it? Classical music?'

Jason sympathised. His parents had taken him to see a few classical concerts at the Birmingham Symphony Hall when he was a young teenager. He'd resented being there for the first two and hated every minute. But by the time he went to the third, he'd recently become interested in hi-fi systems, and the magazines he'd been reading all insisted on testing the quality of the systems by comparing how they performed when playing large orchestral works. About the same time, a music teacher at Jason's school, struggling to get his class to listen to a Mozart symphony, had suggested that they 'forget that you hate classical music for a moment. Imagine that the music is a big comfortable armchair, and all you have to do is lean back into it and let it take your weight.' His words had no effect on the class, who continued to mutter, giggle and flick snot at each other, but Jason had remembered them on his third trip to the Symphony Hall. It was a performance of Gustav Mahler's *Third Symphony* and, satisfyingly for Jason, his parents thought it was 'a bit much'. Jason, however, had loved the wide range of tones and moods that the huge orchestra produced and found even the choral parts were thrilling. He recounted the story to Rita now.

'Aww! I bet you were a lovely lad, going to concerts with your Mum and Dad! Oh! That rhymes, doesn't it? I'll try it, anyway. The music is a big, easy chair, and I'm going to relax into it with my big, easy vodka and my big, easy new friend, Jason!'

The Sacconi Quartet came onto the stage to polite applause. Two men, dressed in dark evening suits, carried a violin and a viola. The two women wore shimmering, sparkling, deep blue evening dresses that echoed the twinkling of the moonlight over the Mediterranean behind them. One carried a violin, the other carried her cello, or 'the big violin that you hold between your knees', as Rita later referred to it.

The audience hushed as the musicians made adjustments to their tuning, and then there was a moment of silence before some telepathic connection caused the cellist and one of the violin players to strike up the opening bars of the first movement. It was a simple, beautiful and calming refrain and Rita settled back into her seat, even though it wasn't quite as comfortable as the big easy armchair that she was envisioning. She breathed deeply and thought how nice it was to be Rita Peru, not Debbie Angelinie. And how nice it was being with sensible Jason, rather than stupid Travis.

Only seconds into the piece, and the music changed. It was suddenly buzzing with ideas and as Rita followed the musical lines with her mind, it seemed like whole new worlds of possibility were opening up. She watched as the four musicians worked together, their eyes locked on each other, passing melodies back and forth. She was astonished, completely gripped, and the music forced everything else out of her mind. At the close of the first movement, the players reached a satisfying dramatic crescendo, and instinctively Rita lifted her hands to clap. Jason was just in time to reach for her hands, and prevent her being the only one to commit the faux pas of clapping between movements. They smiled at each other as the quartet drew breath.

'This is great. I get it. I think I can cope with this,' she whispered to him, and his hand remained holding hers as the musicians started the second movement.

Rita was not ready for the beautiful, delicate force of the *andante*. At times, it was so quiet; she had to strain to hear it. At other times, the music swelled, and she felt her whole body being lifted. Suddenly she was transported ten years or more into her past, to a time before Travis, before all the trappings of celebrity, before she'd even auditioned for talent shows. She was just sitting in her Grandad's house watching the telly, the Christmas after her Nan had died, neither of them knowing what to say. She remembered squeezing her Grandad's hand, and she squeezed Jason's hand hard now. He turned to look at her and saw tears streaming down her face, creating black trails of mascara down her cheek.

As the movement came to its quiet, plaintive end, the emotion became too much and Rita let out a desolate cry. Embarrassed, she stood up and ran as best her high heels would let her down the stairs at the side of the terraces, her loud sobbing masked a little by the genteel applause of the audience. Jason followed her and caught up with her by the stone balustrade, some way behind the stage. He held her in his arms and let her cry into his shoulder. With the moon low over the sea behind them, they made a perfectly framed romantic picture.

Flash.

Too perfect, apparently.

Rita stiffened instantly. Who could do that? Who would take a picture of her now?

She buried her head in the shoulder of Jason's jacket, but asked, 'Did you see who took that? Can you see who it was?' Jason couldn't see anything much, but made out one face, grinning at him from the sidelines: his friend Stuart.

Jason walked Rita back to her apartment along pathways lit dimly by knee-high lights. Cicadas filled the night air with their buzzing. Jason wondered why the sound of them hadn't interfered with the concert. Perhaps they'd found a way of clearing the bugs from that part of the island. Rita had calmed a little.

'I'm sorry, Jason,' she said. 'I've spoiled your evening. Welcome to my world. You'll be famous, now, whether you like it or not. I've got a sixth sense for it. I can tell when the flash is for me. Even when there isn't a flash sometimes, you can sense that someone's snapped you. That picture will be all over the internet any minute. People will be asking, "Who's Debbie with, now then? Why's she crying? Don't she look rough?"'

'It may not happen,' said Jason, 'you never know. And even if it does, just ignore it. Don't read it.'

'Easily said,' she said. 'You just don't know what it's like, Jason. People come up to you... strangers... and they know all about you, where you've been, who you've been with. Imagine never, ever having a moment's privacy.'

They approached the apartment. Travis was standing outside the front door, smoking a cigarette, looking at his phone.

He looked up and said 'Oh, back are you? Had enough of snogging in the moonlight, have you?'

He held up his phone. The picture of them by the balustrade had already reached his newsfeed.

11

The Black Tees were packing up the stage by the time that Jason got back to the terraced garden where the concert had been. He asked after Stuart, and was told that he'd probably be in the comms room in the basement of the old tower. He trudged over to the tower, feeling tired and irritated.

'You'd better have a good explanation,' he shouted as he burst through the door. Stuart looked blankly back at him.

'The photo,' said Jason. 'I could tell by the daft look on your idiot face that you took it. What I can't understand is why you would take it, and why you have posted it already?'

'Hey! Jason,' said Stuart. 'Don't talk bollocks, there's a good chap. I didn't take the photo — of course I didn't! I would never... The reason I was grinning at you was because I figured that photo was probably going to be just what we needed to track down who's been sending pictures of Debbie to the press. And it looks like I was right, too. The picture is already on several news sites and, of course, all over Twitter. The earliest version I can find was posted at 10:15 GMT. That's 11:15 here, just over an hour ago. Now, I can't totally prove this because all the traffic over this island's network is encrypted, so I can't see what is being sent. But I can see a list of the IP addresses that were active within the ten minutes prior to 11:15.'

'Okay, that's good. How many were there?' Jason waited for an answer, but none was forthcoming until he added, 'Oh yeah. Sorry, by the way. I should have realised it wouldn't be you. Whoever it was has caused a shitload of trouble, anyway. I mean, there's Rita's privacy and everything, but more to the point, that photo has put Travis Smak's nose seriously out of joint.'

'Ha! Well,' said Stuart, 'there were three hundred and seventy-five devices sending and receiving information outside of the island during those ten minutes.'

'Oh great! So it could have been any of those? That's a huge number.'

'It seems like it, yes,' Stuart explained. 'But it's only a fraction of all the internet-enabled devices on the island, and here's the clever part. Most of the traffic is pretty continuous throughout the day. This is a high-tech island. Even the fridges are Wi-Fi connected here, sending requests for more milk or heaven knows what. So I can discount about two hundred and ninety of the devices, which leaves eighty-five personal devices, laptops, phones and games devices that come online at different times of the day, especially in the evenings. Eighty-four of those devices have been communicating on and off all evening. People streaming TV from their rooms, that sort of thing. Only three of the eighty-four devices had been silent for the hour immediately before those ten minutes.'

'During the concert, you mean? When people might have their phones switched off, for example. So you think the device that uploaded the photo is going to be one of those three. Now we're getting somewhere! Nice work, techno-boy!'

'Yep. And two of those three were mine.'

'So, whose is the last one?'

'I don't know.'

12

When Jason woke the next morning, his first thought was to go and tell Sarah about what had happened at the concert in the terraced garden last night. He felt bad for Rita; it must be awful to keep having her privacy snatched away at random moments, but he wasn't at all bothered by his own involvement in the incident. So what if, thanks to the mysterious Rara Avis mole, his picture was suddenly being shared across the internet? As he showered, he pictured how people who knew him might react if they saw the photo. Even his own parents would probably just say 'Ooh, he looks a bit like our Jason!' and then 'No way, our Jason's way scruffier than that.' He and his friends would enjoy picking over the incident in the weeks to come, sat round a table at The Pig. He imagined Sarah laughing loudly with the rest and smiled as he pulled on his clothes. Perhaps this business was just the thing to set things back to how they used to be – just good mates. It might put an end to the awkwardness between them.

As he stepped out of his door, he saw Sarah was also just leaving her own door. Followed by Pip Nelson.

'Hey! There he is!' called out Pip. 'Mister Lover-lover! "Debbie Angelinie's Redhead Romance." That's what they're calling you on *Buzzfeed*. Have you seen? Hashtag GingerNuts on *Twitter*. You're famous, buddy! Except no-one knows who you are. Ha Ha! I've just been showing Sarah.'

'Hi, Jason.' Sarah spoke with her head down, looking at her shoes. So much for the end of awkwardness. Then she raised her head and stared directly into his eyes, giving him one of her 'knowing looks'. If only he knew what it meant.

Without anyone suggesting it, the three of them started walking down to the breakfast bar, with a sense that at least two of them were wishing that the third wasn't there.

'How was the jazz concert?' asked Jason, just for something to say.

'Oh, it was good, yeah,' said Sarah. 'I'll tell you about it. Yeah, interesting.'

'So, Jason, you racing today?' asked Pip Nelson. 'Sarah's just agreed to be my co-driver.' Sarah went back to looking at her shoes.

'I don't know.'

'Ah, not much of a one for fast cars, eh? What do you drive at home?'

'Lamborghini Huracan,' Jason answered almost before Pip had finished the question. He saw a tiny smile flit across Sarah's lips and he added, more quietly, '... some of the time.'

'Ha! That's settled then. You're racing. Good man. Just got to get you a co-driver. No Lambos on these roads, I'm afraid though Jason. You'll be in an old Ford Focus WRC. That okay?' Sarah smiled again, knowing that Jason's regular car was a Ford Focus. She said nothing, though.

They reached the breakfast area, which would have passed for a street cafe, if the island had had anything that could be called a street. Only one other person was there, seated at a table for eight. Jason hadn't seen her before, but it seemed rude to sit at a different table.

'Would you mind if we joined you?' he asked her.

'That's fine, Jason,' said the woman, smiling.

'Oh my God! Rita, I didn't recognise you. Your hair tied back, I suppose. Sorry. Are you okay?'

Perhaps it was the concerned way he said it, but she instantly lost the smile. She did have her hair tied back and, even more unusually, she had no make-up, no false eyelashes, and she was wearing just a plain white t-shirt and jeans.

'Sorry, I expect I look dog-rough this morning. I guess that's how I have to be, though, if I want to escape Debbie Angelinie.'

'You look bloody great to me,' said Sarah. 'I wish I could look that good without slap.'

Jason thought how much better that was than 'Are you okay?'. She certainly had the knack of saying the right thing and putting people at their ease when she wanted to.

'I was really sorry to hear about the thing with the picture last night,' Sarah added. 'I can't imagine what it must be like to have cameras intruding on you all the time.'

'Thanks, Sarah,' she said. 'It does my head in, but it's affected Travis more than me. He's not usually bothered by it, but this time he's really angry. I don't think he likes it when he's not part of the story. He'll get over it, though.'

'It's a bummer,' was Pip's contribution.

The breakfast bar overlooked the island's harbour where the *Rara Avis* was moored, shining in the morning sunlight. The breakfast fare of pastries and coffee was simple, but the pastries were warm and fresh and the rich coffee met with Jason's approval. He thought about how happy he would be if he were alone in this spot with either Sarah or Rita, or even both of them. Pip Nelson was really the only fly in his *creme patissiere*.

'Jason needs a co-driver for the race today. You up for it, Deb... Rita?' Pip asked.

'I don't drive. I can't... never learned. Travis neither.'

'It's okay,' said Sarah. 'You don't have to. The co-driver just helps the driver by telling them what's coming up, round the next corner and so on. So the driver knows how fast to go and when to brake. In a proper rally, it's a very skilled job, but here they've got this special app they put on your phone. It tracks where you are on the course and tells you what to say to the driver at just the right time. It's really easy, or at least that's what I've been told. I've agreed to do it for Pip, anyway. You should do it. It'll be a laugh.'

'Yeah, and Jason is a hot-shot driver, so you're bound to win,' added Pip, his mouth in a disagreeable sneer.

At that moment, Helen and Vincent arrived for breakfast, and when she saw the unpleasant look on his face, Helen decided not to sit opposite Pip as she was about to do, but walked around the table and sat on the other side so she didn't have to face him.

'Okay, Helen?' Sarah asked quietly, sensing Helen was upset.

Last night, after the jazz concert and Helen's long conversation with her father-in-law, she had seemed more at ease with everything, but this morning she seemed tense and agitated again. Jason wondered how Vincent coped with his sister's frequent mood swings.

Vincent explained. 'DI Wren came to see us this morning. He told me they had found a body washed up on a beach early this morning. They haven't formally identified it yet, but it matches the description that Jane Fortune gave to the Police yesterday: "middle-aged, slightly overweight male in a white suit, black shirt, and a red scarf". There can't be too many of them washed up on a daily basis. They have taken it away for a postmortem, but it looks like a drowning. No obvious sign of trauma. Wren said that most probably he fell off the stern deck. He shouldn't have been there while the boat was in motion. And of course, there's the fact that he was drunk. So it's likely to be ruled as death by misadventure.'

While he was speaking, Helen had her head bowed. Tears began to fill her eyes and spilled over down her cheek.

'Oh my God!'

'That's terrible!'

The exclamations around the table were awkward and slightly muted. The thought of someone meeting their end in the dark Mediterranean waters somehow jarred with the brilliant morning sunshine.

Sarah tried to make sense of it. 'Well, we know he'd had a lot of alcohol, and if he was on that stern deck when the boat was moving...' but her voice trailed off as she regarded Helen's stern face.

'So that's that,' said Helen. 'Paranoid drunk falls off boat, end of story. Or maybe, just maybe, he was right all along and his past caught up with him. We'll never know.' She took in a long, deep breath, tilted her head back, and looked around the table. 'So! What's everyone doing today? Another fine day on Fantasy Island!'

'It's racing day!' said Pip. 'Fancy a spin, Vince? Jason and I are up for it, aren't we, Jayce?'

Everyone looked embarrassed at Pip Nelson's inappropriate jollity, coming after the tragic news. Jason also looked cross at the unsanctioned shortening of his name to 'Jayce', which always irritated him anyway, but was even worse coming from this clown.

'No,' Vincent said. 'Not today. We're just going to arrange to leave here and get back home as soon as we can.'

'It's okay, bro,' Helen said. 'We're not going anywhere until the postmortem results are in. And I don't mind, really. You might as well enjoy this crazy place. We ain't coming again, you can be sure of that. Go play cars or whatever. It's really kind of you to stick by me, but I honestly don't care anymore.'

'Or you could co-drive for Jason,' Pip continued. 'You need someone, don't you, mate? Sarah's coming with me. And Rita doesn't seem keen –'

'No, I am going with Jason,' Rita interjected, before Vincent could accept. 'There's no way I'm spending the day back with Travis, the grumpy sod.'

Vincent said that in that case, he'd be happy just watching.

Pip told them they needed to find Smethwick and put their names down on the racing schedule, but Sarah said, 'Pip, could you and Rita go and sort it please? I just want to have a word with Jason.'

Jason loved the way she just took charge of a situation in that way, but didn't know where to look or what to say as Pip and Rita ambled off.

As soon as they were out of earshot, Sarah said, 'Jason, look, we've probably only got a couple of minutes and there's a lot to get through. Tell me what happened to you last night, and we'll tell you what happened at the jazz night. Go!'

13

Jason thought he was having a flashback to the narrow alleys around the Strand in London when he saw the leather clad figure of Smethwick walking away from a powerful motorbike.

'I have to admit, Mr Tranter, that is one of the most pleasurable aspects of my job,' he said breathlessly after peeling the helmet off his sweaty head. 'Race Marshall, you see, sir. So I get to check the track is clear before the first race of the day. Quite a thrill, if you don't mind my saying so. Always rode a bike in my younger days. Nothing quite like this, though.'

Smethwick had two new volunteer assistants and, unsurprisingly, they were Sultan and Stuart. Sultan was keeping the register of drivers, co-drivers and race times. Stuart's duty was to make sure the co-drivers were equipped with the Race-Assistant app on their phones and explain its use.

The starting point of the races was next to the 'motor support unit', or garage, down at the harbour. Once again, an unprepossessing exterior belied a high-spec interior, and the garage was staffed by a couple of middle-aged expert mechanics, who reckoned they'd lucked out with their seasonal 'retirement' jobs.

It turned out that Isola Gallinara was a popular place for the world's top motor rally teams to try out new developments in secret, so these teams paid for the upkeep of the island's roads, and equipped this garage with everything it needed. All of which provided the means for the Rara Avis organisation to lay on amateur races, using professional equipment on world-class roads.

'There goes the neighbourhood,' remarked Sultan as the throaty, stuttering sound of a pair of two-litre racing engines suddenly filled the air and the first of the day's races began. 'I'm surprised the millionaires put up with boy racers like that.'

It was an ironic comment; the first two racers were a pair of the older Rara Avis members that Jane Fortune had referred to as 'silver foxes'. Indeed, one of them had proudly given his racing name as 'The Silver Fox', to be entered on the race sheet. When Stuart had asked the name of his young vixen co-driver, he'd earned himself a slap.

Jason and Pip, with their respective co-drivers Rita and Sarah, were up next and they were ushered to the changing rooms to put on flame retardant racing overalls and helmets. They were told that the cars were engineered to be very safe and that accidents on the roads were extremely scarce, but in the event of a fire, the suits might be life savers. Being tall, the only suit that came close to fitting Jason was a slightly worn and baggy one in bright orange — a colour he wouldn't have chosen. Both Sarah and Rita were given brand-new looking white suits that were very flattering.

Rita saw Jason, smiled and said, 'I can't believe I'm saying this, Jason, but safety is more important than style.'

Pip emerged from the changing room, looked very pleased with his black and red suit.

'Woah! Carrot-Man! You look like a convict, ha ha!' he called to Jason.

Sultan came over to enter their details on his list.

'You'd better beat that smug bastard,' he muttered under his breath as he was registering Jason and Rita, which would have been a touching show of support, had he not said the same words when he registered Pip and Sarah.

'How come a Black Tee gets to join in the racing, anyway?' he added.

'Yeah, well. Sometimes I'm a Black Tee, and sometimes I'm a member,' Pip smirked. 'Now hurry up, there's a good chap.' If Sultan was riled, he didn't show it.

Stuart asked Sarah for her mobile so he could install the Race Assistant App. 'Bloody hell, Sarah!' he said. 'It's a bit crap, isn't it? Is this the burner phone you use for drug dealing? I don't think the app will run on that, sorry.'

Pip Nelson had worked out that Stuart and Sultan were friends of Jason and Sarah, but didn't like the banter between them.

'Not appropriate, my friend,' he said, in a voice too old for his years. 'Here, just install the app on my phone and let's get on with the race.'

There was a further safety talk to be had first. Although the two cars would set off at the same time, the drivers should pay more attention to their individual times rather than competing with each other. There were very few opportunities to overtake around the course, but if they both achieved good stage results, they would be entered into races later in the day to determine the fastest driver of the day. The way to get a good time was to keep the car under control by braking before and speeding up after the bends, as indicated by the Race Assistant app, via their co-drivers. That was the gist anyway, but Jason and Pip didn't listen to a word of it. For them, it was a straight race.

Installed in their cars, which still reeked of a mixture of sweat and aftershave from the race of the silver foxes, the two drivers revved their engines, waiting for Smethwick to lower the flag. The very first section of the track was a wide, uphill stretch of road that represented the easiest chance for either driver to get ahead of the other, just by holding a foot to the floor and keeping their nerve. After that, it would be more difficult to find a spot to overtake. Rita was staring at her phone, which was showing a countdown to the start.

The two cars were about two metres apart and, with both accelerator pedals pressed firmly to the floor, they set off neck and neck, side by side. Rita looked at Jason and saw a grim look of determination on his face, his eyes mostly fixed ahead but occasionally darting to the side to see if Pip and Sarah were gaining on them at all. Suddenly, Pip jerked his steering wheel just a fraction and his car swerved fractionally nearer to his opponent. Jason involuntarily touched his brake pedal, and it was all Pip needed to gain the advantage as the road narrowed.

'Cheeky sod!' said Jason, as he took up a following position – a car's length behind Pip and Sarah.

'Don't worry, babe, you'll get a chance to have him later.'

Jason's eyes widened as he noticed Rita had called him 'babe', the term she usually used for Travis. Just a verbal slip in the race's excitement, he guessed. He hoped.

14

Pip Nelson was going to beat Jason; he had no doubt about that. He'd been one step ahead of that lame schmuck ever since their chance encounter on a train to London, and it was important to him to keep that lead. A race like this was the sort of thing he thrived on, and although his experience of racing powerful cars was confined to computer games, he had confidence in his natural ability. He'd already proved he had the advantage over Tranter, plus he had the quick reactions of a young person. He also had no fear.

'Jesus!' cried Sarah, as Pip made the swerve that prompted Jason to apply his brakes. 'Have you got a death wish? Because I haven't, in case you're interested. Right turn, fifty metres, slow to thirty,' she added in a shaky voice, reading from Pip's phone.

Pip smiled. He was going to win this race, and he reckoned he'd won the girl as well. Like taking sweets off a baby. She had definitely been flirting with him last night and she'd jumped at the chance of racing with him when he'd dropped by her apartment this morning. Now, just scare her a little a bit, and show her how skilful and cool you are.

'All under control, Sarah. Have no fear. Just scream if you want to go faster,' he laughed.

15

'This isn't my first time,' said Rita. 'I've only just remembered! What a dozy cow I am! I did this thing on TV, with a real racing driver. It was ages ago. I did all sorts of shit in those days.

I was terrified, I remember. This is a bit slower, though. I can cope with this.'

Jason tried not to feel slighted (it was pretty fast as far as he was concerned), and concentrated on watching Pip's driving style from behind, figuring that he might just learn some trait that could give him an advantage. Rita had worked out how to use the Race Assistant app and was calling out instructions.

'Sharp left turn, seventy-five meters, max speed twenty, brake now.'

Rita's phone buzzed.

'I've got a message. It's from Stuart,' she said. 'It says, "Tell Jason, Pip Nelson's phone is the one." Does that mean anything?'

'Oh man! Yeah, it means plenty,' said Jason. 'It means that Stuart got the details of Pip's phone earlier, when he pretended that Sarah's phone wasn't modern enough to load the app. It means he's been able to trace which IP address it was using last night. It means that Pip Nelson was the person who took the photo last night and posted it on Instagram. The little toerag!'

Rita's nostrils flared in anger.

'I can think of another word for him. Just wait till I get my hands on him, the bastard. Right Jason, we are going to win this race. It's just got personal! Right hairpin bend, seventy-five metres, slow to ten, brake now!'

As well as applying them to his own driving, Jason watched how Pip was reacting to the same messages that he must be getting from Sarah a second or so earlier. Strangely, he noticed that Pip's actions seemed more synced to Rita's instructions. Either he was braking late, or Sarah was taking longer to pass on the information on her screen. Also, Pip didn't seem to have the hang of oversteering, something that Jason had learned a little about on his track lesson in the Lamborghini.

16

They were on a straight stretch of road, just wide enough for Jason to overtake, but they were both going flat out and Pip knew that Jason's car wouldn't have the acceleration needed to take him.

'We've got this!' he grinned and fist-pumped the air, his hand falling onto Sarah's leg briefly, before she quickly brushed it off.

'Keep your hands on the wheel, you maniac. I'm old enough to be your mother... almost.'

Pip flushed. 'My mother was way older than you! She was really good-looking, though. Really classy lady. And very smart. She had it tough, but she was a fighter.'

Okay, thought Sarah, he's working through something here. Let's just let things ride, nice and calm.

'I'm sure she was a wonderful woman. What was her name, Pip?'

'Ingrid.'

17

'This next corner is marked in green. I think that means the road is wide enough for two.' Rita was concentrating hard on the app on her phone. She'd worked out that there was more information available than just the messages that she had to pass onto Jason. 'This is your chance, Jason. Sharp left, one hundred metres, slow to twenty. Try to wang the back end round, babe.'

Jason knew what she meant. Instead of following Pip's line, he went a bit wide of the curve, and braked sharply and oversteered so that the rear end of the car swung round, putting the car in a perfect position to accelerate and overtake Pip and Sarah, as they came out of the bend.

It was a triumphant moment, but both Jason and Rita remained focused. Now that they had the lead, the task was to keep it, and it was harder to choose the right line with no-one to follow. They had reached the highest point of the circuit now and there were breaks in the trees, which showed off impressive coastal views. There wasn't really time to appreciate them, but Jason was just momentarily aware of his situation; racing in a high-performance car on a private Mediterranean island, sitting next to a beautiful girl who was calling him 'babe'. And, even better, he was beating Pip Nelson.

'You're a great driver, Jason,' said Rita appreciatively. 'A great driver, and a nice bloke. If you weren't already in a relationship, Rita Peru would snap you up!'

'Er.. I'm not in a relationship.' Jason's throat was tight and his voice wavered a little.

'Oh, do me a favour, Jason. Sarah's crazy about you. I thought I proved that the other night.'

'What do you mean?'

'At dinner on the boat,' Rita said, 'I saw when I paid you attention, Sarah got all defensive and territorial. Nothing like a bit of competition to fan the flames of passion, eh? I'm not sure it's worked with Travis, though. He just goes all sulky. Never mind, he'll get over it, he always does. Sarah, on the other hand, she's going to stake her claim on you pretty soon, I reckon. She's only joined up with Pip to get back at you for our scene at the concert last night. You see if I'm right. Anyway, this race will crank up the jealousy factor an extra notch. Especially if we win. So stay focused.'

Staying focused wasn't easy for Jason. He may have had the car under control, but his love life seemed to be swerving from side to side rather rapidly. He studied the road ahead, which was now descending the eastern side of the island. Rita told him that there were only minor bends for the next kilometre or so. He checked his mirror. Nelson was a few lengths back.

Something ahead caught his eye. There was a big black bird hovering over the road. No, wait, it wasn't a bird; it was a drone. Stuart and Sultan getting some action shots, no doubt.

'Smile for the camera, Rita,' Jason said as they approached the drone which hung low over the road.

But the payload of the drone looked wrong. That wasn't a camera.

It was a gun.

And then suddenly there was a loud bang and everything went red.

18

Pip Nelson was furious when he lost his lead. 'You said slow down to twenty. I could have easily managed thirty. You've cost us the lead, maybe the race.'

'I'm reading what it says on the screen, Pip.'

'Yeah, right.'

Tosser, thought Sarah, and they were silent for a while.

Then suddenly, simultaneously, they both called out, 'What the ff…!'

They saw the drone hovering just ahead of Jason and Rita's car, which then suddenly went out of control. It swerved to the left, hit the barrier by the side of the road and crashed through it, down a steep slope covered in pine trees. Pip braked sharply, his arm shot out instinctively to stop Sarah from crashing through the windscreen, although the five-point safety harness was doing the same job.

'Call Smethwick — he's on my contacts. Tell him there's been an accident and get someone over here. I'll go see what I can do.'

Pip jumped out of the car and ran towards the gap in the barrier that Jason's car had just made. Sarah flicked through the screens on Pip's phone, impressed by how decisive he was being. Perhaps not a complete tosser then.

Pip scrambled down the hillside, following a path carved out through bushes and scrub carved out by the rally car. He could see that the car had rolled as it had careered downwards, and had ended up lying balanced precariously on the driver's side, all tangled up with a tree. It looked horrific. A low branch had pierced through the front windscreen, and there was blood everywhere.

He couldn't see movement inside the cabin of the car; Jason and Rita both remained clamped in their seats by their safety harnesses; Jason below Rita.

'Okay, I'm here. Help is on its way. Are you able to get out?' called Pip.

'No,' answered Jason. 'Rita's hurt. Be careful!'

Pip clambered over broken trees, looking for some way of getting them out, thinking that there was something weird about the blood on the bonnet, but putting that thought to the back of his mind for now. He knew he couldn't risk tipping the car in case that caused it to slide further down the hill. He climbed up what was left of the tree that the car had crashed into and found a position where he could reach down and open the passenger door. It opened, and he saw that Rita, suspended like Jason by the seat harness, was in a bad way. A branch from one of the broken trees has smashed through the windscreen and was poking at her throat. It had her pinned to the seat headrest and was making her choke. Blood was trickling from her neck and her eyes looked wide and terrified.

Meanwhile, Sarah had called Smethwick and told him that Jason's car had come off the road. She'd been told to stay by the side of the road. Someone was coming to help and would be there in a couple of minutes.

As she was speaking, she saw the drone land in the centre of the road. She left Pip's car and walked down cautiously to get a better look. As she approached, she heard a rustling in the bushes on the right-hand side of the road, and a figure emerged, holding the remote control.

Pip assessed the situation. If he could lower himself down to the car and release her harness, the chances were she'd impale herself further onto the splintered branch.

'Listen, Rita, it's Okay. I'm going round the front to get that branch out of the way. Jason, can you help guide the end of the branch while I pull it?'

He moved round to the front of the car again and, with a powerful tug, pulled the branch clear. Rita cried out as he did so, but it was a cry of relief rather than pain.

'Okay, now I'm coming to get you both out. Don't struggle, stay as still as you can.' Pip's voice was wobbly.

He was worried; someone had lost a lot of blood, by the looks of things. He didn't understand why the blood was over the front of the bonnet, and he couldn't work out why the blood looked such a sickly orange colour.

19

A Range Rover pulled up on the road above where Sarah was standing, and the two mechanics from the garage jumped out, followed by Smethwick. They all looked over the barrier, down to the wreckage of the car. They could see that Pip Nelson had already helped Rita out of the car and was now working to get Jason out.

'Who's that?' asked Smethwick, pointing to another figure who was picking his way down the hillside.

'It's Travis Smak,' said Sarah. 'He's responsible for the whole thing. He's been messing about with the drone they use for the paintball games. He fired paint at the cars. For a laugh, he said.'

'Well, I'm blowed!' said Smethwick. 'If that doesn't just take the biscuit!'

He and Sarah followed the mechanics down the hill to see how they could help. They could see now that Pip had helped Jason to climb out of the car, and that Jason seemed to be able to walk easily and looked relatively unharmed. Rita was on her own two feet as well, but unsteady and appeared to be bleeding. Travis had just reached them.

'Babe, babe! Are you alright? Oh, man! I never meant...,' he shouted in a whiny voice and then, turning to Jason, '... What is wrong with you? Can't you control your fucking car? You're a menace, mate!'

Jason looked incredulously at Travis.

'Someone shot paint at my windscreen when I was doing sixty miles an hour...' and then it dawned on him. 'It was you! You dangerous clown. You nearly killed us! Come here, you... Stop him! Sarah, Stop him!'

But Sarah stood transfixed, looking at Rita. The collar and one shoulder of her white racing suit were both bright red from the blood issuing from the wound on her neck. It held her attention and Travis ran straight past her, up the hill. Jason gave up the chase and turned to Sarah.

'Hey, are you okay? I'm the one supposed to be in shock, you know?'

Sarah flung her arms around him and kissed him urgently.

'Jason,' she whispered 'The Russian. Morozov. I know who killed Morozov! Oh, and in unrelated news, guess who Pip is?'

20

'Do you know, I think part of me has known for a long time?' said Helen, when she had recovered from the initial shock, aided by a gulp of Martini cocktail.

It was several hours after the race, and Sarah had caught up with Helen and Vincent to pass on her news over pre-dinner drinks.

'I just refused to acknowledge it,' she continued. 'Do you remember how I told you his face gave me the creeps? It's because it reminded me of *his* face. Not consciously. It just unsettled me. Oh, my days! Last night, I was on the verge of realising it all by myself. You know, when they were playing all those Billie Holiday songs? There's one, "The Way You Look Tonight" which has a line in it, something about the way his laugh makes his nose wrinkle and how it touches her foolish heart. It's always made me think of David. It was just a look he had when we first met; I found it so attractive and it's how I think of him. Last night that song came on just as I saw you joking around with Pip at the bar, and I went all giddy. He's got the same thing with his nose when he laughs. Exactly the same — it must be genetic. So, he's Ingrid and Brian's son. David's half-brother. Wait! Does Brian know? Does he know his other son is here? Does he even know he has another son?'

'I don't think he does,' said Sarah. 'But I think Pip knows Brian is his father.'

'So how does that work?' Vincent asked. 'There's no way that they're both here by coincidence. That's stretching it too far!'

Jason had entered the bar, looking like he was a man in a hurry, and had caught the last part of the conversation.

'I don't think it is a coincidence, no,' he said. 'We... I... think someone has engineered this situation. Look, it's nearly eight o'clock. We need to join the others on the terrace. I've just been talking with Richards and Inspector Wren. I think it's all going to become clearer. But things may seem a bit weird while we get there, though.'

21

Jane Fortune was there to welcome them as they came down the steps to the terrace.

'Hey guys!' she sang out, 'What a day! Good to see you looking so well, Jason, after the incident. Hardly a scratch on you! It must have been awful, though. The shock alone can take it out of you. You must feel tired. I hope this evening's meal isn't too much for you. I told Richards that with all that's gone on, people may well prefer a quiet meal in their apartments on this final night. But Detective Inspector Wren has specifically asked for a select gathering tonight. He wants to update us with the latest news on his investigation before he heads back home, apparently. It's ridiculous! An email would have been fine, I told him. But no, I've had to arrange with kitchens and the waiters to serve a last minute, exclusive meal out here. They're marvellous, you know,' she said, stroking the arm of a passing Black Tee. 'They never complain — I bloody do, though!' she laughed.

Spencer and Drew arrived in matching plain black tuxedos. The contrast with the rather more garish outfits they'd worn recently was startling.

'We're wearing them as a favour to Smethwick,' explained Spencer. 'He's been hinting that he could supply us with tailored suits from day one at the Hotel Majestic. He's performed a miracle though, hasn't he? We had one measuring session on board the *Rara Avis*, and here they are already! Don't we look gorgeous? Now Jane, is it true? Is this really our last meal together? We heard the police officer said we were all free to leave.'

'Yes, so I hear,' agreed Jane. 'Investigation all done and dusted, I gather.'

Sarah nudged Jason with her elbow and nodded towards the staircase on the opposite side of the terrace, where Rita and Travis were making their entrance. Rita was wearing a neck brace as a precaution after the island's paramedic had checked her over following the accident. Somehow, on Rita, the neck brace looked like a fashion accessory to the expensive-looking white gown she was wearing. Her hair was done up, and she moved across the terrace with the poise and grace she'd learnt from her ex-colleagues on the catwalk but not always employed herself. By contrast, Travis loped behind her, avoiding eye contact with anyone.

'Darlings! How lovely to see you... *both*!'

Everyone was surprised to see them still together, after Travis's stupid antics had nearly cost Rita her life.

'Hello, sweetheart!' Rita looked round the group and smiled. 'I know, I know! I must be crazy. He's my responsibility, though. If I dump him, like I know I ought to, he's just going to go on causing trouble wherever he goes.'

She pulled Travis to her side and put her arm around his waist. He stared down at his trainers.

'It's my own fault,' Rita continued. 'I put him in this spotlight, all the media attention and celebrity shit. Whatever he is, it's all down to me. I've told Richards I'll make good for the damage done this afternoon. I'll find a way of making this one pay in his own way, won't I, babe?'

'Yeah,' mumbled Travis, and a grin flicked across his lips as he wondered what she might mean by 'paying in his own way'.

The Black Tees politely asked them to take their places at the table. It was a huge, circular glass table with sixteen chairs around it. Under the centre of the table, a collection of red, yellow and orange lights shone upwards into the evening air, creating the impression that the guests were sitting around a campfire. Jason found his place marked with a printed label and saw that he was next to Smethwick. He asked him about the table.

'Quite a history, sir. It was made to seat the G8 group of world leaders and their "plus ones". In 2014, they suspended Russia from the G8 and the group became the G7. We got this table for a song, sir. Imagine, you may be sitting where Barack Obama, Angela Merkel, Vladimir Putin or even David Cameron once sat.'

It was a thought. The diners tonight were a less well known set. Next to Smethwick was Jane Fortune, followed by Richards and DI Wren. Next to Wren were two empty chairs, followed by Pip Nelson. Then came Spencer and Drew, followed by Travis and Rita. Helen was sitting between her brother, Vincent, and her father-in-law, Brian. Sarah sat to Brian's right, and next to her was Jason. There was a little stilted chatter around the table. Everyone except Sarah and Jason, perhaps, seemed to feel a little apprehensive about the change to their dinner arrangements and the fact that they were dining with the policeman who had interviewed each of them the previous day. Richards tapped his glass.

'Ladies and Gentlemen, our guest of honour, Detective Inspector Wren has requested two additional guests this evening. Mr Stuart Diall and Mr Jamil Ahmed.'

Stuart and Sultan stepped forward and took the two empty spaces. There was a brief murmur of surprise which Jason and Sarah traced to Jane Fortune, who clearly hadn't been informed that two of the service staff, three including Pip, would be joining them for dinner.

Richards continued, 'It's extremely gracious of DI Wren to extend this invitation, even though, ha ha, he's not paying for his own meal yet alone anyone else's.'

He possibly meant it as humour, though as usual it had a feeling of menace about it.

'They've joined us, apparently, because of the help they've given the Detective Inspector while he's been here, which is most commendable of course, although what it says about his own detective skills that he has to rely on our serving staff, I'll leave for him to consider.'

There was a polite chuckle from Sultan and Stuart.

'Anyway, I give you Detective Inspector Jeremy Wren.'

Wren said, 'Oh, I didn't expect to make a speech, but while I've got the chance, yes, I would like to thank Mr Diall and Mr Ahmed. They have made my work considerably easier. As you know, I was called out here because there was a report of the alleged attempted poisoning of Mrs Yarnley. However, by examining their aerial drone footage, these clever gentlemen found that the unlucky seagull that ate Mrs Yarnley's cheese sandwich had previously eaten some dodgy fish. We are now pretty certain that this caused the bird's untimely death. Which I'm sure is a great relief to Mrs Yarnley and to Mr Pip Nelson who made her the sandwich!'

It got a bigger laugh than Richards' efforts, anyway.

'So, any of you who may have thought that I'd called you all here to the terrace to make a dramatic revelation of the identity of the poisoner are going to be disappointed, I'm afraid.'

'Shame! Shame!' called Drew and Spencer together in mock disappointment.

The mood around the table was lightening.

'However,' Wren continued, 'Perhaps no-one will mind if I take this opportunity to reveal the identity of a different culprit.'

There was a hush around the table once more. Wren paused and looked around at each diner's face. This evening was a career highlight for him; an opportunity to gather suspects together for 'the big reveal' — something he'd always wanted to do. Two of the faces, he noticed, looked satisfyingly anxious.

'Mr Diall also helped solve another mystery today,' said Wren. 'Now, this is unrelated to my presence here on the island, but I feel I should celebrate such a smart piece of detective work. As you may know, Miss Rita Peru, formerly Miss Debbie Angelinie, has had her privacy invaded in recent days by someone sending pictures of her to social media platforms and the popular press. The consequence of this has been that, having learnt that Debbie Angelinie was on board a ship, somewhere in the Cote d'Azur, the paparazzi photographers started following the *Rara Avis* and even, at one point, boarded the ship. Mr Diall... Stuart here... using his technical wizardry, has identified the phone that was used to take those pictures. The owner of that phone is sitting here with us, around this table. Stuart, would you like to name and shame that individual yourself?'

Stuart declined, lowering his head and covering his eyes with his hand. There was hardly any need to identify the guilty party anyway as he was sitting right next to Stuart looking red-faced and tearful.

'Fair enough,' said Wren. 'The owner of the phone was... Mr Pip Nelson. No poisoner perhaps, but a wrong'un in my book. He might think... any of you might think... I've overstepped the mark in publicly shaming him like this. But I agreed with Mr Richards that this little performance might teach him what it's like to have your privacy stripped away. Have you got anything to say to Miss Peru, young man?'

Pip tried to speak, but his mouth refused to make the shapes that would make comprehensible words. His throat was tight and a high-pitched warble was the only sound he could make.

Rita spoke instead. 'It's okay, Pip. I was really cross with you when I found out, but I've already forgiven you. This afternoon, when the car I was racing in with Jason was forced off the road by the idiot on my left here, you could have driven past and won the race, but you stopped, came down a steep bank and got me out of that car, when I was about to choke to death. You may have saved my life.'

The high-pitched warble rose an octave higher. Hot tears ran over Pip's cheeks.

'When I came to Rara Avis,' said Rita, 'It was to start a new life. It's not an easy thing to do, but I think people should be given second chances. So make sure you learn from this and don't be a prat in the future. Okay? And that goes for you too, Travis Smak.'

There was general relief around the table.

Stuart offered Pip Nelson his napkin to dry his eyes and said, 'Sorry about that, mate. You going to be alright?'.

Spencer and Drew congratulated Rita on her magnanimous gesture of forgiveness to the two young men who had let her down. Everyone felt thankful that an awkward scene seemed to be settling down again nicely. A waiter checked that everyone's glasses were topped up. One glass required a complete refill.

Richards said, 'Very good. Now I expect we can continue with our meal without anymore dramatic revelations.'

'Maybe, maybe not,' interjected Sarah.

She wasn't used to speaking up at events like this, and the sound of her own voice, projecting loudly so that all the table could hear it, surprised her. A discreet wink from Detective Inspector Wren gave her the confidence to continue.

'There is something else that could do with bringing out into the open,' she said. 'Something very serious, I'm afraid. It's great news that it turns out that no-one was trying to poison Helen. I'm sure it's a relief for all of us. But that's not the only weird stuff Helen has had to put up with these last few days. Y'alright with me saying this, Helen?'

Helen looked horrified, not knowing exactly where this was going, but nodded her consent, as keen as anyone sat around the table to hear what Sarah was going to say next.

'When Helen came aboard the *Rara Avis*, three days ago,' Sarah continued, 'there were a couple of people she met who made her feel like she wasn't welcome, or spooked her out in some way that she didn't quite understand herself. Even worse, she found a message in her cabin the other night, written on her newspaper, saying "*I'll never forgive you for what you did*".

Between us, I think we've pieced together what's been going on.

'There's a rule in this club that we don't discuss people's back stories, but I'm wondering who that rule is supposed to protect. Anyway, I'm going to ignore it. Helen is here because her late husband, David Yarnley, was a member of Rara Avis, even though he never told her about it when he was alive. David Yarnley had joined the club when his father wanted to pass on a huge pile of money to David, but it was all kept hush-hush because they didn't want to upset David's mother. Long story... suffice it to say that Helen had been estranged from her father-in-law for many years, which is why she didn't recognise him when she saw him on board the ship. He tried to keep out of her way. It annoyed him that his secret hideaway in the sun had been exposed, and he was afraid the news of it would soon reach his wife. So there was Brian Yarnley... yes, he's seated here, ladies and gentlemen, ... so there was Brian Yarnley, ducking and weaving around the decks of the *Rara Avis*, and here was Helen, wondering who the hell was this jerk who seemed to resent her presence so much. Anyway, thankfully, the penny eventually dropped and we see the two of them together pretty much reconciled. So that's one more mystery cleared up.'

'Yes, well, I didn't really mean this to be a general free for all, show-and-tell...' interjected Richards.

'Hear, hear!' cried Jane Fortune. 'Can we let the staff serve the food, please? I'm starving!'

'Sorry,' said Sarah, 'but I'm going to continue, I'm afraid, because my friend's been very upset these last four days, and she needn't have been. The other person who made Helen feel uncomfortable was Pip Nelson. Sorry to make you the star of the show again, Pip.'

Pip had regained some of his composure and now just stared vacantly, letting it all roll over him.

'Pip knew a bit about Helen, even before he met her,' Sarah continued. 'He knew she was David Yarnley's widow, and Brian Yarnley's daughter-in-law. It surprised him to discover she was a black woman, coming from such a very "white" family as the Yarnleys. He'd done some research into them. He knew, for instance, that Brian had made his money through some smart investments in the early nineties. And he knew Brian had been in an affair with his secretary, Ingrid, and that they had been on the verge of running away together, but they had split up over some jealous quarrel. He also knew what Brian didn't know... that Ingrid had had a son. He was told all this by Ingrid herself, because Ingrid was his mother.'

Now Brian Yarnley was staring disbelievingly at Pip Nelson, growing redder and redder. Helen reached and held his hand, while Sarah continued.

'So Ingrid had brought up Pip single-handedly — no easy task. But from her days as Brian's secretary, she had copied some of his lucky investments in early internet start-ups. It was on a more modest scale than Brian's fortune, at first, but she found she had a talent for the stock market, and gradually her pile increased as well. Sadly, Ingrid passed away last year, leaving her fortune, of course, to Pip.

'Then Pip gets a job on the *Rara Avis*, but who does he bump into, on board? His father. The father who had left his mother, to go back to his wife, and who had been absent throughout his life. No wonder he's angry with the man. It wasn't a great idea to leave an anonymous, threatening note for him — "*I'll never forgive you for what you did*" — especially as it ended up in Helen's cabin and scaring the lights out of her, but he's a young lad, and this is a strange set-up, what can you expect?

'A bigger question is, how is it that Pip ends up working on a boat, or later on an island in the Mediterranean, with his father and the widow of his half-brother, without either of them knowing anything about them? I mean, it's quite a coincidence, isn't it? But of course, it isn't really a coincidence at all. Is it, Mr Richards?'

'I don't know what you mean,' said Richards.

'I mean,' replied Sarah, 'that fathers don't get re-united with unknown sons and estranged daughters-in-law on luxury superyachts, just by accident, do they?'

Richards coughed and said, 'Of course, there is no such thing as coincidence, but I fail to see what business it is of yours, Miss Headly.'

'Well, it's certainly *my* business,' said Helen angrily. 'Thank you, Sarah. I'll take it from here. I'm glad this is all coming out in public, because I think people need to understand how this organisation of yours operates. So here's what I think... I think you engineered this situation, bringing Pip, Brian and me all together like this without us knowing. I think you did it simply because it amused you. And that's what you do, isn't it? You watch people, put them in situations, and see how they get on. Like at the Casino, watching who would go for the high stakes, and who would go for low. A nice little social experiment. And watching what would happen when you recruit Jason's two best friends as deckhands for his luxury cruise. Switching people's choices when deciding whether to go to a jazz gig or a classical recital. It's all a game for you, isn't it?'

'Mrs Yarnley, I assure you it's no game.' Richards lifted his hands, as if to halt an oncoming vehicle.

He turned and signalled to the waiters that they could start serving the first course of the meal and then continued.

'I take all that goes on in and around the Rara Avis organisation extremely seriously. It's my job to understand our members' circumstances and tastes, not out of idle nosiness, but so that my colleagues and I can create the environment and experiences that our members value. We all do it. Mr Smethwick takes a keen interest in our members' personal aesthetics, how they like to dress, what they like to eat. Ms Fortune has an instinct for laying on memorable occasions, such as the concerts we've enjoyed, as well as being able to call on her vast range of contacts in the worlds of investment and philanthropy. Between us, we all try to understand as much as we can about our clients so we can help them use their wealth wisely and live well. I think we do it pretty well, but none of this expertise is god given. We are all constantly observing and learning'.

The Black Tees silently distributed plates of grilled langoustines with a chilli and garlic butter to the diners, who had once again become quiet and tense as they listened to Richards's explanation. One person asked for yet another refill of their glass of chilled *fino* sherry.

'My colleagues and I don't have enormous fortunes like the members of Rara Avis, but as you see, we do share in the luxuries that they enjoy,' Richards continued. 'However, like many of you, I have learned that the luxuries of life are superficial. They get boring after a while. The only thing that is constantly interesting is people... oh, and birds. So yes.. I confess.. It seems to be a night for exposées and confessions after all... I do enjoy watching "life's rich tapestry", and perhaps once in a while, I do a little weaving myself. In my defence, I would say that as a trustee of Pip Nelson's fortune, I thought that employing him was an excellent way of introducing him to some of the pleasures and pitfalls of the high life. I wasn't aware at that time that Brian Yarnley was Pip's father. Had I been, I may have made other arrangements to prevent their meeting. Pip recognised his father's name from the ship's manifest, and I took pains to keep the two apart as best I could. As far as you are concerned, Mrs Yarnley, when you applied to join Rara Avis, I wasn't in a position to know that you and your father-in-law weren't on speaking terms. So you can hardly hold me accountable for any awkwardness, can you?'

Richards's voice was raised, and he glared around the table defensively, and everyone stopped eating momentarily. It was obvious from the diners' raised eyebrows that no-one was really buying this. Clearly, just by his haughty manner, he was accountable for quite a lot of 'awkwardness'.

He paused and then, in a lower, more contrite voice, said, 'Hmm. Alright then, *mea culpa*. "My bad", as the young people say. Look, I'm sorry things have worked out the way they have, and I'll try to avoid that happening in future. Now please, everyone, enjoy your food. *Bon appétit*!'

22

Tentative, polite chatter resumed. In normal circumstances, langoustines would have presented too much of a challenge for Jason. Fiddling about with body parts of alien-looking creatures was not his thing, and he would have requested an easier dish, such as a bowl of tomato soup — Heinz if they'd got it. But these langoustines had been so expertly prepared that it was very easy for the diners to remove the meat from the shells and this allowed Jason to concentrate on the conversation and wait for his turn to lead it, as arranged. He did briefly notice that the sweet taste of fresh shellfish in his mouth was really rather agreeable and that the way it complemented his wine was very satisfying too. He reckoned his time had come.

'So, Mr Wren,' he said casually, 'The cheese sandwich turned out to be a red herring then, eh? Bit of a distance for you to travel, to find that out, eh? Still, it's good to know that no-one was trying to kill Helen, that's the main thing. The Russian guy, Mr Morozov... will his death be put down to misadventure then? Got drunk and fell off a dangerous part of the boat?'

DI Wren dabbed his mouth with his napkin. 'Well, no. There are some suspicious circumstances, actually. The investigations will continue.'

'Oh, great! Not a wasted trip for you then. Nice one!' said Jason. 'Am I allowed to ask what those suspicious circumstances might be?'

'Probably not, but since we're among friends...'

Jason and Wren were talking across the table and others left their own conversations hanging so that they could listen in.

'... the toxicology report on the seagull identified an unusual substance. A nerve agent, in fact.'

'A what?' exclaimed Jane Fortune, joining in the conversation.

'A nerve agent, similar to the one that was used in Salisbury last year by Russian agents. Not as strong as Novichok, I might add, but deadly all the same... and of Russian origin.'

Helen Yarnley started breathing rapidly, her eyes wide and angry, but unable to speak. Her father-in-law tried to comfort her.

'I stress again, Helen,' said Jeremy Wren calmly, 'we're certain that your cheese sandwich wasn't poisoned. They found the nerve agent to be concentrated in the fish inside the bird's stomach. We found no traces of it on the plate that had held the cheese sandwich or in the kitchen where Pip Nelson prepared it. However, we found traces inside Mr Morozov's cabin.'

'So wait, what? Was someone trying to poison Morozov... or was he the poisoner?' asked Jason.

He felt like he was hamming his part a little, but no-one seemed to notice.

'Well, that's interesting, Jason. You see, this nerve agent is of a specific type that we have encountered somewhere else recently.' Wren glanced nervously at Helen, as he had more news that was going to shock her.

Nevertheless, it had to be done.

'We found it on the lips of Mrs Yarnley's solicitor, Mr Arthur Jarrold,' he said. 'At first, we put Mr Jarrold's death down to a heart attack or massive stroke, but an autopsy detected the nerve agent and that's where the West Midlands Counter Terrorism Unit... my unit... came in. Our forensic team was puzzled. The chemical traces were there on his lips, but they couldn't trace how it had been administered. The man was found sitting in his armchair. It looked like he'd been having a morning cuppa and reading his post, but they couldn't find any of the poison on the cup, or anywhere in his kitchen. He'd been spraying his roses earlier in the day, and we checked his sprayer, but they found nothing. So that was all a bit of a mystery.

'But now we learn a seagull has died on the deck of the *Rara Avis*, and we identify the same nerve agent as the one that killed Arthur Jarrold as the cause. Interesting! And there's another link. Helen Yarnley witnesses the seagull's death, and Arthur Jarrold is Helen Yarnley's solicitor. Now that is very interesting! Suspicion *almost* falls on Mrs Yarnley.'

'Now, hang on, mate!' exclaimed Vincent. 'That's outrageous...'

'You're quite right, sir,' interjected Wren. 'I was being a bit fanciful there. I did say "*almost*". There is really no reason to suspect your sister. I apologise. But there had to be a link between the seagull, your sister, and Mr Jarrold, and we soon found what it was. Helen had instructed her solicitor to investigate a charity that her late husband had supported. A charity project, to set up a school in the Democratic Republic of the Congo. Now it turned out that the letter that Mr Jarrold had been reading on the morning he died contained a report about that same charity. In fact, he'd just put a receipt for that report into a reply-paid envelope. This afternoon I've had the labs check that envelope and they've found the nerve agent on the glue that sealed the envelope.'

There was a shudder around the table, as people thought how the innocent act of licking an envelope seal could be so fatal. Meanwhile, Jason had been listening carefully and something was bothering him. How exactly had the police made the connection between Helen and Mr Jarrold? The connection was obviously there, but he wondered what line of questioning had led to the revelation that Helen had a solicitor called Mr Jarrold? He wanted to ask DI Wren about this, but that wasn't what had been agreed, so he kept to his script.

'So, you're saying whoever poisoned Jarrold did it by getting him to lick the gum on an envelope? So... who sent him that report?'

'The letter attached to the report came from someone called Guillaume Bertrand, care of the Rara Avis organisation,' said Jeremy Wren and turned to Richards.

'One of your team, Mr Richards?'

'No, he's not actually,' Richards answered. 'Monsieur Bertrand is the director of the Belgian charity that's building the school in the DRC. He's joined us at some of our meetings to present the work of the charity to our members, and to recruit donors. He's not part of Rara Avis and I've no idea why he'd sign a letter in a way that suggested that he was. Back in April or May, I received an email from Arthur Jarrold, asking for information about Yepi-Kasai and so I asked Jane who the contact for that charity was. Then I forwarded the email to Guillaume Bertrand. That's the extent of my involvement with him. Jane handles all contacts with the charities and entrepreneurs. That's her line.'

Richards turned to Jane Fortune, with a look that invited her to speak next.

'Yes, well,' she said, 'Bertrand probably used our covering address, as we tell all our partners to be very careful about any requests for information. This is a very discrete organisation, you see. Strictly speaking, he should have sent the information back to Richards so that he could reply back, but he probably just did what came easiest. If he's out building schools in Africa, he's probably a very busy guy.'

'He's very busy indeed,' said Jeremy Wren. 'We did a bit of a search on Monsieur Bertrand. Couldn't find much about him, although there is a picture of him on the Yepi Kasai Foundation website, a brief description of the aims of the school project and contact details that lead to a "number unobtainable" phone and an unanswered email address.

Nothing else anywhere. But when we ran an image search on that photo, we found he has another string to his bow. We found his face on the talent register of a Belgian theatrical agent. On that site, however, he's listed as Yves Rambert. Star of some soft-porn films, apparently. Which is odd. I've got the Belgian Police tracking him down for questioning right now.'

'Oh my God!' Jane Fortune was clearly shocked. 'I mean, are you sure? There must be a mistake! Perhaps they're twins? Perhaps Yves... whatsit is just a stage name?'

'It's a possibility, Miss Fortune. Yes, or maybe the charity worker, Guillaume Bertrand, had a second life as Yves Rambert. There's also the possibility that Guillaume Bertrand was bogus... I mean to say that he was an invented character, representing an invented charity, and conning members of Rara Avis out of their money. And when Arthur Jarrold started investigating that charity, Mr Bertrand or Mr Rambert sent him a poisoned letter, designed to silence him for good. How does that possibility sound?'

Jeremy Wren finished with a flourish, and looked round the table to see the impact he was making, his gaze eventually resting on Jason, a trace of a smile on his lips.

Jason hoped he was the only one who noticed the smile. Clearly, Wren was getting into the swing of this performance just like Jason.

Now it was his own turn again, and he said, slowly, as if he were just thinking of it for the first time, 'But surely... that's a bit odd. I mean... it's ingenious to use a poisoned reply paid envelope, yes. But it's plain daft for the murderer to sign the letter and identify themselves as the sender. Surely the poisoner must be someone else, other than Bertrand?'

'You're right, of course, Jason. Smart lad, this one,' said Wren. 'So, we have to ask who else is involved in this charity?'

Helen was quick to reply. 'Anatoly Morozov also donated to the charity. And he –'

'That's correct,' interrupted Jane Fortune. 'And now I come to think of it, it was Morozov who originally introduced Bertrand to us at Rara Avis. Morozov had been supporting the African school project before he joined us... or so he said! Do you think that the charity could be a scam, cooked up between Bertrand and Morozov?'

'It's a strong possibility, yes,' said Wren. 'Let's suppose that some time last year, Morozov and Bertrand saw an opportunity to defraud members of Rara Avis. Let's say they came to hear about a charity building a school in a war-torn, dangerous part of Africa, a small village called Yepi, in a remote part of the Kasai region of the Democratic Republic of Congo. They just had to create a shadow, twin charity, to take donations just from Rara Avis members. They could have been quite open about this. The official charity, the Yepi-Kasai Foundation, doesn't take donations from anonymous donors, for ethical reasons. The way round this was to create this shadow charity, registered in Belgium, perhaps. *La Fondation Kasai Developpement*, for example. That way, anonymous donors could give money to the Belgian charity, which then passed the money on to the original African charity. But of course, they did not pass the money on. Instead, it lined the pockets of the Belgian charity's proprietors, Guillaume Bertrand and Anatoly Morozov. This is all just conjecture, you understand — I'm just hanging a story on the few facts we know. But now, suppose they persuaded David Yarnley to donate to this charity, and then he did something that they hadn't expected. They would have been pretty certain that the comfortably off Rara Avis members would never dream of visiting the dangerous backwaters of the DRC to check on how their money is being spent. But David surprised them all. He was a teacher, and he'd encouraged the pupils at his school in Nebberton to make their own donations to the African school project. He wanted to "twin" the two schools and set up a lasting relationship between them. And David and Helen Yarnley are adventurous world citizens — they're not put off by the idea of roughing it a little — so David went out to visit Yepi.'

'That's interesting,' said Jason. 'He was right. That evening, I spent some time in the comms room with Stuart. He showed me the radar and sonar displays. He reckoned there were two boats following us. That's right, isn't it Stuart?'

Richards didn't give any time for Stuart to answer.

'I asked Stuart to track those two boats,' he said. 'I'd noticed them earlier. Sure enough, they came right up to the stern of the ship later that night, after Stuart had been relieved and Mr Smethwick was on watch. I believe he was on the stern deck to greet the boarders.'

'That's correct, sir,' said Smethwick. 'Two gentlemen in frogman suits joined us briefly. They were paparazzi, after pictures of Debbie Angelinie, Miss Peru, I mean. I pointed a distress flare gun at them and they seemed to change their minds, suddenly.'

There was a little chuckle around the table.

Jason pressed on. 'So what time was that, then?'

'That was nearly four o'clock in the morning, sir.'

'And there was no sign of Morozov on the stern deck then?'

'No sir, I saw the boats were closing in, and I rushed down to the stern deck. I was there a couple of minutes before the frogmen, if I'm allowed to call them that, sir, climbed aboard. But the deck was empty, sir.'

'I see,' said Jason. 'So was Helen the last person to see him alive, then? At about eleven-ish, wasn't it Helen?'

Richards interjected, rather than allow Helen to answer Jason's question. He was impatient to move the conversation on, in the way they had agreed beforehand.

'Well, I hadn't seen him since breakfast. He was drunk then, and I guess he kept himself topped up all day. Oh, but you took him back to his cabin, didn't you, Jane?'

'Yes, Pip and I took him back to his cabin,' said Jane 'I confiscated his hip flask of vodka and put him to bed to sleep it off.'

'What about the fish?' said Jason. 'You know, the fish he had for breakfast, the same fish that was dangled under my nose when I was playing VR games on the sports deck, and the same fish that eventually ended up poisoning the seagull. Was that in Morozov's room when you left him?'

'I don't remember,' replied Jane.

'I can help you there,' piped up Sultan. 'Stu and I delivered the *selyodka...*,' he paused while he looked around the table inviting people to be impressed at his use of the Russian name, '...to Morozov's cabin while you were sorting him out. He was already asleep when we arrived, so we left it on the side.'

'Yes, if you say so. That sounds right,' admitted Jane, and Pip nodded in agreement too.

'And you didn't see him again, after you'd taken his hip flask and left him in his room?' asked Jason.

'No,' said Jane Fortune with emphasis.

'Did you see the fish being prepared, Sultan... I mean, Jamil?' asked Jason, already knowing the answer.

'Hmm, yeah,' said Sultan. 'The preparation of selyodka is obviously the work of a trained master-chef. Basically, it involves taking a piece of fish out of a cling film-covered dish in the fridge, and plonking it onto a plate with some bread and butter and five salad leaves. We took the plate on a tray, with one of those silver dome thingies on the top.'

Stuart, head down, fiddling with his phone under the table but still listening, grinned to himself.

Wren took over quickly. 'As I said earlier, there are no traces of nerve agent in any of the galleys, including the Stern Bar. There were traces in Morozov's room, however, and following our hunch that Morozov poisoned Jarrold, it's reasonable to assume he prepared the envelope in the cabin, so it's likely that the fish also became contaminated there. This stuff is very dangerous and lingers round for weeks.'

'Where did he keep it then, Inspector?' asked Jason.

'We didn't find his store. We checked his toiletries, aftershave et cetera, but no sign. It would have been in a small glass bottle.'

'Or a hip flask? Like the one Jane confiscated?' Jason stared at Jane Fortune.

'You mean I confiscated nerve agent?' she cried. 'Oh my God! Oh no! I don't know why... I was cross with him... I'm sorry if I've unwittingly destroyed evidence. *I threw it over the side!*'

'After you put a few drops onto his fish?' said Jason coolly.

'Don't be ridiculous!' Jane Fortune looked furious.

She reached for her glass, but it was empty once again.

'It's not ridiculous though, is it Jane?' said Richards, in his best cold, threatening way. 'What is ridiculous is the idea that anyone could have been running a fraudulent charity scheme under the auspices of Rara Avis, without your knowledge. You're too good at your job not to spot that. I hired you, remember? No. You had to be in on the act. Perhaps it was all your idea. A way of increasing your benefits from this organisation – that might explain your constant supply of new Gucci shoes and handbags.'

'I can't believe this!' Jane exclaimed. 'Lock me up then! "She must have been on the fiddle, m'lud. She bought herself a new handbag!" Get real Richards! Is that all you're basing your suspicions on?!'

She stood up to leave, a little unsteadily. Jane Fortune was clearly rattled. A swift succession of accusations and revelations this evening had played havoc with her nerves; each time threatening to expose her own secret. Exactly as Wren, Richards and Jason had planned.

Jason prepared another blow. 'It's not all, no. There's something else, isn't there? You've claimed that the last time you saw Morozov was after breakfast in his cabin. But Sarah has spotted a flaw in that, haven't you Sarah? Proper detective, our Sarah,' he said, smiling at her.

'Well, I don't know about that,' she said in an embarrassed voice. 'But no, it's just that something occurred to me earlier. It happened this morning, at the accident on the car rally. Mr Smethwick and I were watching Jason and Rita getting out of the car and coming up the hill. Rita's neck was bleeding, and there was red blood round the neckline of her white racing suit, and all over one shoulder. For a moment, it looked like she was wearing a red scarf. And then something went off in my mind, and for a second I thought about the way Detective Inspector Wren described how Anatoly Morozov's body was found – in a white tuxedo with the red scarf round his neck. They'd identified him based on the description Jane had given the police when he was noticed missing. But I realised Jane couldn't have given that description to the police unless she had seen Morozov *after* Helen had given him the scarf.'

'Exactly,' said Jason. 'Now, Helen, you reckon you last saw Morozov on the Stern Deck at about a quarter to midnight, which is when you gave him the scarf. So Jane couldn't have given that description of Morozov unless she'd seen him after that time. And that's just twenty minutes before I was watching the sonar and radar screens in the comms room with Stuart. That's when he showed me blips on the tracking system that turned out to be paparazzi boats. But we also saw sonar traces which showed something bulky being dumped off the back of the boat. Something that could well have been the body of Anatoly Morozov.'

Stuart looked up from his phone and said, 'Five minutes and seven seconds after midnight. I could show you a replay of those sonar traces as well if you like?'

'No thanks, Stu,' said Jason, with an indulgent smile, 'I think it would spoil the moment. The thing is, at ten minutes after midnight, Sultan, who was keeping watch outside Pip's cabin, saw you, Jane Fortune, returning to your own cabin.'

Jane Fortune stood frozen, breathing in short, asthmatic gasps.

Sultan added helpfully, 'You told me off for not clearing up the fish from the Sports deck, if it helps you remember. I noted the time because I'd actually been dozing on the job until you came stomping along the gangway. I wanted to check how long

I'd been asleep. Sorry if that makes me seem like a bad employee.'

Detective Inspector Wren took over.

He started quietly, and calmly. 'So let's see if I've got this. You took a flask of toxic nerve agent off Anatoly Morozov on Friday morning. Whether or not you knew it was nerve agent, we can't be sure. You say that you didn't know. Okay. What we do know is that quantities of that nerve agent found their way onto his favourite fish breakfast. And you admit yourself that you threw the flask into the sea. God help the fish population if and when that flask starts to leak.' Wren was speaking louder and more forcefully now, piling the pressure on. 'Anyway, regardless of that, later that day, at a quarter to midnight, Helen gave Mr Morozov a scarf. You must have seen him after that time, because you included the scarf in your description of him. It seems likely that Morozov fell off... or was pushed off... the stern deck at five minutes past midnight. Then, five minutes later, Mr Ahmed saw you returning to your cabin. And yet you didn't mention any of this in your statement. You said the last time you saw him was just after breakfast. Which can't be true. Why is that, Jane? Why would you lie to us? One reason would be if you pushed Morozov overboard. Is that right? Is that what happened? Because poisoning the fish hadn't worked, so you had to resort to another method of eliminating your partner in a fraud scheme that was unravelling before your eyes, so that you could pin the blame on him and deny any involvement yourself.'

Wren had reached his crescendo.

The rest of the diners sat bolt upright, alarmed at the scene that was unfolding — except Stuart, who was still playing with his phone, under the table.

Jane Fortune gripped the back of her chair to steady herself. The wine was making it difficult for her to think clearly.

'No!' she said. 'It wasn't like that. I didn't... you don't understand... he was a vicious... it wasn't... I mean, I didn't...'. She bowed her head and paused for a few moments while she caught her breath.

The diners watched silently.

'Anatoly Morozov was a dangerous man,' she continued. 'It was all his idea. The whole thing. Bertrand didn't know what was going on. He was just an actor playing a part. You're wasting your time going after him. Morozov was responsible for it all.' She looked directly at Helen. 'You have to believe me. I didn't know anything about any hitmen killing your husband in Africa. I didn't. Or Mr Jarrold! Morozov was a maniac. He could have killed us all, keeping that nerve agent in his cabin! I thought it was vodka, honestly. Yes, I saw him on the stern deck, wearing that stupid scarf. I was just checking round the decks before I went to bed and stumbled upon him down there. I must have surprised him, scared him. He acted like a lunatic. He tried to kill me, he tried to push *me* overboard. In the struggle, he must have slipped and fallen himself. That's what happened. You have to believe me!'

'Oh yes! Get in there!'

The unusual interruption came from Stuart, who stood up and brandished his phone proudly.

'Here you go. I've just been doing a bit of Googling on old Guillaume Bertrand. Or rather Yves Rambert. These actors often have a few names they go by, especially porn stars. I mean, you're not going to use your own name in the credits to a porno, are you? But if you do a bit of searching on social media, you can usually find all their aliases. One of their Twitter accounts follows another, you see, just to boost their number of followers. And do you know who Yves Rambert and Guillaume Bertrand both follow? *Simon Fortune*. Ring any bells..., Jane... Mum?'

23

'Something's wrong here,' said Wren, an hour later in the basement bar. 'Here I am on an island jam-packed with millionaires and I'm the one getting the drinks in! Still, I think you've earned them tonight.'

He was carrying a tray of five beers and a glass of water. The beers were for Jason, Sarah, Stuart, Sultan and himself. The water was for Richards, who said he didn't touch alcohol.

'Cheers mate, I wasn't sure that was going to work!' said Jason.

'It very nearly didn't,' said Wren. 'The evidence we had against Ms Fortune was always going to be circumstantial. Alone with Morozov on the deck at midnight, it would be impossible to disprove her account of events. I thought we did a good job though, ratcheting up the tension, first with that stuff about Pip Nelson, then all that business about you, Richards — the great manipulator, toying with the lives of Pip, and Brian and Helen Yarnley. You could see Jane Fortune was uncomfortable. Did you see the way she was putting away the sherry? By the time it finally came to accusing her outright of murdering Morozov, I thought she was in a state to confess. But blow me, even though she could see she'd been cornered, she had enough in her to insist that the Yepi school charity fraud was all down to Morozov... nothing to do with Bertrand, did you hear her say that?... and that Morozov had tried to throw her overboard. Anyone could see it was a load of cock and bull, but we'd have had a hard job proving it.'

'And then Stuart plays his blinder and saves the day!' said Jason.

'To Stuart!' toasted Wren and took a good draught. 'The man's a hero. When he discovered that Guillaume Bertrand is one of Simon Fortune's aliases... Simon Fortune, son of Jane... the game was up. Did you see her collapse? You were quick to catch her, Robin.'

'It's Sarah,' Sarah said.

'Yeah, sorry... Sarah. I don't know why... Anyway, thank you. And thank you for helping me get Fortune down to the *Carabinieri* at the harbour. Good to have another woman there.'

'So Jane is being whisked away to the Italian mainland now, is she? Is she okay?' asked Stuart.

Richards tutted, and then in explanation said, 'I'm sorry if I don't seem overly concerned over the welfare of an ex-employee responsible for the murder of two of my clients.'

Wren ignored him. 'Yes, she's fine. The walk helped her regain some composure. She was talking quite a bit, wasn't she, Sarah? I read her rights to her before handing her over to the Italian police, and they read them again, in Italian, but while they were getting the boat prepared, she was giving chapter and verse on the entire story. We'll have to see how it compares with her son's version of events when we apprehend him, of course, but she's admitted that she was party to the initial fraud scheme. She still claims that she knew nothing of the business in the Congo when David Yarnley was shot. When she heard he was dead, she believed the official line that he'd been caught up in local violence. She only became suspicious that Morozov was involved a couple of days ago when she heard that the Yarnley's lawyer, Jarrold, had been killed. She said she was horrified, that she hadn't realised what a monster Morozov was. Somehow she found out about the poison in his possession, and she admitted putting some on his fish. That backfired, with the seagull and everything, so she searched the ship for Morozov and eventually found him, drunk on the stern deck. She now says that she just walked towards him as he stood on the edge of the deck and he fell backwards before she could even touch him.'

24

'Piggin' hell, Jason! I swear it wasn't this far back to the apartments yesterday. I'm bushed, I'm fried and I'm wasted. I can't take any more days like this. I'm going to need a holiday when I get home!'

Sarah and Jason were slowly making their way back from the basement bar, where Stuart and Sultan were making the most of a night off duty, at the expense of DI Wren's bar bill.

'Come on, it's not far now' said Jason, and slipped his arm around Sarah's waist.

She leaned into him. 'I have to say, Jason, I'm impressed.'

'That's good. What with?'

'The way you and Wren did a double act to wear Jane Fortune down bit by bit. I mean, Richards and I played our part as well, but the heavy lifting was you and Wren. It was all very smoothly done. Have you had actor training or something?'

'Hey, we all just made it up as we went along,' said Jason. 'Wren knew we'd need to put the pressure on to get her to confess, so we worked out a rough idea where we were going with it, I suppose. It didn't feel smooth. It felt really amateur, but it was fun though... I must admit, I'm still buzzing a bit.'

'I wish I was. I'm dead beat. Point me in the direction of bed.'

They continued along the path without talking. The island was quiet now. They could just about hear the sea throwing lazy waves against the shore. Jason was thinking about what Rita had told him that afternoon during the race just before they crashed.

Do me a favour, Jason. Sarah's crazy about you.

But just like the other night, on board the *Rara Avis*, it felt like the wrong time to think about taking things further. Sarah was too tired. She needed rest. There'd be other times.

But would those times be on a moonlit night, on a balmy Mediterranean island? Or on a drizzly evening down The Pig in Hambourne?

They reached the apartments. Sarah turned and faced him and said, 'Jason, there's something I want to say to you.'

'Yeah?' said Jason.

'I really like you. I mean, I *really* like you.'

'Um. That's good. I really like...'

'But I can't be with you,' she interrupted. 'I'm afraid there's one more revelation tonight.'

Suddenly, Jason felt he wasn't buzzing any more.

'First of all, my name isn't really Sarah Headly. It's Robin Towers.'

'What? Wait... hang on. Wren called you Robin, briefly. How did he know your name?'

'He's my boss. I'm a policewoman.'

'No, you're not! You're a... you're a social worker or something, aren't you?'

'No, Jason. I'm not. I'm Detective Constable Robin Towers of the West Midlands Counter Terrorism Unit and I'm... an undercover officer.'

'You're bloody joking! Nice try Sarah. Really nice try. Try it on Stuart and Sultan in the morning.'

'It's no joke, Jason. Please, let me explain. It's not easy. So, a while ago, the CTU got to hear a rumour about a suspicious group operating around Hambourne. It sounded like a possible terrorist cell. It was three guys, one of them was a foreign national, Asian, and they all had beards... look, I know it's lame...'

'I don't understand.' Jason looked puzzled.

'It was you. You, Stuart and Sultan. Someone heard that the three of you were known in The Pig as The Taliban, on account of your beards, and they actually reported you to the hotline. It wouldn't normally have gone any further than the first brief check, but it was noticed that one of you had recently bought an aerial drone. Our Super is really twitchy about Birmingham Airport and there had been some business with drones at Gatwick... anyway, they sent me to check it out. This was last year, when I first started going to The Pig.'

Jason looked at her incredulously and then started laughing.

Sarah continued. 'No, listen. Straightaway, it was pretty obvious to me that someone had got their wires crossed. Just sitting at the bar and earwigging your conversation, I could see you were a right bunch of twerps.'

'Thanks, none taken,' said Jason.

'Look Jason, I trust you. That's why I'm telling you this. But you've got to promise not to tell another soul. Promise?'

'Hmm, yeah.' Jason didn't sound certain, but that didn't seem to bother Sarah.

'The thing was,' she said, 'I'd just come off a pretty awful op where I'd had a bloody rough time. I was thinking about quitting the Force completely. I needed time to cool off. So I did something I should never have done. I wouldn't do it now, but I guess I was suffering from stress or something. So I kind of swung the lead a bit. I filed a report saying that I thought that there may be something going on, and I needed time to get closer. Jenny was fine with it. Jenny is Jeremy Wren's nickname. Jenny Wren, see? It's not important.

'It was a really stupid thing for me to do, because once I'd started, I had no way out. I'd have to file an exit report at some point and someone would ask why the hell I'd ever thought there was anything suspicious about you three. I was bound to get found out eventually. I still am. But I have to admit, I started to enjoy myself. Especially when you won your money. Oh my God, I sound like a dreadful freeloader. I suppose I am, but I promise I'm not after you for your money, Jason.'

'That would be okay...'

'No, Jason. I'm not after you, I can't. It's bad enough making up a false investigation. When they find out about that, I'll be fired for sure. But if I get in a relationship with a suspect while acting undercover... that's a whole different ball game. I'd be facing criminal proceedings. It's against the law.'

'I'm jail bait. I knew it!' said Jason with a sigh.

'No, look, the thing is, this business with Jane Fortune and Anatoly Morozov may have just saved me. Okay, it's nothing to do with terrorism, but one way or another we've uncovered some serious criminal activity. My copper instincts were alerted as soon as Helen told us her solicitor had died. Then minutes later there was Boris doing the dance of the dying seagull... too much of a coincidence. That's when I messaged Jenny and got him to come over. He seems pretty pleased with the result, anyway.'

'So, are you going to come clean with him, then? About there not being a terrorist sleeper cell in Hambourne, I mean?'

'I've no idea. I need to think about how to play it and I'm too tired. Oh, Jason, I'm sorry. *So* sorry.'

25

Six weeks later, on an evening in early September, Jason, Sarah, Sultan and Stuart were gathered around a table at The Pig. Another evening discussing the merits of various Netflix series, the latest Bon Iver album, and Brexit.

'The beer's not been great tonight,' said Stuart. 'My stomach is feeling a bit ropey.'

'Yeah, new barrel, I reckon. Not settled properly. Sleep with the windows open and keep your head outside the duvet tonight, mate,' Jason advised.

They laughed, but after a short while, Sultan suddenly looked serious.

'Sorry man, I've got to ask. Does it bother you?' asked Sultan.

'What do you mean?' asked Jason.

'Well, I know you don't like to make a big thing about your money,' said Sultan. 'For instance, we all still have to get our rounds in.' He coughed pointedly, and Stuart and Sarah smirked. 'But take this dodgy beer: it bugs me, but hey, you know, that's part of life. But you don't have to put up with that, do you? I mean, you could afford to have the finest beers flown in, or employ a master brewer to serve perfect beer, at the perfect temperature at a purpose-built bar in the grounds of your own mansion. But here you are, roughing it with us plebs, putting up with a pint of gut-rot at The Pig.'

'Yeah, but it's real, isn't it?' Jason explained. 'It's rough tonight, but usually it's okay, and sometimes it's bloody brilliant. Out on Isola Gallinara, for all its posh food and fine wines, you couldn't get a decent beer, could you? I mean, that Czech lager was great, and it certainly hit the spot on a hot afternoon after plunging down a hot and dusty cliff-face on that bloody car race... but it can't really compare to a pint of Hank's Best, sat round this table with a bag of pork scratchings, can it?'

'That's no way to refer to your friends,' joked Sultan. 'Alright. Anyway, listen, drink up Stuart. I'll drive you home. It's a school night tonight, term starts tomorrow. I need to get some sleep.'

'And I've got an early start too,' said Stuart. 'I'm going down to Surrey to see our old friends, Rita and Travis. I'm installing infrared cameras at their new place.'

'Ooh, that reminds me... before you go... look at this!' exclaimed Sarah.

She showed them an Instagram message on her phone. There was a picture of Helen Yarnley opening the Yepi-David School in Kasai. She was a changed woman from the nervous and angry Helen they had known from earlier in the summer.

She was standing with a group of children in front of the smart-looking school. She was smiling and looked relaxed and confident.

'Nice to see. Right, off we go. Cheers, Jason,' said Sultan. 'Cheers, Sarah. You working tomorrow? Didn't you say your job might come to an end soon?'

'No, I was wrong. Looks like I'm sticking round for a while. Goodnight, lads.'

Stuart and Sultan left, and Jason and Sarah were alone.

'Sticking around?' Jason queried. 'Haven't you come clean with Wren yet, then?'

He looked sternly at her. He didn't like that he was now complicit in her subterfuge and he felt he was betraying his mates by not letting them know that there was a copper in their midst. Even if she was a slacker, pretending that she was investigating a non-existent terrorist cell.

'Yes. Thing is, Jason, remember our last night on the island? We left Stuart and Sultan trying to drink Jeremy Wren under the table. Well, that's what they thought was going on, anyway. Actually, Wren was working a number on them. Plying them for information. He was getting them to talk about their backgrounds. And since then, he's been following up leads, tracing their backstories and looking for links with radical organisations. I've been expecting to get found out and be handed my P45 any day. So, anyway, he called me today, checking that my cover is still intact. It is, isn't it, Jason? I mean, you haven't told anyone, have you? Good... because he said he'd found something... something really important. *Really* important. But he's not telling me what...'

The End

Did you enjoy this book?

When I first came up with the idea of *The Secret Millionaires' Club*, I held onto the hope that a generous publisher would usher me into their fold with a lavish advance, allowing me to immerse myself fully in the millionaire lifestyle for the sake of research. So much for that plan. Instead, I'm trying to grow my readership organically, one reader at a time. To each new reader, I extend my heartfelt gratitude.

I really hope you enjoyed this book. If so, you have the power to make a profound impact. Leaving a review, or even just telling your friends may seem like a small action, but a handful of positive words can make all the difference to prospective readers.

Jason Tranter will return

For those curious about what lies ahead, a glimpse into the next installment of the Secret Millionaires Club series, '*The Secret Burial*', awaits at authorfrost.com. I'll be honest, I'm trying to get your email address so that I can let you know when the next novel is available. But I promise I won't send lots of annoying spam emails and I'll never pass your address on to anyone else.

Acknowledgements

This book was partly inspired by a regular discussion I used to have with my work colleague, Tony, about what it would be like to win the jackpot on the National Lottery. We're both still part of an occasional syndicate.

I'd like to thank Mai Black and her Suffolk Writers' Group for all sorts of support and advice, and particularly Muriel Driver who gave me such encouraging feedback.

Even more thanks must go to David Taft, who not only gave me encouragement, but also pointed out some areas for improvement, which were most valuable.

Finally, thank you to my family for being my first readers and constant supporters.

About the author

Adrian Frost was born in Wolverhampton and can still just about do the accent, but now lives in Suffolk with his family and three imaginary cats.

Printed in Dunstable, United Kingdom

82422811R00211